THE MAN ON THE
END OF THE ROPE

A Thriller Novel

Thriller

HIGH on the vertical north face of the Eiger a helpless figure is suspended in space by a rope. That he is a mountaineer in distress is enough for the intrepid rescue parties who set out, in terrible conditions, to bring him down. But the man is destined to hang there a long time—long enough for sensation-seekers to jam the valley and bring an unexpected wave of prosperity in their wake which is strangely unwelcome to some of the inhabitants. Among the assembled crowds is the Press. The drama on the Eiger is News: meat and drink to the reporters, commentators and cameramen who flock in to record it. Foremost among these is Chipperfield, the arrogant, self-styled "Torch-bearer of Truth," a man whose single-minded pursuit of his career makes him hesitate at nothing and whose coverage of this story is so complete that some of his colleagues are not only irked but suspicious.

Throughout Paul Townend's outstanding new suspense story the reader is kept fascinated; compelled to read on to discover the answers to the questions which are tantalising the world: who is the Man on the End of the Rope and can he survive his dreadful ordeal on the Eiger?

By the Same Author
DIED O' WEDNESDAY

Travel
AMATEUR HOBO
SWISS VENTURE

THE MAN ON THE END OF THE ROPE

by
PAUL TOWNEND

COLLINS
14 ST JAMES'S PLACE, LONDON

FIRST PUBLISHED   MAY, 1960
REPRINTED   OCTOBER, 1960

AUTHOR'S NOTE

The North Wall of the Eiger exists, and this novel is as accurate topographically as I can make it. The rest, however, is fiction. Although I have drawn from certain aspects of the Stephan Longhi tragedy of 1957, I must make it clear that the events depicted in my story are entirely imaginary and that no parallel with real people living or dead, is in any way intended.

PAUL TOWNEND.

CHAPTER I

CHIPPERFIELD drove into Interlaken in an ugly mood.
Switzerland bored him to tears, and the prospect of a
further four hours' drive to Geneva in order to report the
dreary platitudes of a handful of politicians filled him with
gloom. Politics were strictly for egg-heads, and there were
very few of those amongst the vast public for whom
Chipperfield wrote.

He drove at considerable speed down the wide boule-
vard towards the centre of the town, not bothering to
glance left at the glorious view of the Jungfrau across the
meadows. At the crossroads the traffic was congested.
It was mid-August, and the tourist season was at its height.
He nosed his car impatiently through the narrow street
and veered right at the West Bahnhof. The red and white
railway-barrier poles were just dropping, and he tried
to cross the track before the road was closed, but at the
last second knew he could not make it and with an oath
stamped on his brakes.

As he waited for a goods train drawn by an electric
locomotive to trundle through, he suddenly realised he
was hungry. When the barrier lifted he was the first
across, and cut boldly left in the face of the slowly-moving
line of traffic coming in from the Thun-Berne road.
Several horns sounded in annoyance but he paid no
attention.

With difficulty he found a place to park near the station,
locked his car and made his way through jostling crowds
towards a sign announcing Restaurant.

Once inside he was inclined to regret his lack of
selectivity. It was hardly the sort of place he was accustomed to. But the sour, dispirited mood that had hung
over him all that morning robbed him of the initiative

7

to seek something smarter. And, he reflected, minor economies such as the difference between the price he would have to pay in a third-class restaurant and the heavy lunch expense-account he would later charge up to Global Features was one of the meagre satisfactions likely to be garnered from a dull and pointless journey.

The restaurant was divided into two sections, with a ground-glass partition separating the room into two more or less equal halves. Figures could be seen vaguely silhouetted through the glass screen, their outlines indistinct. Through a swing-door the journalist caught a glimpse of the other section: bare tables and bone-handled cutlery, beer mats and baskets of tired-looking *pretzels*. It appeared to be a kind of *Bierstube* frequented by men of the working classes, many of them probably from the nearby railway. He was thankful that he had at least hit upon the section of the restaurant that boasted table-cloths. The food when it came was wholesome and plentiful, and the waitress an amiable, elderly woman dressed in neat clean black. She seemed inclined to linger and gossip, but he quickly made it clear that he was in no mood for that.

As he drank his soup he glanced out of the window and noticed that quite a large crowd appeared to be milling round the approaches to the station. He did not pay much attention; his mind was gloomily concentrated on the coming political conference in Geneva which Global Features had sent him to report.

Suddenly the elderly waitress who was serving him moved to the window and, standing on tip-toe said excitedly to no one in particular:

" Oh look, here they are! "

Chipperfield glanced up, only slightly interested. Two young waiters had joined the waitress and were gazing eagerly out of the window.

" *Lueg emal da*," said the waitress. " How young they are! "

" They look in pretty good shape, when you consider——"

" *Isch nit wahr*, they're worn out if you ask me. Look at
the cuts on the big fellow's face."

" That's from the stone-fall. They say the rocks came
down like hail."

" Not only rocks, ice as well, the papers said. Those
fellows have really been through it."

" Get a paper, there's a picture of them in it, we can
tell which is which."

Chipperfield watched, by now mildly intrigued, as one
of the young waiters darted to a newspaper-rack and took
out of its pigeon-hole a paper curled round a thin wooden
frame. He caught a glimpse of its title: *Der Bund*. It was
a local newspaper printed in Berne, and a copy of it lay
on his table, left there by a previous diner. The waiter
flipped the pages over and stabbed a finger excitedly.

" There they are. The big fellow with the cuts must be
the Austrian climber—no, wait a moment, it's difficult to
tell them apart when they haven't got their gear on."

The newspaper was snatched from him and the
conversation was lost in a babble of confused comment.
Swiss newspapers do not carry many photos and Chipperfield, by now interested, was easily able to find the object
of their excitement. Page two carried a three-column
story and two photos under a modest sixteen point headline
recording " *Die vierzehnte Eigernordwand Besteigung gelun-
gen*." He glanced rapidly through the columns, then laid
the paper down and carried on with his meal. A bunch
of enthusiasts had succeeded in climbing the north face of
some mountain or other, it seemed. Since they were
apparently the fourteenth party to accomplish this, it
was hard to see what all the fuss was about. At any rate,
it was not his line of country. He was not interested in
two-day wonders with happy endings, in " local boy
makes good " and stories of similar ilk. He continued
with his main course and only glanced up once, surprised

to see flash-bulbs popping; the successful climbers appeared to be receiving some kind of send-off.

When the elderly waitress had calmed down sufficiently to clear his plate away, he inquired casually, in good High German:

" What was all the fuss about just now? "

The woman's eyes were sparkling as she replied:

" They've just climbed the Eiger. It was in the papers this morning—there, you've got it in front of you."

" *Hiesiger Bursche?* " he inquired.

" No, they are from Germany or Austria, I believe. Ever so young, no more than mere boys really. They're *verrückt*, of course, but you can't help admiring them."

" Why? "

She gazed at him with eyes wide with surprise. He added:

" What's so special about the Eiger? It's been climbed before, hasn't it? "

Her mouth opened and shut twice before she could find a suitable answer.

" Yes . . . but, well, you see, it's not just the Eiger they climbed, but the North Wall. It's the most terrible climb in all Switzerland, nearly two thousand metres, and almost vertical all the way up."

" How high is the Eiger itself then? "

" Four thousand metres."

He made a swift calculation and said, " Thirteen thousand or so feet. High enough. But I still don't get it. Why all that circus outside? " He waved a hand towards the dissolving crowd at the railway station. " They got there, didn't they? Nobody was killed? "

" Oh yes, they got to the top," she answered, her voice charged with admiration. " Forty-two hours' climbing, it says in the papers, and they——"

" Then the story's finished, I should say," he cut in. " Now, how about a little of your delectable Swiss cheese to finish off with. Not Emmentaler, have you a nice ripe Tilsiter, not too sharp? "

The waitress nodded, gave him a puzzled look and went off to the kitchens, somehow conveying, by the manner in which she walked, her disapproval at his lack of enthusiasm.

Chipperfield glanced at the newspaper once more, making a more or less instinctive check to see that he had missed nothing important. A moment's perusal convinced him that he had not. It was a typical local story, of interest solely to the district and perhaps to climbing circles in a few neighbouring countries, nothing more. Matters might have been otherwise, he mused idly, if the climbers had been swept away by an avalanche or a rope had broken. That would have been news.

Various items of knowledge stored at the back of his retentive brain floated to the foreground. The Eiger North Wall . . . it certainly rang a bell. Was it the Whymper story? . . . no, that was the Matterhorn, and nineteenth-century stuff, anyway. Mountains were strictly old hat now that Everest had at long last been conquered. There had been, he seemed to remember, some fuss about the Eiger way back in the thirties: a lot of people had died in a series of attempts on the north face, and eventually it had been climbed by a bunch of Germans and Austrians just before the war.

Mountaineering, from the standpoint of news-value, was out. Nowadays it was the private lives of royalty and well-rounded film *divas* that made headlines. Of course, if some bright publicity boy could persuade Brigitte Bardot or Marilyn Monroe to take up mountain-climbing, that *would* be news. He grinned inwardly and dismissed the topic from his thoughts.

In four hours he would be in Geneva. The big brass were due to arrive on the following day. That would give him the evening to set up, or rather renew, his contacts and obtain the services of one or two willing legmen (for the glamour of being allowed to associate with a name as powerful as his was generally sufficient to lure a couple of pink-cheeked " errand boys " into his service); there was no point in making hard work out of a routine political jamboree. The legmen could pick up the wordy, meaning-less hand-outs at the end of each day's talking session, and he would be free to nose out anything that smelt faintly like a real story. Not that there was much chance of that. Politicians were growing increasingly cagey about their private lives, and there was scant hope of an assassination, a suicide or any other kind of healthy scandal. It would be dull routine work, with only the compensations of the Casino at Evian over the border and perhaps the atten-tions of a ripe young innocent from the over-crowded UNESCO offices to while away the tedium.

You couldn't deal in headlines all the time, of course. Three or four big stories a year were all that the most forceful newspaperman could hope to unearth. He had certainly squeezed all that could be got from the Soraya-divorce story, and his handling of the famous Peter Townsend romance had been unrivalled in its audacity. On the whole it had been a good year, and Global Features had secured him a handsome price for both these stories and the more recent one on Rita Hayworth. True, the latter was suing for libel, but that was to be expected, and provided nothing untoward occurred, even added to the size of his reputation.

It had been a good year, but that was nothing to be complacent about. When you had reached the top of the tree, you could not afford to rest there. He felt himself itching to get his teeth into something big once more; not just the perennial round of double axe-murderers, scandalous parties at St. Tropez and the illiterate con-fessions of champion boxers who had thrown their fights, but something really big, something only he could handle and only Global Features could splash around the world. He had reached the heights in his profession, he could file a story under a thick by-line in a chain of top news-papers at the drop of a hat: he was Paddy Chipperfield, ace news-hound, the " Torchbearer of Truth "—but there did not seem to be any story to be unearthed, any truth to be revealed. At least, not his kind of truth.

Four seconds later he had changed his mind.

He happened to glance up to check his watch with the restaurant clock, and his eye was caught by a profile silhouetted against the ground-glass partition. For the space of perhaps two seconds Chipperfield stared un-believingly. The owner of the profile turned away, took some kind of headgear from a hat-stand, and disappeared from view.

Then the journalist leapt from his chair and made a headlong dash for the swing-door. A waiter carrying a full tray blocked his progress between two tables. Chipper-field swore, wheeled back and ran down another lane through the restaurant, nearly tripping over a dog leashed to a table. Cries and angry comments followed him. But by the time he reached the swing-door leading to the *Bierstube*, it was too late. Of the handful of people sitting at the bare tables, none resembled the man he had seen—or half-seen.

He glanced quickly round the drab room. The corner where he guessed the man to have been sitting was empty. The door to the street rocked slightly and then settled to a standstill. Chipperfield thrust his way roughly through the tables regardless of the confusion he caused and reached the street. He was just in time to see a small green sports car, its hood down, drive out of sight past the West Bahnhof. It disappeared too quickly for him to read the number plate; he had only time to note that there was a D in it somewhere. For a wild moment he thought of giving chase by foot, then realised the foolishness of doing so.

He came in from the street and gazed unseeingly for a moment at the dingy *Bierstube* in which—unless he had been mistaken—one of the most fabulous figures of world society had been eating. The idea was scarcely possible. If such a figure were to stray from the traditional circuit prescribed by High Society (Fifth Avenue-Claridges - Paris - Cannes - Capri - Ischia - Taormina) and somehow arrived in a bourgeois holiday-Mecca like Interlaken, then he would certainly not be found eating at a seedy clothless table in a third-class restaurant. Unless . . .

Unless he wanted no one to know he was there.

His pulse quickening, Chipperfield strode swiftly to the table where he calculated the silhouetted figure had probably sat. The remains of an ice-cream and an empty cigarette packet were the only signs that someone had eaten there. He picked up the packet and examined it closely. The brand was Astor Filter, and had contained ten cigarettes, made in Germany. He pocketed it and called a nearby waitress. The young girl came over.

" Did you serve this table, *Fräulein*? " he demanded.

" *Jawohl.*"

" A single man sat here? "

" *Ja.*"

" What language did he speak? "

The waitress, who was young and pretty, eyed him suspiciously and Chipperfield realised it was necessary to turn on the charm. Thinking quickly, he said:

" It is very important, *gnädiges Fräulein*, you see, I am looking for a friend of mine and I thought I saw him leave a moment ago. I should be most grateful for anything you can tell me about the man you served at this table. Very grateful indeed," he added, producing two five-franc coins and slipping them deftly on to the edge of the table. He accompanied this action with one of his all-stops-out smiles which had so often, aligned with hard cash, produced results before.

The girl blushed, and answered guardedly:

" Well, if he was a friend of yours, there's really no reason . . . the gentleman spoke High German, though he hardly said any——"

" Without an accent? "

The waitress considered this for a moment, then replied:

" None that I noticed, but I'm not very good on matters like that. He didn't say much, it's hard to tell. He was very charming, though."

Chipperfield nodded encouragingly: the charm part fitted, even if the language was not what he had expected. He said:

" Was there anything unusual about him, anything that struck you as being out of the ordinary, *Fräulein*? You did not think you had seen him somewhere before, perhaps? "

The girl shook her head slowly. " No, I don't think so," she replied. " But he was rather strange—for example, he wore sun-glasses the whole time. You'd hardly think that necessary in here——" she indicated the gloomy room, " though of course a lot of tourists do wear them, especially the Italians, indoors and out."

" Did anything else about him strike you as strange? His clothes, perhaps, or any mannerisms? "

" No. But what was odd was the meal he ordered. He must have been terribly hungry."

" What did he have? "

" Soup, two *Bratwurst*, and five soft-boiled eggs."

" Five! Are you sure? "

" *Natürlich*. Mind you, I couldn't believe my ears at first; but he ate the lot. And he had a double portion of ice-cream, with whipped cream on top."

" Anything to drink? "

" Milk. Cold milk."

The journalist shuddered at the thought of such a meal. It did not fit, but there might be an explanation which he could puzzle out afterwards. He asked:

" Could you describe the man, *gnädiges Fräulein*? "

The girl knitted her brows with concentration and then answered: " Tallish, about thirty-five years old, rather on the thin side, fair-haired, good-looking—what one could see, with those big black sun-glasses."

Chipperfield's heart-beats quickened. There was nothing in her description that did not fit. He pressed her with more questions but soon became convinced that she had told him all she could. He withdrew his hand from the partially-covered coins, thanked the girl and returned quickly through the swing-door to his table. There he ordered coffee, lit a cigarette and tried to set his racing thoughts in order.

Could it be " the phoney Baron "?

It was a very long shot indeed. Almost entirely un-believable. What on earth—supposing the split-second glimpse through the ground-glass partition had been accurate—was a celebrity of his calibre doing in the middle of Switzerland, eating off bare tables (and consuming a fantastic meal to boot)? Supposing that his intuitive reaction at the imagined sight of that famous profile had been right, supposing it *was* the playboy Baron himself, why all the mystery? Why the dark glasses? What on earth was the man up to, in this benighted neck of the backwoods? What possible place had a hot-house plant like the Baron Wendelin Mandoza amongst the worthy, prosaic Swiss and hordes of middle-class tourists? It just didn't make sense. The more he thought about it the more far-fetched the idea seemed. He must have been mistaken. Infallible though his eye for famous faces usually was, this time he must have slipped up. He had very nearly made a fool of himself.

Or had he? Would he be making a bigger fool of himself by not checking up? He could put a call through to the syndicate in London and find out where the young Baron was supposed to be. That should settle the matter decisively. If there was nothing in it, then he had missed nothing. But if the playboy Baron was not at one of his favourite haunts, if there was the slightest mystery concerning his whereabouts, then he, Paddy Chipperfield, ace news-hound, had stumbled across a very interesting item of news. For it was not every day that the rejected lover of a queen went tramping incognito through Central Europe, eating weird meals in workers' restaurants.

*   *   *

When the call from London came through Chipperfield asked immediately for Bernheim.

" Listen, Bernie, and listen hard. I want two pieces of information, double quick. There's not a second to lose. First, find out where Mandoza is . . . yes, ' the phoney Baron ' himself . . . and make sure your facts are dead accurate. Secondly, see if you can find out what brand of cigarette he smokes. Got that? . . . no, I'm not crazy . . . I can't say yet, just do as I ask. Now, here's the number, phone me back as soon as you can . . ."

Bernheim's reply seemed to take an eternity to come through. A fever of anticipation mounted in him. If his hunch were right, Geneva and its banal conference could go overboard; he had something potentially far bigger on his platter.

In Paddy Chipperfield's world, certain personalities made news. It did not matter how trivial the action or saying of such personalities was; they were, in the expression of the trade, " hot." If one of the Italian *divas* such as Loren or Lollobrigida, if Ali or the Aga Khan, or one of the Gabor girls, or ex-Queen Soraya, Grace Kelly, Rubirosa, Rita Hayworth, certain royalty, a few names in Hollywood and one or two members of London's upper crust, drank a cup of tea with the left hand instead of the right—that was news. One could deplore the fact, or seek to explain it, but one could not deny it. In this

B

strangely mixed company, often referred to loosely as High Society, the handsome young Baron Wendelin Mandoza held a prominent place. If it had not been enough that his claim to the title of an old Spanish-German family was considered by experts to be dubious, his choice of dancing partners, recklessness at the race-track, behaviour at night-clubs (where in the small hours he frequently took over the saxophone) and his love of fast cars (with attendant rumours of several hushed-up accidents) would alone have earned him a secure niche in the gossip columns. It had not yet been recorded that the carefree, fabulously rich young man had ever done a day's work, but this fact in no way diminished his appeal for millions of readers. All this, however, was not all that there was to be said about him.

Fate had stepped in and in a matter of a few weeks raised the Baron from mere playboy to international celebrity. For he had fallen in love with a queen.

It was true she was only a minor queen, and her kingdom an unstable and rapidly diminishing one; but that did not alter the heavily romantic facts. The lady of his desire was the lawful queen of a minor European monarchy, she was unmarried and disarmingly beautiful into the bargain. Since the moment she had reached her late 'teens the public had never tired of speculations concerning suitors for her hand. The popular press of many nations had rejoiced in this fact, and seldom let a month go by without producing possible candidates. And then the Baron had openly declared himself, with apparently favourable response from the royal château. For a while all was great excitement, until the Baron's name was mentioned in connection with some unpleasant scandal on the Riviera. Then rumour began to cancel rumour, Crown, Church and Parliament conferred and disputed, and the public was invited to take part in polls of mass opinion for and against the marriage. Eventually a discreet communiqué from the royal château wrote finis to the romantic fable. The handsome young Baron had wooed and lost.

Thereupon the public really took him to its heart.

There was nothing so universally beloved as the tragic figure of a rejected lover. Derisive nicknames such as " the phoney Baron " and " the sexy saxophonist " were pushed by prudent newspaper editors into the background; Mandoza was respectfully referred to as " the royal suitor," and no photographs that even hinted at a smile on his stricken face were allowed within yards of a feature-editor's desk. " Why does the Baron look so sad? " became a catch phrase in New York and along Fleet Street; various ribald answers were devised, but, needless to say, never printed.

The end of his great romance had not, however, meant the end of Mandoza's career. All his activities continued to fall into the same eye-catching, news-making mould. It was announced by his apparently indispensable press agent that he was engaged upon writing his memoirs; the film rights had already been sold for a formidable sum. He was also conducting two libel suits against newspapers that had dared to ridicule him. And as certain quarters in London and New York had shown signs of turning cool towards him, he had obtained an obscure diplomatic post somewhere in Europe, where he had retired, purely for the time being, " in order to forget." If the fickle public had any intention of forgetting him, several shrewd editors amongst the popular press could be relied upon to see that this did not happen. It was on this fact that Chipperfield was placing his hopes. He was not to be disappointed.

" I don't know what you're up to, Paddy boy," Bernheim's voice crackled over the wire from London a short while later, " but here's the gen you were asking for. The ' phoney Baron ' has left his post in Bonn——"

" He was stationed in Germany? " Chipperfield yelled frantically.

" Yeah. Left Bonn and gone on leave, destination unknown."

" You mean you don't know *where* he is! "

" That's about it. Seems he drove south through Germany in the direction of the Austrian border. That's the best I can do for you, Paddy boy. What's the panic? Something may turn up in the next few hours——"

" It had damn' well better! And make sure your facts are spot-on. I'll phone you this evening. What about his brand of cigarette, could you find that out? "

" He's a non-smoker."

Chipperfield gripped the receiver with crushing force, fury and frustration surging up inside him.

" Like hell he is! What about that time they caught him with reefers down on the Riviera? "

" It was never proved, Paddy boy, don't you remember? That was how he got out of the charge, by proving he'd never smoked a cigarette in his life."

" Not many people believed it then and I don't believe it now. The man's a phoney."

" Of course he is, through and through. But he sells newspapers, what more do you want? Now you just toddle along to Geneva like a good lad and see what you can dig up on the conference, and I'll——"

" You'll be hearing from me," Chipperfield snapped, and slammed down the receiver.

He stepped angrily from the phone booth and lit a cigarette, then noticed that the pretty young waitress who had answered his questions was loitering as if to catch his eye. She came over to him, her face slightly flushed. She wants another tip, he thought sourly.

" *Bitte um Entschuldigung*, but that friend of yours, the one——"

" Yes? "

" Do you think you will be seeing him again? I wouldn't ask, only——"

" Quite possibly. Why? "

" Well it's just that . . . I don't like to mention it but he paid his bill with German money and the——"

" With German money? Are you quite certain? " Chipperfield interrupted her excitedly.

" Yes, I have it here. You see, it is no longer valid . . . Oh, I don't mean it's a forgery or anything like that, but I was changing it into Swiss francs a moment ago and the *Herr Direktor* told me these notes have recently been withdrawn from use. I was wondering if perhaps . . ."

" Certainly, *Fräulein*, most certainly." He snatched the note eagerly out of her hand and gave the girl an equivalent amount in Swiss currency, plus a liberal tip.

Only when he sat trembling with keyed-up nerves at the wheel of his car a few moments later did he realise he had no idea where to start hunting for Mandoza.

It was not going to be easy to find him. But he had undertaken trickier manhunts than this before, and run his quarry to earth. Of one thing he was now certain: it was not a waste of time to search for the owner of the green sports car. It was true that he had only the slenderest shreds of proof with which to support his incredible theory. It was scarcely a theory, more a wild hunch. But an experienced newspaperman scented a big story like a well-trained field-dog smelt the hidden beast. And if the worst came to the worst, if it proved to be a dead end, then little time or expense had been wasted; Geneva and the prattling politicians would still be there on the morrow.

He drove slowly down the road past the West Bahnhof and several imposing hotels, till he came to the corner where the road swung right towards Spiez. This was the critical point, the literal dividing of the ways. If he took the wrong road here he would never hunt down the man he believed to be Baron Mandoza.

It was most likely that the man had branched right, along the shores of Lake Thun. The road led to Berne, after it had passed through Spiez and Thun. That was the logical thought to follow. A left-hand turn would only have brought him back on his tracks, into the heart of Interlaken once more. The final alternative was a narrow road directly ahead that appeared to lead somewhere up in the mountains, obviously to nowhere important.

Then he caught sight of a garage. There was nothing to be lost by asking. He swung off the road and drew up at a petrol pump.

Three minutes later he slammed his car into gear and stamped hard on the accelerator. The garage-hand had been sharp-eyed and worth the big tip he had received. Not only had a green sports car driven by a man with smoked glasses stopped for petrol and oil a little less than an hour earlier, but its driver had inquired for the route up the Lütschine valley to Grindelwald. And his car had carried a German licence plate, alongside the large letter D which is used by German cars abroad.

Chipperfield slipped into top gear and headed at maximum speed up the narrow road that led into the heart of the mountains.

CHAPTER II

By PURE CHANCE John Bellman saw Chipperfield arrive at Grindelwald.

Try as he would he could not succeed entirely in quelling the wave of irritation, almost dismay, that surged over him. He could not imagine what had brought the self-styled Torchbearer of Truth to this tranquil mountain village. Grindelwald with the lid off would look very much the same as Grindelwald with the lid on, and it was scarcely the sort of place someone like Chipperfield would choose for a holiday; it was not nearly smart enough.

He tried to shrug the matter off, as well as the distinct

impression that the famous journalist had seen him as he drove slowly into the village—seen him and cut him dead.

Since the occasion when they had clashed bitterly in New York, their paths had happily not crossed, and Bellman for his part would have been content if things had stayed like that. To be fair, it was just possible that the man had not seen him. Judging by the slow, peering fashion in which he had driven past the spot where Bellman was standing, one might have guessed that Chipperfield was searching for something or somebody; he had perhaps been looking so hard that he had been unable to see anything except the image of his search. It did not matter. Fate would hardly be so unkind as to send the man up to the ridge of the Kleine Scheidegg where he, Bellman, was staying.

He strolled down to Grindelwald station and along the open platform towards the waiting green and cream train, stubby and somehow toy-like, that would take him up to his hotel. It was too early to get in, as it would not be leaving for the Scheidegg until at least another fifteen minutes, so he strolled on towards the end of the platform where the cog-rail, dipping abruptly, crossed the Grindelwald road and swung down to the floor of the Lütschine valley.

He stopped and gazed contentedly at the soft green panorama spread out before him. The afternoon sun had begun to break through after a dull morning, and the thin silver ribbon of the Lütschine river glinted joyfully as it ran past Grund Station and on down the valley out of sight. He was able to trace some of the walks he had done during the past two weeks over the alpine pastures that rose steeply from either side of the river.

On his right the green fields rose swiftly to the white-powdered peaks of the Faulhorn and the Schynige Platte, and across the river, to the west, more gently towards Männlichen, and the ridge of the Kleine Scheidegg. Almost with reluctance, for he felt he had spent too much time during the previous few days gazing at it, his glance swung slowly left to the massive grey-black flanks of the Eiger.

Its upper half was shrouded by thin cloud, but curiously enough this seemed to enhance, rather than diminish, its overwhelming bulk. Like an egoist greedily sprawling across a group photo, its brooding great flanks spread from west to east over a distance of some four miles, shutting out a glorious view of Mönch and Jungfrau which would otherwise have been obtained from where Bellman was standing. The base of the mountain was so vast, so all-engulfing, that it seemed to defy one's right to look at anything else which the lovely valley had to offer. For the hundredth time or more, Bellman stared at the Eiger, fascinated by its sheer enormity, and for the hundredth time the impression it had first made upon him was restated: it was not a beautiful mountain.

Then suddenly, stirred by some freak of wind sweeping up the Scheidegg ridge, the clouds began to shift. Bellman watched spellbound, knowing what was to come but fascinated as though for the first time: clouds parted, sealed, shifted and then opened, revealing section by section the black ugly face of the famous *Nordwand*— the North Wall. The east and west flanks of the mountain sliced razor-sharp lines against the blue vault of the heavens, thrusting for thousand upon thousands of feet, rising, soaring upwards to the mighty summit to form the near-symmetrical sides of a time-worn pyramid thirteen thousand feet high. A plume of purest white cloud streamed like a long thin pennant from the apex, as if announcing to all the world some kind of challenge or symbolic victory. It was a breathtaking sight.

Breathtaking, beautiful, and yet somehow dreadful, a kind of beauty that had nothing in common with the gentle charm of the green valley below, with its scattered clusters of flower-decked chalets and wandering herds of placid, bell-hung cows. It was a harsh beauty that had something of the awesomeness of great, grotesque music, or the fearful grace of an atomic explosion in the desert— beauty and terror combined in unholy harmony, both fascinating and repelling.

With a slight inward shudder Bellman turned away and walked slowly back to the train, his thoughts centred yet again on the drama of the previous few days, when three young climbers from Austria and Germany had pitted themselves against the North Wall and emerged, scathed but alive, its fourteenth conquerors.

He had not come up to Grindelwald in order to watch them. He had not even known an attempt was being made. He had come in search of rest and peace of mind and had chosen the Swiss village not only from nostalgia for a boyhood holiday but because he could think of no better place in which to wash the taste of cities and hectic newspaper life from his system.

And he had enjoyed every moment of his holiday, including the gratis drama that had been thrown in. It was a story he would hardly have been able to ignore even if he had not been a reporter by profession. There had been little point in telling himself that he was on holiday when an interesting theme suddenly cropped up right under his nose. He had followed the climbers' progress with the aid of a powerful pair of binoculars and had filed a short, factual account back to his office in Hamburg, not really caring if they made use of it or not. Aside from this brilliant feat of climbing, the walks he had done, the good food, the keen mountain air and the magnificent scenery had been all he had hoped for. He would be sorry to return to the Press Agency office in Hamburg when the remaining days of his holiday had expired, but at least he felt fit and rested, ready to start work once more.

People were beginning to board the train by now, and he secured himself a window-seat on the left-hand side. Gradually the carriages filled up with a colourful collection of tourists from many nations: young sun-tanned girls, several middle-aged couples, and a few hardy young climbers in heavy hob-nailed boots, each laden with weighty rucksacks and coils of rope. Bellman eyed these young men with special interest. Were they a breed apart, these quiet, muscular, weather-beaten young giants, was it pure fancy to imagine a distant, almost fanatical look in their eyes? What made them risk their lives in the pursuit of their sport? Not money, that much was certain. There were no competitions or leagues, no fat prizes to be gained, no tempting targets such as a professional boxer, footballer or tennis star strove for. There was not even the roar of an appreciative crowd to sound like music in their ears. For the most part, with very few exceptions, they went about their dangerous pastime with a quiet dedication, oblivious to whether their achievements were seen or ever heard of. A great deal of fatuous nonsense had been written about the sport, of course, but even so it was impossible to deny that its exponents possessed a great deal of courage, formidable stamina and a queer, admirable devotion—qualities noticeably absent in a great many other fields of athletic endeavour.

Lost in these thoughts, Bellman hardly noticed the gentle bite of cogwheel into toothed-rail as the train moved smoothly off. It crossed the road, dropped down to Grund Station on the floor of the valley, then crawled like a cautious green caterpillar up steep flanks towards the massive base of the Eiger. For a while the lower glacier and the two great cathedrals of Schreckhorn and Wetterhorn remained in view, then the massive eastern humpback of the Eiger—the Mittellegi Ridge—cut them off, and the brooding great mountain absorbed all that Bellman could see from his window. They passed a gaunt, aged farmer in battered felt hat and knee boots, emptying *Mischt* from wooden panniers lashed to the back of a patient mule, both man and beast lodged at weird angles in order to retain their balance on the steep slopes. From time to time groups of hikers were seen on the narrow, twisting footpaths up the slopes, making brief, vivid splashes of colour against the uniform green of the crisp turf. Then the train nosed slowly into woods of mountain-maple and spruce-fir, emerging a short while afterwards at the tiny station at Alpiglen.

Whilst they halted, Bellman opened a window and craned his neck upwards to gain a thrilling close-up view of the vast North Wall that soared sheer above the tracks. Alpiglen was generally the starting point from which attempts on the north face were made. It consisted of no more than the tiny station, a few chalets and a small *pension*.

After a brief halt the train ground slowly forward on the final three-mile stretch up to the Kleine Scheidegg. They entered a long one-sided tunnel, built to protect the tracks from rock- and snow-fall. As they emerged, the face of the Eiger continued to shut out all view to the left, so that Bellman was impelled to look at the bare stretch of rather desolate ground that fell away in uneven undulations on his right-hand side. Not for the first time he stared curiously at the gloomy hotel which stood on a small knoll in the centre of these windswept, almost treeless slopes. The building had a forlorn air about it, despite its pretentious title which, in large black and white lettering, could just be read from the train: GRAND HOTEL NORDWAND. It had struck him as a strange place to build a hotel, grand or otherwise. If people wanted to take a holiday in the area, they either stayed down in Grindelwald itself or else came up to the Scheidegg. The latter, with its fine hotel, superb view of the Eiger, Mönch and Jungfrau, and unique position at the junction of the cog-rails from both Grindelwald to the east and Lauter-brunnen-Wengen to the west, was a great attraction in both summer and winter. But it was hard to see the point of a large hotel in this particular desolate spot, except perhaps for the unparalleled view it must command directly on to the Eiger North Wall.

A narrow cinder track across swampy-looking ground connected the hotel with Alpiglen Station. As if to point the loneliness of the scene, no one had got out at Alpiglen and taken this path. But there was a solitary figure on it. He was walking away from the hotel towards the tracks, and appeared to be wearing an incongruous black bowler hat and carrying a black brief-case. A second tunnel cut him off from sight, as Bellman's train began the final gentle ascent to the Scheidegg.

*　　　*　　　*

Klaus Borgwand hated that bowler hat and shiny black brief-case, truly hated them with all his soul.

He picked up a pair of field-glasses and stared out of his bureau window, focusing not on the bowler-hatted owner of the brief-case so much as the bulging piece of leather itself. Other men had come to him over the years, carrying brief-cases along the narrow cinder track, and he had watched their arrival with equanimity, for they had only been doing their duty—that of asking him to meet his debts. Some had been paid with promises, the more forceful with part or even full payment, but though it had often come to sharp words, he had never really disliked callers of this kind. Klaus Borgwand was an hotelier and a business man and he understood well enough that the butcher and baker had to be paid, inconvenient though it often was. But this nasty little man with the absurd *Melonenhut* (it was currently the fashion in Zürich to ape London modes) had come not to demand money, but to offer it . . . at a price. That was his unforgivable sin. The agreement had been signed, the harsh terms of the *Wechsel* accepted, for there was no other way to save his hotel from the auctioneer's hammer; but though they had smiled tightly at one another and shaken hands on departure, it had been an infinitely more distasteful interview than any he had been forced to undergo before.

Binoculars in hand he left the hotel and stepped out on to the terrace, leaning in his favourite position against the giant telescope that dominated the centre of the terrace. Unwillingly his eyes were drawn to the ridge of the Scheidegg less than two miles away, to the cluster of buildings thronged with tourists; it was a sight that never failed to cause him a pang of bitterness and honest envy. Why should they always be so full, so successful, and he so empty? He detested self-pity, and fought back the temptation to put it all down to ill-luck. Somewhere along the years, perhaps right back at the beginning, he had heavily miscalculated.

He had known he was taking a big risk, to build his hotel where he had. In the valley they had mocked him, called his house " Borgwand's Folly." But he had gambled on the North Wall, gambled on its spreading fame, and at first his efforts had seemed bound for success. He had worked like a coolie and people had begun to spread the word about the new hotel with its incomparable view of the Eiger North Wall. Then disaster had struck: war broke out, at the end of his third summer season. No further handfuls of brave young men had come to pit their skill against the north face, and no throng of interested tourists had come to watch them.

By the time peace came, his debts had reached a formidable total, and people seemed to have forgotten about the Eiger. It was almost as if the world's appetite for danger and spectacle was temporarily satiated. A few climbers came, some conquered the *Nordwand*, and then left, with little to show in the hotel books that they had even been noticed. His two rivals, Kleine Scheidegg to the west and Grindelwald to the east, had crushed him as though in a vice. Under the burden of debts and growing ill-health he felt himself slowly going under. The *Wechsel* he had signed was ruinous in its terms, he could not hope to meet it unless a miracle happened. In a few months they would take his house, and his life's purpose, from him, leaving him nothing, not even good health.

He stood there for some time, lost in the complex web of past, present and future. Finally he heaved a sigh and was on the point of putting his binoculars down and returning inside when something unusual caught his eye. It was not the afternoon train crawling slowly up the final gradient to the Scheidegg, nor the small dissolving stir of movement at Alpiglen station: something else, on a rocky slope above and to the right of the station . . . a tent, and two indistinct figures bent over a camp fire. They were partly hidden by a thin copse of spruce-firs, and it was impossible to make out anything very definite about their appearance. There might even be more than two figures, it was difficult to say. To almost anyone else, viewing the scene through binoculars, they would have presented no more than an everyday picture of holiday campers preparing their evening meal. But Klaus Borgwand saw them with other eyes.

He turned into the hotel and, averting his eyes from the sign on the lift that read " Temporarily out of action," climbed laboriously to the fourth floor, his heart beating alarmingly at the effort. He walked down a carpetless corridor and entered a dark, musty-smelling mansard room which had once been used as a staff bedroom. He opened the window, paused to regain his breath, and focused his binoculars once more.

He gave a grunt of satisfaction. He did not think he had been mistaken. One could not live for twenty years at the foot of the Eiger North Wall without acquiring a fine instinct, as well as a great deal of technical knowledge. From the nature of their clothing, from the rucksacks and scattered objects of equipment visible only from where he now stood, he knew beyond doubt that these were no

mere tourists fond of outdoor sleeping. They were men
planning to climb a mountain, and there could be no
doubt, from the spot where their tent was pitched, which
mountain: the North Wall of the Eiger.

His reactions were the same each time it happened:
wonder, pride, admiration—and fear. It was twenty
years since the impossible had been achieved and Heckmair had led the way up the mile-high wall of ice-
covered rock. Twenty years, and as many lives for-
feited, not to speak of the more fortunate ones who had
been plucked from the mountain in the nick of time,
half-dead from exhaustion and exposure. Twenty years,
twenty deaths, yet still they came, lured as though
hypnotised by the mountain's challenge.

For a long time he stood watching the two men, hoping
that they might glance in his direction so that he could
get a good look at them. But both figures—there appeared
to be only two—remained squatting round the fire,
eating steadily, occasionally putting fresh coffee over the
flames to boil, their backs half-turned towards him.
Eventually one of them got up, stretched himself and
turned to examine the weather prospects. His was a
stocky, broad-shouldered, powerful figure, and though
he wore a knitted stocking-cap and the slanting rays of
the setting sun impeded perfect vision, Borgwand was
able to recognise him. It was a local man, named Hans
Albrecht, a former mountain guide. There had been
some scandal about him, and he had been removed from
the list of officially accredited guides, for reasons which
Klaus Borgwand could not precisely remember.

The hotelier brought his glasses to focus on the other
man, but his luck was out. The man rose to his feet and
without turning disappeared swiftly into the screen of
trees with cooking utensils in his hands, apparently bent
on washing them in a nearby stream.

Borgwand stayed as long as he dared, though it was well
past the time when he had to go down to the kitchens to

supervise the evening meal; but the stocky guide, finished with his survey of the skies, had ducked into the tent, and the second man showed no signs of reappearing. He glanced at his watch, muttered a mild imprecation and closed the window. In the old days, before the war, an immaculately dressed chef had knocked respectfully on his bureau door each morning and submitted suggestions for the day's menus. He, Borgwand, had merely had to read carefully through them and make an occasional amendment. Now he could not afford the expense of a chef; the menus came from his own tired brain, with frequent assistance from Claire when he was stumped for new ideas, and, with the aid of two unskilled Italian kitchen boys, he himself had to prepare all meals.

Grimly he descended the stairs and made his way down to the kitchens.

*   *   *

Claire was making a depressing inventory in the bar when Papa Borgwand went past. He had not glanced up and given her his customary smile. That meant he was more than usually worried. She had a fairly shrewd idea whom the director's visitor from Zürich had been that afternoon: certainly not one of the habitual, dogged tradesmen in search of money—the slick little man had been much too obsequious for that.

She sighed and continued checking the bottles left at her disposal. They made a fairly bold array, but only she and the director knew how little there was in the cellar to back them up. Unless one of the wine merchants could be persuaded to unbend, there would be no further supplies coming up from the valley. Matters were indeed desperate if stocks in the bar ran out, for that was the only section of the hotel that could be counted on to show a profit. Not that the handful of modest, middle-aged guests staying at the hotel at that moment showed much

sign of stampeding her; but one never knew what unexpected demands a bar might have to meet.

A small, nagging voice at the back of her mind told her
that she was foolish to stay in her job. But she had
vowed to herself that she would see the season out. It was
the least she could do in return for the kindness Papa
Borgwand had shown both her and her family in the past.
Several merchant travellers and not a few guests had asked
her why she did not seek a better job. Two offers from
night-club proprietors—one in Geneva and one in
Zürich—lay gathering dust on her bedroom table at that
moment. But one could not always run away from an
inconvenient situation, she had decided; sometimes one
had to stay and see it through.

She finished the inventory, took her keys and went
down to the wine cellar, hoping against hope that she
might discover an overlooked bin, or even a single bottle
of liqueur or spirits put aside for some special occasion.

She had to pick her way carefully: the steps to the
cellar were beginning to rot with mould in one or two
places; there was no money to spare for repairs to those
parts of the hotel not generally seen by guests. At the
locked door to the wine cellar she tried the light switch,
but nothing happened. The bulb had not been replaced,
probably because there were no more—even in the empty
rooms of the disused wing. Claire reached for the shelf
on which a reserve candle always stood stuck in a saucer.
She lit the candle, unlocked the door and entered.

Her search in the gloomy vault by the light of the
flickering candle unexpectedly produced results. Acting
on a whim she took a step-ladder and examined the
innermost recesses of each bin; she was about half-way
through when the weak candle-light suddenly revealed
six squat bottles heavily coated with dust. Carefully she
scraped the grime from their labels and then uttered a
cry of delight at her discovery: she had found six pre-
war bottles of bonded Kentucky bourbon. This was a

find indeed. Their value lay not in their appeal to the handful of modest gentlefolk staying at the hotel at that moment: it was their trading value down in the village which caused her to gasp with pleasure. With their aid, and perhaps a crate of vintage wines for which the demand at the hotel was equally scant, she would be able to replenish more vital stocks in the bar.

She was just about to climb down from the ladder when she felt a pair of hands grasp her ankles. She let out a short scream and clutched the bars of the bin to prevent herself from falling. Turning, she saw the grinning face of Ludwig, the head waiter, raised to her in owlish satisfaction.

" That surprised you, didn't it? " he said with a guffaw.

" Let go of me, you fool," she said furiously.

He tried to take her in his arms as she reached the ground but she hit him on the face with the sharp point of her elbow, both hands being occupied in possession of two precious bottles.

The waiter stepped back crestfallen, rubbing his chin.

" What have you got there? " he demanded truculently, " the old man's private store of booze? "

" It's none of your business. Instead of standing there why don't you put those wandering hands of yours to some use? No, on second thoughts I don't trust you, I'd rather get them myself."

She climbed the steps again and fetched two more bottles, conscious from a prickling of her skin that he was behind her, ogling her legs.

" I don't really know what you're doing here in any case," she said over her shoulder. " You know the cellar's out of bounds for all staff——"

" You seem to forget, I'm the head waiter now. I ought to be allowed in here, as well as the old man's little piece of fluff."

She whirled on him, her body tense, anger darting like

flint-sparks from her eyes. The waiter stepped back, thoroughly alarmed.

" Listen, you jumped-up *commis*, if you ever say a grubby thing like that again I swear I'll claw your tongue out. And you're only the head waiter because all the other rogues walked out."

" And why did they walk out? " Ludwig jeered.

" Because they were all a bunch of spineless tip-chasers."

" Because Papa Borgwand couldn't pay them, you mean."

" They would have been paid," she said flatly.

The waiter gave a snort of derision.

" Yes, but when? " he said.

In silence she fetched the remaining two bottles.

" You don't imagine I'm going to stick this dump much longer, do you? " he went on, growing bolder at the success of his last shot. " If Borgwand doesn't cough up soon, *and* with the sort of salary I'm worth, then I'm off."

" Why don't you? There'd be no tears, I assure you."

" You couldn't manage without me."

" We'd have a very good try."

Ludwig laughed incredulously and stalked off.

Claire hunted by the light of the candle for some means of carrying the six valuable bottles, and eventually found a small crate containing empties.

She locked the cellar door behind her, snuffed the candle and went back via the kitchens, eager to tell her employer of her lucky find.

She entered the brightly-lit *Garde-Manger* where the director, clad now in white jacket and sweat scarf, was skilfully trussing chickens. She was on the point of speaking when something about the drawn look on the old man's face stopped her.

He looked up and said dryly:

" I've just sacked Ludwig. Or he resigned, I'm not sure which."

" Oh dear . . . what happened? "

" He demanded more money; and wanted it now."

" He's not worth it. And he wouldn't get it anywhere else."

" Quite. That is something I couldn't convince him of. He will have to find it out himself. But it does leave us rather shorthanded, even with so few guests as we have."

" I'll come into service for dinner," she said.

" Would you? I should be most grateful—just until we get a replacement, of course."

The old man and the young girl looked at each other, and a small smile of understanding passed between them. Both knew they would be unlikely to get hold of a new waiter at this stage of the season, but there was no point in mentioning it.

Then Claire held up the crate containing the six bottles for him to see. The old man's round little face brightened for an instant.

" Well I'll be blowed . . . I'd clean forgotten about them. I must have been saving them for a very special occasion—the end of the war, perhaps. What a pity we haven't any American guests to enjoy drinking them."

" I don't plan to put them in the bar. I'm going to bargain with them down in the village. May I telephone from the bureau? This is liable to be a delicate transaction."

He raised his eyebrows, then broke into a slow smile and handed her the keys to his office.

" I don't know what I'd do without you, my dear," he said.

He watched her go, forgetful for a moment of his work. It was always a pleasure merely to look at her walking. Then out of the corner of his eye he caught sight of the two Italian kitchen-hands sniggering to each other. They did not know how wrong they were in their cheap surmise, and there was no point in trying to tell them. You could not possibly explain to young Italian men that there were other emotions beside the animal instincts. He gave them a cold glare and they hastily got on with their work.

*   *   *

Ten minutes later Claire put down the phone, a smile of triumph lighting up her pretty features.

She had been right about the bargaining powers of half a dozen pre-war bottles of bonded Kentucky bourbon. By adding some vintage Bordeaux to the bait she had made a good exchange. Fresh supplies of brands which had been urgently necessary had been promised by the evening train from Grindelwald. The loss of Ludwig was forgotten. Already the future looked a bit rosier. What was needed now was the arrival of a few unexpected guests; it was Sunday, the week-end not quite at an end, so there was a faint chance of this. They were due for a spell of luck.

Glancing into the *Saal* before going up to her room she noticed several errors in the way the tables were laid. She corrected them quickly, chiding gently the two remaining waiters and making unashamed use of her feminine appeal in order not to send them off in a huff in the wake of Ludwig. Then she ran up to her room and changed into her best black dress.

It was cut a bit low at the neck (she mentally called it her " vamp costume ") but somehow she had the feeling that Fate needed only a jog in the ribs for something really fortunate to happen and thus seal the day. She fastened her two best silver clips to the corners of her bodice, brushed her short dark hair vigorously until it seemed to gleam and, after a moment's hesitation, added a touch of scent behind the ears. She glanced swiftly in the mirror and tried not to feel complacent at its reflection.

" *Fräulein* Claire, there's no two ways about it," she said to her reflection, " in this dress you're a hussy."

Outside in the corridor she nearly bumped into Gerda,

the chief chambermaid, arms laden with a pile of pillow-slips. They exchanged a quick friendly greeting and Claire was startled to hear the old lady give what could only be meant as a low wolf-whistle as their paths separated.

"Thank you, Gerda," she called gaily, and ran lightly down the stairs.

A tall, powerfully-built stranger stood at the reception desk, his back half-turned towards her as she passed through the foyer towards the bar. As she broke ice from the tray inside the bar-refrigerator she heard the stranger raise his voice. He was speaking High German with an accent—English or American, she was fairly certain. He was making inquiries in a manner that was rather domineering, and Heinrich, the concierge-cum-hall-porter, was doing his best to cope. Claire did not pay them very much attention, for arrogant guests were hardly something new.

The cubes of ice arranged in their silver bucket, she picked up a cloth and began polishing some of the glasses that had come inadequately cleaned from the office. As she did so she hastily checked her supplies of olives, maraschino cherries and lemons, and debated whether to switch on the lights behind the bar. It was a gloomy spot without lighting, and normally she switched them on at about this time; but none of the hotel guests appeared to be loitering nearby in search of an apéritif, so she resolved on economy.

Her mind still on the successful bargain she had struck over the telephone, it was some time before shreds of the conversation at the reception desk filtered through to her.

"I've been tramping all over this blasted valley for hours," the big man was saying irritably, "and yours is the last hotel on the list."

"You have been up to the Scheidegg, sir?" Heinrich asked.

" Yes, of course I have—and I phoned up to the hotel on the Jungfrau Joch. I give up. This just isn't my lucky day. Now what in heaven's name do I do with myself until the next train leaves back to Grindel-wald? "

Scarcely believing that it was she who was acting so boldly, Claire switched on all the bar lights with one quick movement and said:

" You could always have a drink, sir."

The stranger turned and stared arrogantly at her.

Claire felt herself blushing under his scrutiny. Even to American or British guests, who were by far the most informal and friendly hotel-guests in her experience, one did not speak in quite such a carefree manner as she had done. The " vamp costume " had indeed inspired her with rashness—or perhaps it was the unexpected discovery of the six bottles and the elation of striking a good bargain that had loosened her tongue.

The foreigner hesitated for a moment, then crossed the foyer with powerful strides and came up to the bar. He was well over six feet tall, broad-shouldered, handsome and expensively dressed. The hint of a smile lurked at the corners of his large, mobile, clean-shaven mouth. Slowly the smile broke wide over his face, revealing large white teeth of perfect symmetry.

" Well, now maybe I could do worse than that," he said in strangely musical English.

He stared boldly at her, making her uncomfortably conscious of the low square-cut bodice of her dress; but her job had inured her to this aspect of male behaviour and she composedly returned his gaze with a friendly smile.

" You wouldn't happen to have any whisky, would you, *Fräulein*? " he asked.

Without thinking her hand went out to the six bottles waiting to be collected and sent down to Grindelwald as her part of the exchange. The man standing at the bar followed her movement and stiffened perceptibly, as if unable to believe his eyes.

" No, it just isn't possible! " he almost breathed. Stretching out an immensely long arm he took hold of one of the bottles and inspected the label closely.

" Is it real? Are all six of them true, or a mirage? "

" Yes . . . at least, I think so."

" You think so! You mean you don't *know*? Then there's only one thing to do, isn't there? "

Before she could prevent him he had ripped the foil from the bottle's head, picked up a handy corkscrew and carefully drawn the cork. The damage was done now, so automatically Claire set a glass in front of him, and watched with surprise mingled with anger as the over-bearing stranger poured himself out a small measure.

For a moment he savoured the liquid with the theatrical care of a connoisseur. Then he set down his glass and turned on her a smile of huge contentment.

" Nectar of the gods, *Fräulein;* the real McCoy."

He swung a lanky leg over a bar stool and sat at the bar, his powerful head hunched between two hands; she shifted her position slightly, to increase the distance between them.

" To be honest with you, *Fräulein,* I was wondering why you called this seedy great mausoleum a Grand Hotel. But now I know. Would you have the kindness to write my name on this noble flask and reserve its contents entirely for my use? I shall be staying the night . . . that is, if you have a room free? "

Claire ignored the hint of sarcasm in his last remark and said that she was sure they had.

" Splendid. Here is a pen. Will you do the honours? The name is Chipperfield. P. Chipperfield. My friends call me Paddy. And your name, dear *Fräulein?* "

" Claire," she said, then forced herself to add a smile; they needed guests badly.

The journalist raised his glass as though proposing a

toast. He said, grinning broadly and showing once again his perfect teeth:

"To the owner of a green sports car—wherever and whoever he may be—who led me to Claire and to this godlike, golden liquid."

A small shiver ran down Claire's spine as she poured him a second measure.

CHAPTER III

DINNER in the semi-deserted dining-room proved, to Chipperfield's surprise, to be excellent. With the prospect ahead of him of a pleasant evening spent in the company of an astonishingly attractive young girl called Claire and an equally-astonishing bottle of pre-war Kentucky bourbon, the journalist found himself in prime humour. It was only fitting that at least a part of the day should hold out some promise, considering the fruitlessness that had preceded it. He no longer had much faith in the fantastic notion that had hit him in Interlaken. His imagination had led him on an absurd wild goose chase. There was about as much chance of his having really seen the Baron Mandoza in a seedy workers' café in the middle of Switzerland as there was of finding the Archbishop of Canterbury in an opium den.

He glanced at his watch. The call that he had placed to London should be through in a matter of minutes. By now, with the aid of their "spies" dotted all over Europe, Global Features Syndicate would have succeeded in tracing the errant playboy. Bernheim's news would set his mind completely at rest and leave the evening free for carefree dalliance and serious drinking. All work and no play, he reflected, could make Paddy a dull boy.

In the background above the faint murmur of conversation in the room he detected the shrill clangour of a telephone, and a moment later he saw Claire hurrying towards his table. He studied her appreciatively; that was some girl. What on earth was she doing in a tumbledown hotel at the back of beyond? She was like a gleaming pearl amongst ashes; she ought to be shown off against a smart setting—Ciro's, perhaps, or the Stork, some spot where she would be seen by people who counted. He had several connections in that sphere, he would be only too willing to help her, with no other motive in mind than a simple desire to give another fellow-being a helping hand up the ladder of success. Of course, if she showed signs of wishing to express her gratitude, as was sometimes the case. . . .

" Your call is through to London, sir," Claire announced breathlessly at his elbow.

He gave her a lingering smile, uncoiled himself from his chair and languidly rose to his feet; she would be impressed if he did not hurry to take the long-distance call.

" Where do I take it? " he asked.

She pointed out a public phone-box adjoining the bar. Chipperfield made a grimace of distaste.

" No chance of anything more comfortable and . . . er . . . private, I suppose? "

The girl hesitated for a second and then answered:

" I'm afraid we don't have phones in the rooms." She was about to add " any more," for they had once had them, until the telephone company ran out of patience.

" Is there perhaps one in your director's office? " the journalist asked. " I'm sure he wouldn't mind my using that for a few minutes—my call is of rather a private nature."

He scarcely gave her time to reply, but strode purposefully to the director's bureau, knocked on the door and entered. Claire quelled her irritation with the overriding logic that they needed guests, needed them badly.

*   *   *

Chipperfield locked the door of the empty office behind him and picked up the phone.

" That you, Bernie? Paddy here. What's the word on ' the phoney Baron '? "

Bernheim's voice crackled thinly over the wire. " Nothing very definite yet, I'm afraid. All right . . . all right, stop swearing, we've managed to trace him to a little village on the German-Austrian border, a place called Kufstein, not far from Salzburg."

" What the hell's he doing there? "

" The official word is still the same, he's on holiday."

" More likely sweating out a hangover. Is he alone? "

" He was—four days ago."

" Four days ago! You mean . . . what's happened since then? "

" He's disappeared into the blue."

Chipperfield swore expressively. " Fine pack of bloodhounds you've got. In other words you haven't got a clue where he is at this precise moment? "

" No, but keep your shirt on, we're working on it. You want me to float a story? How about ' Broken-hearted Baron disappears on mysterious holiday '? The papers would like it."

Chipperfield's brain raced in an effort to make a decision. Bernie was right, the popular press would snap it up. But he wasn't ready yet. It would be fatal to let even a hint of the story leak out till he had it tied up—always supposing there was a story.

" You still there? " Bernheim's anxious voice came. " What are you on to, Paddy? You got something hot? "

" I don't know yet. Listen, don't float it yet, Bernie, give me another twenty-four hours, and I'll let you know. O.K.? "

" Whatever you say, genius. Where are you phoning from, Geneva? "

" No, some crummy place called Alpiglen, in the Swiss Alps, up the hill from Grindelwald. You'll have to send somebody else along to Geneva till I can get there. In the meantime you can contact me at this joint . . . Grand Hotel Nordwand, Alpiglen . . . here's the number, note it down and call me back the moment you get anything definite on Mandoza."

He gave the number and rang off before Bernheim could shoot any more questions at him. He did not know the answers and there was no point in airing his wild theory until he had given it more substance.

He sat for some considerable time at the hotelier's desk, head in hands, trying to force his mind through the tangled puzzle to a possible solution. Some sixth sense, some deep-rooted reporter's intuition, urged him that a story hung in the air. Not everyone could sense it. A fool like John Bellman, for example, who was apparently dozing away on holiday in the near neighbourhood, wouldn't know a big story unless it got up and hit him between the eyes. That was why they had fired him from his desk in New York.

But he was Paddy Chipperfield, ace news-hound, trained to spot the unbelievable and splash it across the world's headlines one jump ahead of any other writer in the game. A tiny corner of his brain kept nagging him, telling him that he was already that one jump ahead; all he had to do was worry it until the tumblers clicked into position and turned the incredible into the possible.

He left the bureau and strode thoughtfully back to the bar, only one part of his mind on the crusty bottle of bourbon and its charming administrator that awaited him.

*   *   *

At approximately the same moment John Bellman left

the lounge of his hotel on the Kleine Scheidegg less than two miles away, crossed the foyer, bade the concierge and the hall porter good night and was on the point of taking the lift up to his room when he heard his name called.

He turned and saw one of the reception clerks making signs at him, his pale hands fluttering in the air like a Balinese dancer. He was a paunchy Swiss, sparse of hair and inclined to garrulity; for some reason he had taken a liking to Bellman and enjoyed cornering the latter in cosy chats whenever possible. Bellman did not dislike him, but he thought him rather an old woman. He waited patiently as the clerk paddled across the thickly-carpeted foyer, his face creased in a smile that was almost conspiratorial.

" Ah, Mr. Bellman sir, I thought you might like to know that a gentleman was here this evening, just before dinner, asking after you."

Bellman frowned. As far as he was aware there was no one in the district who knew him. Unless it was Chipperfield.

" Did he leave any message? "

" No sir."

" What did he look like? "

The clerk gave a fairly accurate description of the famous journalist, then added in his heavily discreet voice, " He only checked with us as to how long you have been staying here, sir. I thought you might like to know."

" Thank you very much. I had no idea that Mr. Chipperfield—that's the gentleman's name, I think — knew that I was staying here."

" Oh, he did not, sir. He was quite surprised to see your name on the guest list."

" Then he wasn't looking for me, then? "

" I should say definitely not, sir. And as soon as I told him you have been staying with us for over two weeks he seemed to lose interest. Almost, I might say, as if he were

relieved. He was much more anxious to find someone
else."

The clerk looked disappointed when Bellman failed to
ask who this might have been. But he was in no particular
mood to encourage further gossip, so he thanked the man
and took the lift to his room.

He undressed slowly, his thoughts toying idly with the
curious fact that the celebrated Torchbearer of Truth
appeared to be searching the Bernese Oberland for
something—or somebody. Judging from the questions
which the clerk had been called on to answer, it was
almost as if Chipperfield had been momentarily worried
about competition from rival journalists. The information given him by the clerk, that he, Bellman, had been
staying on holiday for some time in the area, appeared
to have put his mind at ease on that score.

It would be mildly interesting to discover just *what* it
was that had brought the powerful journalist up to the
mountains. He was hardly the type to have come for his
health or from a love of scenic beauty. What possible
" truth " could there be for the Torchbearer to unearth
amongst the alpine pastures, what could he find interesting enough to expose in a quiet village in the Alps?

Bellman got into bed but to his annoyance found that
the incident would give him no peace. Eventually he
switched on the bedside light and phoned down to the
reception desk, knowing how much his friend the clerk
would enjoy imparting further discreet information.

The clerk's voice purred over the phone with ill-
concealed pleasure: " What was the gentleman looking
for, Mr. Bellman? Yes, I think I can tell you that. He
asked me if we had staying with us, or if I had seen, a tall
fair man speaking German with a slight accent, possibly
wearing black-rimmed sun glasses."

Bellman could scarcely restrain a laugh.

" There must be hundreds of people on the Scheidegg
who answer to that description."

" That's what I told him, Mr. Bellman sir, but he was very insistent. He had a fixed idea that the person in question might have driven up here in a green sports car with a German licence plate, but of course I told him that was impossible; as you know, there is no motor-road up to the Scheidegg."

Bellman sat upright in bed, a brief image flickering on to the screen of memory.

" Would you say that bit again . . . about the sports car? "

The clerk repeated his message.

" Thank you," Bellman said, " you've been very helpful. Good night."

" Good night, sir. You can always rely upon me, sir, at any time."

Bellman thanked him again and hung up.

His curiosity was now aroused. The incident was developing in rather an intriguing fashion. It was true that he was still on holiday, but if one of the world's most forceful reporters was hounding out a story right under his nose, it would be interesting to discover what that story was.

In one sense, he was even a step ahead of his rival. He might not know whom the object of Chipperfield's search was, nor why that person had to be found, but he did know where he was likely to be found. On his way up from Grindelwald in the train that afternoon he had caught a quick glimpse of a green sports car parked behind a hedge near a smoke-blackened chalet. The chalet, which had struck him as poor and rather neglected, did not have a garage, so when a thin woman dressed in black had come out and covered the bonnet with a rug, he had taken it as a normal precaution against the cold of the night. But the action of throwing the blanket over the bonnet had drawn his attention for a moment to its number plate. A large black D on a white shield had told him it was German. The train had climbed slowly the gradient towards Alpiglen and he had given the matter no further thought.

Now it came back to him, with significant clarity. As he switched off the bedside light he resolved that if he had nothing better to do on the morrow, it might not be a bad plan to take a stroll down to the chalet and engage its owner in a little friendly conversation.

*   *   *

Chipperfield sat at the bar, ignoring the small group of guests who were keeping Claire spasmodically occupied. There would be time enough for intimate conversation later, when the old crones had toddled off to bed. The girl was on ice anyway, she could hardly run away. He lit a cigarette and let his thoughts circle once more around the puzzle of Wendelin Mandoza.

If Bernheim's information was correct, as it usually was, the sad young Baron had driven incognito from the Rhineland four days earlier to a small village on the German-Austrian frontier, destination and purpose unknown. He had apparently been unaccompanied. This did not mean that the possibility of a secret rendezvous with some between-divorces film star or famous Parisian mannequin was entirely ruled out, but apart from a rumour that the Baron had been consoling himself with the attentions of a beautiful model named Jasmine, of which he had been unable to get confirmation, Chipperfield had nothing to go on as far as that line of speculation was concerned. In fact there had been remarkably little publicity about Mandoza for some weeks, which in itself was very strange.

Chipperfield had seen them come and go, the names that made the headlines, and he knew one thing: once a man or woman had savoured the sweet taste of being in the public eye, had blinked at the flash-bulbs and seen their names in a chain of newspaper gossip columns, they became trapped. Like an animal trained on only one diet, they soon found they could not do without it. They would rather die than no longer be courted, reported, criticised and observed. Least of all " the phoney Baron." If once during the years of fame Mandoza had failed to catch the public eye for more than a week or two, had failed to have his presence reported at this or that fashionable spot, then he had committed some extravagance or minor infringement of the law—fast driving, or punching a head waiter—which had brought him immediately into the news once more. Editors loved him, for the simple reason that the great bulk of the public never grew tired of him.

Yet now Mandoza had slipped quietly from his obscure post in Bonn, driven without word to anyone down to the Austrian border, and taken apparent pains to surround himself in impenetrable obscurity. It was a story in itself, and Chipperfield would have told the syndicate to let it run, were it not for the brief tantalising glimpse he had caught of a profile against a ground-glass screen that lunchtime.

What was the name of that village Bernheim had mentioned . . . Kufstein. Kufstein and Grindelwald. Was there a connection? What would anyone, be they socialite or plain man in the street, wish to do in those two insignificant villages? He had studied a map, seeking some kind of link between them. He had learnt nothing more than the bald fact that eight to ten hours' fast driving was all that separated them. From the geographical standpoint, viewed in terms of mileage and time, his original hunch, however, fantastic, was perfectly feasible.

What else had he to go on?

A packet of cigarettes, a car, and some money—all of them German. They did not prove anything. The man who ate the formidable meal in Interlaken could have been almost any tall, fair-haired and charming German tourist. But, it did not *dis*prove his theory. It could just

D

as easily have been the young Baron, en route from
Austria to Switzerland, from Kufstein to Grindelwald.

It all came back to the accuracy with which he had
reacted to that snap-second profile silhouette, and to the
unknown link which stretched invisibly between two
small Continental villages.

*   *   *

An hour later Claire was at last alone in the bar. His
opening remark after she had poured him a double
measure from his bottle more or less baffled her.

" Tell me, Claire, why do people come to Grindelwald?"

As she sought for an answer he added impatiently:

" Like they go to Nice for the sun, Africa for the
elephants, and so on. What does anyone come to
Grindelwald for? "

" For a holiday," she answered. " Ski-ing and winter
sports when the snow's here, and——"

" All right, a holiday; that's obvious. But is there
nothing else? No thermal baths, no sanatoria, no music
festivals, no intellectuals' get-togethers? Is there any
hunting? All right, don't laugh, I'm just exploring every
avenue . . . is there a gambling casino here? "

" No. There's one in Interlaken, but I think the highest
stake is two francs. You have to go outside the Swiss
border if you want to gamble."

" Yes, I know. Well, describe to me, spell it out as if
I were a child, exactly what people find to do with themselves here in the summer."

" Do? . . . well, just what anyone else does on holiday,
I suppose. They make excursions, some like to pick
flowers, take long walks along the mountain paths, have
picnics and so on. Then there's shopping in the village,
and swimming, and tennis, and of course, mountain-
climbing. But mostly people take trips on the different
railways and enjoy the scenery."

" It all sounds madly exciting," said Chipperfield with thinly-veiled sarcasm.

For a while he sipped his whisky in gloomy silence. It was quite out of the question to imagine the socialite Baron indulging in any of these humdrum pastimes.

He began to ply the girl with more intimate questions concerning herself, and tried to persuade her to take a drink with him, which she politely refused. After a short while Claire was relieved to hear a door shut and the familiar jingle of keys as the lock was turned. Papa Borgwand often possessed an uncanny knack of knowing when his presence was necessary or welcome at any point in his hotel. Claire was, by nature of her job, fairly experienced in coping with most types of guest, but all the same she had not much fancied a session alone in the deserted bar with this admittedly handsome but rather overpowering new guest.

The director came into the room, greeted Chipperfield and drew up a stool at the bar.

A worried old man, Chipperfield thought, and not without reason, if you took a good look at his crumbling hotel. He supposed it was expected of him to offer the hotelier a drink.

Borgwand demurred but the journalist insisted.

" Very well then, but you must allow me to stand the next round," Borgwand said. He wondered how much longer this new fellow was going to keep Claire up. She looked tired. No wonder, it was a long day she had, as long as his, and she was only a young girl.

" Tell me, Herr . . ." Chipperfield began.

" Borgwand," Claire supplied.

" Herr Borgwand, what does one find to do in Grindelwald, why does anyone come here in the first place? "

It was the director's turn to appear puzzled, till Claire in rapid dialect explained as much as she understood of the journalist's line of questioning.

Chipperfield listened carefully as the Swiss listed the attractions which the district had to offer. It scarcely differed from what the girl had told him.

When Borgwand had finished Chipperfield said:

" All right. Now here's another question. Ever heard of a village called Kufstein? It's somewhere near Salzburg, on the——"

" Yes of course, I know it," the hotelier interrupted.

" You know it? You've been there? "

" Yes. I would know it, or of it, anyway, whether I had been there or not. It happens to be connected with a sport that lies very dear to my heart."

" What sport is that? "

" Mountaineering."

" Is that so? Well now, that's very interesting. And in what way is Kufstein connected with——"

" It is the village from which one climbs in the *Wilde Kaiser.*"

" The what? "

" The Kaiser mountains. A particularly difficult and challenging range for all lovers of alpinism. It is a spot beloved by German climbers above all, for it is only a short distance away from Munich, where they are all keen climbers."

All at once, the tumblers began to click into place.

Chipperfield felt his pulse quicken, and unconsciously, until he realised the others were staring at him, he began pounding his glass gently on the bar-table. He said through clenched teeth:

" It couldn't be. It's impossible . . . much too far-fetched."

Borgwand motioned to Claire to pour out another round. He signed a chit for the drinks, handed it to the girl and then said to his guest:

" Are you interested in mountaineering at all? "

The journalist appeared not to have heard him, for he said:

" You say one goes to Kufstein in order to climb these Kaiser mountains: any particular one? "

" Not especially. It is more the area as a whole. They often refer to it as the climber's high school, because of its excellence as a training area for sheer rock climbs."

" Sheer rock climbs? Herr Borgwand, you grow rapidly more and more interesting. Tell me . . . Grindelwald is quite a place for climbing, I believe. Which mountain in particular does one come to Grindelwald for? "

The director exchanged a wry glance with Claire and they both smiled.

" There are many worthwhile tours, of course, but you will only get a biased answer from me, I'm afraid. Others would tell you about the Wetterhorn, the Schreckhorn, and of course the highest of them in these parts, the Finster——"

" Which mountain is tops with you, Herr Borgwand? " the journalist cut in harshly.

Borgwand paused, slightly taken aback by the man's abrupt tone of voice. Then he said simply:

" The Eiger."

Chipperfield's eyes narrowed, and when he spoke his voice was tense.

" That's the one they succeeded in climbing a few days ago, isn't it? What's the part people talk so much about? —the North Wall."

" That is correct. *Die Nordwand*. I named my hotel after it. In fact I built my hotel on the exact spot where it stands because of the Eiger North Wall. I have looked at that mountain night and day for twenty years and I honestly believe that there is no other like it. It is probably the most dangerous climb in the whole of the Alps."

" You interest me, Herr Borgwand, you interest me more than you will ever know," said Chipperfield tensely, his eyes strangely bright as though he were feeling the effect of a stimulant drug.

Claire looked at him curiously and said:

" Do you do much climbing yourself, Mr. Chipper-field? "

If he noticed her persistent refusal to use his Christian name, he showed no signs of it.

" Me? " he answered with a rough laugh, " Good God no, I'm a newspaperman, not a lunatic."

Claire flushed and glanced with embarrassment at her employer; Borgwand had flushed too, but made no comment.

" No sir, you'll never find these precious bones of mine preserved in ice down some glacier-crevasse. I've got much too healthy a regard for my own skin. But I *am* interested in people who are bitten by the bug—at least, certain people."

Borgwand said:

" In that case you must go to-morrow morning to the foot of the Eiger and have a talk with the two men who are there now. I'm fairly sure they plan to climb the North Wall in the next few days, before the weather breaks."

" Oh, I didn't know——" Claire began.

" Wait a moment! " Chipperfield cut in excitedly, " you say there are two men there *now*? Since when? "

" I saw them for the first time this afternoon through my binoculars."

" What did they look like? "

" It was hard to tell. One of them I recognised, a local guide by the name of Hans Albrecht."

" And the other one? "

" I could not see very well, on account of the trees."

" Was he tall or short? Dark or fair? " the journalist rapped out eagerly.

Borgwand shook his head, inwardly disturbed by the man's sudden, almost hysterical interest. He wondered if the journalist had had too much to drink. He was convinced of this a second later as the stranger slipped off his stool and gripped him by the coat-lapel, his voice taut with urgency:

" Come on, man, you must have got some idea, some
fleeting impression? "

" Whether he was dark or fair I couldn't say, he had his
back turned to me all the time. Once he stood up . . ."

" And? "

" Rather on the tall side, I should have said."

To his relief Chipperfield let go of his lapel and began
pacing the room. The two Swiss watched him with
concern. It was clear he had drunk too much.

" It can't wait till the morning," Chipperfield suddenly
snapped. " I must go now."

" Go? Go where? "

" To those two men, of course."

" Now? But it's pitch darkness outside. And they will
be sleeping."

" That doesn't matter. Lend me a torch. How far is it?
Ten minutes, twenty? "

" At least half an hour."

" But the damn' mountain's only a stone's throw away."

" Distances are deceptive. It is much farther than it
looks. I would not recommend it in the dark, especially
when you don't know the way."

" All right, who does? Get me a guide, I'll pay anything he asks. It's a matter of vital importance."

Borgwand looked at Claire and shook his head in
bewilderment. In more than thirty years of hotel life he
had never had a guest quite like this one.

" You could not get a guide at a time like this, no
matter what you offered to pay—unless there had been
an accident," the hotelier said. " Why don't you wait till
morning? "

Chipperfield threw his hands in the air and let out a
shout of despair.

" I keep telling you, it's vitally important, man. Good
grief, can't you get that in your head? "

Borgwand flushed. He needed guests, but not that
badly.

" I think you should go to bed," he said evenly.

" Go to bed? At a moment like this? You must be crazy. Wait, I've got it . . . *you* could take me. Yes, you! You know the way, you know better than anyone how to find them. You've been telling me that you've spent twenty years looking at that blasted mountain: all right, lead me to it! "

The hotelier slipped from his bar stool and shook his head stubbornly. He said:

" Mr. Chipperfield, I will do anything within reason for the guests of my house, I will serve them in any way I can; that is my job. But I will not disturb the sleep which those two men vitally need in order to build up their strength for the arduous task ahead of them."

Chipperfield gave a groan of despair and muttered, " Oh my God, ethics at this time of night."

" I regret. No doubt I sound pompous to you. I will willingly take you there in the morning. The men will still be there, do not worry. Claire, I think it is time we shut the bar."

The girl switched the lights off one by one, surprised to find that her hands were trembling slightly. It had been a strange scene, with a great many undertones which she had not understood. Mechanically she handed her employer the cash-box, but her eyes were on the rangy, powerful figure of the journalist, who was pacing the room once more like a caged beast. She was far from certain that he was drunk; if so, it was from some other stimulant than plain alcohol.

Chipperfield's brain was like a whirlpool. He had to find out who the second climber was. Every minute counted. By the morning someone else might have picked up the trail, and the startling story that had been his, his alone, would become world property within a few hours.

If he could only find out for certain now, he had at least a seven-hour start. On the face of things it was a wild notion, but the facts fitted. Mandoza had been traced four days earlier to a village famous for climbing—famous, above all, for sheer rock climbs. He must have gone there to limber up, to get into the required state of training before attempting something bigger. Then he had driven incognito into Switzerland, hired a local guide, and was now bent on undertaking the most dangerous climb in the whole of the Alps.

Why?

Why on earth would an elegant star from the ranks of High Society want to do such a crazy thing?

To draw attention to himself. The answer flashed across the journalist's brain with glaring certainty. It was just the sort of thing Mandoza would do. It was the action of a vainglorious man, a grandiloquent gesture flung in the face of his public, a gauntlet thrown at the feet of the queen he had wooed and lost. He could not do something small, it had to be grandiose.

And Borgwand, the maddening old fool, couldn't see what such a story right on his front doorstep could do for his bankrupt, decrepit hotel. It would become famous overnight: he, Chipperfield, could make it so.

The door to the director's bureau was ajar, light streaming from it. The journalist entered without knocking, shut the door behind him and started to speak.

Five minutes later the two men emerged. Their faces were set, and each carried a powerful torch. They made towards the steps out to the terrace. Claire watched them leave in blank surprise. She could not imagine what had passed between the two men to have made Papa Borgwand change his mind.

At the hotel entrance Borgwand paused, and though he was considerably shorter than his companion, he seemed somehow possessed of a new stature, a queer kind of dignity.

" I must remind you of our agreement, Mr. Chipperfield. I will lead you to the tent, but it is understood that you will in no way disturb the men in their sleep. If there are any signs of life, then you may do what you wish, but if they are asleep, you have given me your promise that you will not intrude until the morning. Is that quite clear? "

" Yes, yes, come on man, do stop pontificating, we haven't got all night."

CHAPTER IV

CHIPPERFIELD kicked at the remains of a camp fire and swore with concentrated fury.

" Too late! And all because you had to waste time sermonising about some asinine code of ethics. Half an hour earlier and we would have been in time."

Borgwand ignored the fuming journalist and craned his neck upwards, searching for some tiny speck of light that might reveal the whereabouts of the two men. Were they up there? It was by no means certain. Quite possibly they had abandoned their plans due to poor weather prospects, or had decided on an alternative route up the mountain.

If they had gone up, in pitch darkness, it was a bold but by no means foolhardy plan. At night the ice which covered the vertical face of the North Wall was less dangerous than by day; pitons held more securely, and there was no chance of a thaw unseating an avalanche or easing the daytime hail of rock, ice and loose stones which was one of the Eiger's greatest dangers. But a climb at night demanded two things: an intimate knowledge of the route, and a reliable lamp—for preference one fixed to the forehead like a miner's helmet, leaving the hands free for belaying and work with the ice-axe. It was some indication of this light which Borgwand was seeking, but he could see nothing. The huge black wall towered above them, soaring swiftly out of sight, a faint inky outline merging at no fixed point into the indigo, moonless sky. Any sound the climbers might have made was drowned by his companion's flow of curses and the scuffle of his movements as he poked about the deserted camp-site.

"Are you quite sure they were here?" Chipperfield snapped angrily for the tenth time.

"You can see the signs yourself."

"It could have been anybody."

"I'm quite sure of the spot. It has been used on other occasions by *Nordwandkandidaten*."

"Do all these lunatics start at night?"

"Many of them. Generally a little later than this, but always before dawn."

"Why? Isn't it safer to wait until daylight when you can see where you are going?"

"Not if you know the route." He added a brief explanation about the firmness of the ice during the cold night-hours.

"How long does the climb take?" Chipperfield asked.

"That depends. If it is successful, about two days is a fair average. Some have done it in less, but most have taken about that, and many have needed more. It depends on the weather and on the skill of the climbers."

He could have told the journalist a lot more, but it was hardly the time or place, and it was obvious that the man was not listening. He gave a grunt, as though he had discovered something. Borgwand shone his torch, and saw the journalist bend on one knee, lever up a heavy stone and begin poking amongst the refuse that had been neatly buried there. Suddenly Chipperfield gave a cry of satisfaction. He stumbled towards the hotelier, an object in his hand. It was a flattened piece of carton, pale brown in the amber light of their torches.

"Look, man! Astor cigarettes. Astor Filter. Made in Germany."

The crushed empty packet shook in the journalist's hand.

" It's a fairly common brand, on sale in Switzerland too," said Borgwand evenly. " Does it prove anything? "

" Yes, man, it's the last piece of evidence I needed. Now I'm sure! The man climbing that mountain is the Baron Mandoza."

" It seems a very slender thread to go on, but that is your business. Let us return to the hotel and go to bed."

For answer Chipperfield thumped him across the back and shouted:

" Go to bed, man? Not on your life! The day's work has just begun: yours and mine. We're seven hours ahead of the rest of the world, at the very least, and we're going to use those hours up to the hilt."

*   *   *

Claire had waited up for them. She brought them coffee in the director's bureau; Borgwand thanked her and insisted that she went to bed.

" Mr. Chipperfield promises us a heavy day to-morrow, dear. Get some sleep."

" Get all the sleep you can, *Fräulein*," Chipperfield added. " You won't get much during the next few days, I assure you."

The girl gave him a puzzled look and left the room.

" What makes you so sure? " Borgwand asked.

The journalist banged the desk with the flat of his hand, then reached for the whisky bottle and topped up his coffee. His eyes gleamed like a man with fever, and his face was flushed.

" Because this is my profession, the profession I understand, in the same way that you know about food and wine and all the tricks of your trade. This is going to be a big story, Herr Borgwand, very big indeed."

" Is it so important that a man tries to climb a mountain? "

Chipperfield grinned, baring his perfect white teeth.

" What mountain, Herr Borgwand? And what man? There's the difference. You've told me yourself, the Eiger North Wall has killed more men than any other mountain——"

" I only said it had claimed a lot of lives," protested the hotelier. " I didn't say anything about——"

"Details, Herr Borgwand, details for petty-minded pedants. The Eiger's a killer mountain, a murderous mountain . . . that's a good line, maybe I can use that. And the man who's climbing it? Number One on the sob-stuff hit parade: the handsome young Baron, scion of an ancient European family, darling of society, the lover who lost a queen and is now seeking to find his soul on the cruel face of Murder Mountain. Don't you see, man, it's got everything! "

Borgwand said, without looking up:

" Including the truth? "

Chipperfield shot the old man a sharp glance and frowned with irritation.

" Don't you think it's a bit late for weighty philosophy?"

The hotelier was silent for a moment before replying. Then he looked his guest in the eyes and said quietly:

" I didn't mean it that way, though it is an aspect perhaps worth considering. What I meant was, are you sure of your facts? From what you have told me, it does not seem to me that you have very much to go upon."

" I'll chance it. In my profession you take a risk every time you put pen to paper. Write that Princess Margaret wore a red hat to some wedding or other and you get several hundred letters telling you the hat was pink. But it doesn't matter; it's not the piddling little details that count, it's the big truths that we go after, the stories that stir the hearts of men. And women."

" Well, of course, it's your affair what name you give to the man you've been hunting all day for. But I must warn you, it is by no means certain that those two men have begun to climb the North Wall. There was nothing at that abandoned camp-site to prove which way they went when they packed up their tent."

" You mean——"

" They might have changed their plans."

" Why? They get scared? "

Borgwand frowned with distaste.

" You have a lot to learn about the mentality of mountaineers, Mr. Chipperfield. No, there might have been sudden illness, or an impending change in the weather—I don't know, I did not have a chance to listen to the forecast."

" The weather looks settled enough."

" I am not so sure. It has held now for two weeks, but otherwise it has been a bad year. This may be the only really good spell of the whole season. I personally doubt if it will hold much longer."

" O.K., we'll play it your way. I say it's the Baron all right, but you say he's not definitely on the mountain yet. But we should know by first light, shouldn't we? "

" If there are no clouds, yes. The Eiger is one of the few mountains in the world where one can watch the climbers cutting their steps one by one up to the very peak."

" With the naked eye? "

" No. But with the aid of binoculars, or the big tele-scope on my terrace."

" Right. Now here's what you do. Buy up every pair of binoculars in the district. Double the price of using your telescope, and——"

" What are you talking about? " Borgwand interrupted. " The telescope is free, for the use of all my guests."

" *Was* free, Herr Borgwand. From to-morrow on-wards it costs plenty. They'll pay a pound a minute for its use once they learn who it is up there. The next step: double the price of your rooms. Get in more staff. Treble the prices at your bar—there'll be a bunch of hard-drinking newspapermen descending on this joint within twenty-four hours, and scores of sensation-hungry tourists eager to use your hotel as a grandstand. You could even charge an entrance fee for the use of the terrace out there, with easy chairs at extra cost. Rooms with balconies facing the North Wall will be twice the price of others, naturally. Borgwand, you're on the rocks with this hotel—don't try to deny it, a blind man can see the place is falling to bits; but with my help you can get it on its feet again. I'll plaster the name of this hotel all round the world. It will be on the by-line of every article I write, and I write for millions. I'll bring you more publicity than you ever dreamed of, scot-free, and you'll never look back, even after the story is over."

Chipperfield paused for breath, his face flushed with excitement.

Borgwand said coldly, " And my contribution to this astonishing nightmare you are suggesting? "

The journalist burst out laughing.

" Good for you. You weren't born yesterday. All right, it's not so bad, in fact your side of things is very simple. Get your hotel ready, get everything on top line . . . staff, food, and so on, all ready for the word go. And just one little favour to me: give me the twenty-four hour use—the monopoly you understand?—of your private telephone. Let the latecomers quarrel over the public call-box. I want this phone here, and I want it all the time, any time of the day or night. I'll pay for all my calls, don't worry. Most of them will be long-distance, so that's only fair. But I want that phone."

The journalist stood up, and then added:

" One more thing. I want to charter a small private aeroplane to-morrow. You can tell me how to get hold of a pilot."

He watched with enjoyment as the hotelier's eyes widened at his request. He gave a short, rough laugh and said:

" Never mind what for, just get me a plane, no matter

what the cost. Round about midday would be suitable,
if you can arrange it."

The old man rose wearily to his feet. He felt desperately the need of sleep, and the chance to digest some of the
astonishing things he had heard that night. At the door
he turned and said:

" I have a feeling I am not going to like this affair, Mr.
Chipperfield. There seems to be something . . . unhealthy about it. Of course I cannot stop you writing for
your newspapers——"

" You cannot, Herr Borgwand, that you cannot," said
the journalist smoothly, a hint of menace in his voice.

" I am a desperate man, near bankruptcy as you have
already guessed, so I shall be glad of any increase in trade
that your articles may bring me. But I want to make one
thing quite clear: I will co-operate with you to the best
of my ability, I will continue to run my hotel and to offer
hospitality to anyone who seeks it. But I will not be
swayed into doing anything which I consider . . . indecent.
Good night."

" Pontificating ass," muttered Chipperfield to his back,
then reached for the phone which had begun ringing.

" That you, Bernie? I know, I know, a godawful hour
to haul you out of your pit, et cetera, but wait till you hear
this. Grab a pencil . . . come on, man, rub the sleep out of
your eyes . . . you ready? . . . right, here's the headline,
and I want front page treatment: ' Socialite Baron
defies death on Murder Mountain.' Got that? Yes, it's
true . . . the Eiger, right across the fields from where I'm
sitting. Here's the story . . ."

When he had finished dictating he listened impatiently
to the other man's startled comments, then cut in:

" I know it's a risk, but I'm willing to take it on my own
neck. You've said yourself nobody knows where the
Baron is. I say he's here, right under my nose, I'm dead
certain I saw him in Interlaken this morning. There's
only one thing, Bernie: hold the piece for another . . ."

he glanced at his watch, " another six hours or so. If you don't hear from me by then, let it run. Yep, London, New York, Germany, the whole works. I want Number One treatment, Bernie, this could be the story of the year. So long."

Replacing the phone he poured himself another drink and gulped it down. Then he wrenched the hotelier's typewriter towards him and began drawing up his plans for the coming battle.

*   *   *

Of the three men most directly concerned with the events of the following day only John Bellman slept well. Chipperfield worked through until shortly before dawn, having discovered where spare supplies of coffee and an electric percolator were to be found. Klaus Borgwand spent an uneasy night tossing and turning in his bed, his brain a vortex of conflicting emotions. He needed several good hours sleep each night, a fact which several worried doctors had told him; the knowledge seemed only to aggravate the tautness of his nerves and muscles.

But Bellman slept the sleep of the just and awoke early. Gazing out of his window, which normally commanded a magnificent view of the Mönch and Jungfrau, he thought he detected a pending change in the weather. The mountains were the colour of steel. The skies were uniformly dull and over towards the Lauterbrunnen valley he saw clouds forming with a greyness that threatened rain.

Glancing at his watch he saw that if he hurried over breakfast he could just catch an early train down to the Grindelwald valley. He would go as far as Grund station, then climb back from there and see if he could find the large black chalet where the green sports car had been parked.

He caught the train with a few minutes to spare. As it

descended towards Alpiglen he glanced across the desolate ground to his left and detected two figures standing on the terrace of the Grand Hotel Nordwand half a mile away. One of them was engaged in peering through a large telescope mounted on a stand, apparently trained on the vast mountain which towered directly above Alpiglen— the Eiger, he realised. There seemed to Bellman to be something vaguely familiar about the second figure on the terrace; perhaps because the famous journalist occupied a front place in his mind at that moment, it struck him that the second, taller figure could easily have been Chipperfield. It was difficult to tell at that distance, and he dismissed the idea as improbable; wherever the Torchbearer had spent the night, it was hardly likely to have been in that somewhat derelict-looking palace.

Reaching Grund station at the bottom of the valley without having been able to identify the large black chalet, Bellman alighted, recrossed the Lütschine river and began climbing by a narrow road back in the direction of Alpiglen. Shortly before the road petered out he noticed a path that branched left towards the railway. It was a stiff climb, and he rested several times, for there seemed no particular need to hurry. It would of course be interesting to know why Chipperfield should be searching so energetically for the owner of a green sports car, but he doubted if the information, should he discover it, would prove valuable in any way. It was only mild curiosity, and want of anything better to do, that had prompted him to this early-morning jaunt.

After perhaps half an hour he found the black chalet. It was connected to the road that had petered out by a rough cart track; tyre-marks were still visible in the soft earth.

The chalet was a large, smoke-blackened wood building, badly in need of repair. It had an air not merely of age and poverty but of neglect, which, amongst Swiss peasants, was unusual. There were no curtains, no window-boxes of scarlet geraniums, the shingles needed patching and the small vegetable patch which served as a garden was clotted thickly with weeds. At the bottom of this patch stood a clump of beeches largely concealing a green car with a rug thrown over its bonnet. The car had been moved, but it was undoubtedly the same one. The beech trees obscured it from all sides except from where Bellman was now standing. Perhaps, he reflected, that was why Chipperfield had not seen it from the train when he had come up to the Scheidegg a few hours after Bellman on the previous afternoon. He eyed the car now with keen interest. He would have liked to have pulled the blanket away, to make quite sure, but he feared to do so in case he was seen by someone in the chalet.

He had to think up some plausible reason for knocking on the door. If they saw him snooping around and became suspicious he would learn nothing. It was a tricky situation. He did not even know what he was looking for. But he had not been a reporter for twenty years without having acquired some ingenuity in these matters.

He took a bumpy, stone path to the front door and knocked. He heard a scuffling, almost as if someone had hastily scrambled from a vantage post at one of the dark gaping windows, but no one came in answer to his knock. He tried again, louder. This time slipper-clad footsteps approached from within, a wooden bolt was shot free and the door creaked open a few inches. The combined stench of bad sanitation, washing and the odours of a thousand meals that is common to most alpine chalets met his nostrils.

" *Ja ?* " inquired a gruff, suspicious woman's voice.

" *Grüss Gott,* " he said, waiting for the door to open wider. It did, but only the fraction of an inch.

" What d'you want? " came the same unfriendly voice.

" I . . . er . . . I'm looking for a house—the *Verkehrs-*

verein in Grindelwald told me its name but I have lost the piece of paper they gave me."

" What house? "

" Er . . . well, one where I could stay for a few nights—on holiday, you understand."

" We don't take visitors," came the blunt reply, in awkward High German.

" I'm sorry, I must have the wrong place. They described the way to me very clearly. Isn't your name . . ." he thought quickly, it would have to be a name common to the district, " isn't your name Kaufmann? "

" *Nein.*" And she obviously had no intention of telling him what it was.

" Then perhaps you could direct me? There must be a chalet near here where they take visitors."

Grudgingly the woman opened the door and came slowly into view. She was thin, pasty-faced and middle-aged, and her wispy hair was tied in a tight bun that did nothing to relieve the stoniness of her features. She wore a stained apron over a threadbare black dress.

She gave him clipped directions to a nearby chalet and turned abruptly to go. Bellman realised he would have to take the bull by the horns. He had found out nothing, almost as if the woman had not intended him to, as if she had something to conceal. The people of the Bernese Oberland were normally friendliness itself, especially towards tourists.

He began to walk purposefully towards the green car half-hidden amongst the trees, saying:

" That's a smart car you have parked over there."

" It's none of your business! " the woman called out sharply behind him.

He quickened his pace and threw back the blanket, revealing a strange number plate, definitely not Swiss. At the rear of the car was a large white and black D. D for Deutschland. It was the same car all right.

The woman stumbled towards him, shouting angrily.

" You leave that alone, it's none of your business."

Bellman replaced the rug, disliking the ugly scene but refusing to let the matter drop now that it had developed so strangely.

" I must apologise, *gnädige Frau*, I was only checking up; you see, a friend of mine owns a car like this and I was wondering if it could be his."

She glared at him with disbelief, anger pointing two red flecks in her pasty cheeks.

" You couldn't tell me where I am likely to find the owner of this car, could you? " he asked, striving to keep his voice gentle and polite.

" *Nein*," was the curt reply.

They wheeled as a voice spoke in English behind them. " *But I think I can.*"

Bellman stared incredulously at Paddy Chipperfield standing a few yards away, a menacing smile lurking at the corners of his mouth.

" *Nicht wahr, Frau Albrecht*," he said in German, " the owner of this car is off for the day, climbing mountains? "

The woman jerked backwards as though she had been struck by a blow.

" I don't know. I know nothing," she muttered.

" But your husband Hans knows, doesn't he? "

" My husband is not at home."

" Of course not. How could he be, when I've just been watching him through the telescope scrambling up the North Wall of the Eiger? "

The woman appeared lost in confusion. Eventually she stuttered lamely, " A guide has to earn his living."

" But of course, my dear *Frau* Albrecht. Even an expelled guide. But I have not come about him, and don't worry, I shall not breathe a word to anyone that he has taken a client on to the North Wall . . . that is, provided you are co-operative and tell me the name of the man your husband has with him. Wait! It is not something for the ears of everybody. Mr. Bellman here was just leaving, weren't you, old man? "

The woman spoke before he could answer.

" I don't know who it is. Hans wouldn't tell me."

" Oh, come now," Chipperfield said, " you must have a pretty shrewd idea? No? Then perhaps this will help your memory."

He opened his wallet and took out a five-franc note.

The woman turned on him with sudden ferocity.

" Keep your filthy money! You're wasting your time, both of you. I don't know who my husband's client is, and if I did I wouldn't tell you. Now get out of here and leave me alone! "

" Just a moment, don't be so hasty," Chipperfield cut in, " Perhaps I am willing to believe you when you deny knowing this climber's name—but surely you can tell me what he looked like, when he came, and so on? "

" I never saw him. It was all arranged behind my back. Hans knew I would be against his going, no matter what the price was. When I saw what he was up to I tried to stop him, but he said we needed the money. That's all I know. Now *in Gotts Namä* leave me alone."

She turned back along the path and slammed the chalet door behind her.

The two men stood looking at each other in a silence broken only by the bellowing of a distant cow.

Bellman was at a loss for words. Too much had been revealed, or half-revealed, during the bitter altercation for him to have grasped the significance of each point in one flash. He needed time to sort it all out.

Chipperfield lit a cigarette and said with a cynical smile:

" Well, well, if it isn't Little Tommy Tittlemouse. I'd never have thought you'd be the first on the scene."

" What precisely does that mean? " Bellman asked.

" Oh come, you know the rhyme, surely?——

> " He caught fishes
>   In other men's ditches."

Bellman answered acidly, " I didn't see any sign saying
' Fishing Prohibited: Switzerland belongs to P. Chipperfield! ' "

" Then you must look closer next time, old man. So
long. Don't work too hard."

He gave the sports car a brief but careful inspection,
noted its licence number and strode out of sight, whistling
contentedly.

*   *   *

Klaus Borgwand came into his bureau—it was absurd,
he was already beginning to feel that he ought to tap on
his own door before entering—and watched Chipperfield at work, heavy fingers flying with unexpected dexterity over the typewriter keys. Not for the first time since
the thrusting, heavily-built journalist had marched into
his hotel, he felt a twinge of misgiving, almost fear, as he
looked at him. The man reminded him of the Hindu
idol Juggernaut, crushing all before him as he pressed
ruthlessly down his path.

He quelled his misgivings and tried to look on the
bright side of things. Already seven newspapers had
cabled for rooms for their correspondents, proof that the
article Chipperfield had telephoned the previous night
had attracted immediate attention in several countries.
A small knot of curious tourists was sitting on his terrace
drinking coffee and watching from time to time (without
charge) through the giant telescope the slow progress of
the climbers up the North Wall: many of them would
stay to lunch and some had even inquired about accom-
modation for the night. Business was picking up, and
only he knew how essential that was. The journalist's
high-sounding speech of the previous evening seemed to

contain an element of accurate prophecy. But still he did not like the flavour of the whole affair.

Chipperfield finished typing and ripped the sheet from the machine.

"Take a look at that," he said, grinning up at the hotelier.

Borgwand took the piece of paper. It was headed with the date, and the name of his hotel—misspelt, he noticed. He read:

"In a sweet little olde-world chalet garlanded with flowers, not a stone's throw from the sumptuous hotel where I am staying, I have just experienced one of the most harrowing interviews of my career. I have been speaking to a pretty, tear-stained little woman with nervous white hands, a woman distraught with worry. Her name is Louise Albrecht. Even whilst she was talking to me, those bright, tearful eyes would stray every so often upward at the cruel face of Murder Mountain where her husband, one-time crack guide, Hans Albrecht, is risking his life at this precise moment. Biting her lips to force back the sobs, she told me: ' I begged him not to go, I begged him on my bended knees before Almighty God, but I could not hold him back. The call of the North Wall was too powerful, he said, as he kissed the children good-bye and in the first light of dawn . . .' "

Borgwand read no more. He could not imagine the stolid and far from pretty *Frau* Albrecht behaving in this fashion, and there were at least half a dozen factual errors in the report, but he contented himself with remarking dryly:

"You have a remarkably powerful arm if you can throw a stone from here to Albrecht's home, it's at least two miles away."

Chipperfield beamed a large, artificial smile at him.

" Petty details, my dear Borgwand. I've already told you they don't matter. My task is to stir the reader's heart. He wants to feel that he *knows* that ugly old trout —what's her name—Albrecht; knows her and can take part in her despair, suffer her agony . . . at comfortable second-hand, of course.

" Now then, if my call to London doesn't come through before I leave, I should be more than grateful if you would despatch this for me: you speak admirable English, I'm sure you will have no trouble. Tell me, how's business? Things are looking up, eh? I promised you they would. And this is only the beginning, by to-morrow you'll be swept off your feet. Now I must be off to the airfield. Sure you've got everything lined up? "

The old man nodded stolidly, and flinched as the hefty journalist smote him between the shoulder-blades.

" Cheer up, dear fellow. You've got your head above water already, soon you'll be swimming—positively swimming." He strode out of the office and slammed the door.

Borgwand was still standing at his desk sunk in a gloomy study when Claire knocked and entered. He asked immediately:

" How are they coming on? "

She knew what he was referring to. One half of his mind was on the hotel and its administration, the other half with the two men on the Eiger. It was always the same whenever an attempt on the North Wall was being made.

" Very fast indeed, I should say," she answered. " They are about half-way up the first icefield, you can see them cutting steps."

He nodded. They were indeed making good progress. Albrecht knew his craft, and evidently the client roped to him was no dead weight or they would not have been able to cross the Hinterstoisser traverse successfully during the hours of first light.

" Does Mr. Chipperfield still believe it is this Baron something-or-other? " Claire asked.

" Apparently. Though he doesn't seem to have got much out of *Frau* Albrecht this morning."

Borgwand had confided in the girl what was going on, after he and the journalist had spotted the climbers soon after dawn through the big telescope. The journalist had in fact forbidden him to talk about it to anyone, but the hotelier knew he could rely on Claire's discretion.

" I thought Mr. Chipperfield knew what this Baron looks like? Wasn't the telescope enough for him to be quite sure? "

" You could tell which was which, that was all. I know Albrecht's build, and the other man is somewhat taller. But both men are wearing helmets and goggles, and of course their backs are turned towards us most of the time. It was quite impossible to pick out faces. To tell the truth I don't think Chipperfield has anything more to go on than before, but he seems determined to stick to his theory."

He switched his mind back to the hotel.

" How many for lunch, do you guess? "

Claire gave him her estimate.

" As many as that? Has the extra staff turned up? "

" Some of them." She gave him details.

" Good," he said at length. " Our friend Mr. Chipperfield won't be in to lunch, by the way. He's gone down to the airfield at Interlaken to pick up a private aeroplane."

" Whatever for? "

" He did not tell me, but I have an idea we shall know before long."

CHAPTER V

As JOHN Bellman left his hotel on the Scheidegg and turned down the path towards the Hotel Nordwand at Alpiglen, his mind was only partly on the coming clash with Chipperfield. It was a sour trick of fate that had thrown him once more into conflict with his old enemy— almost as if he were being offered a return bout, a chance to avenge the defeat which he had suffered at Chipperfield's hands in New York. The setting was in sharp contrast, but the conflict was oddly similar. John Bellman was almost certain that the other man, for all his powerful connections and undoubted ability, had somehow got hold of a false story.

Mondial P.A., the press agency for whom he worked in Hamburg, was of the same opinion. Chipperfield's sensational despatch had broken that morning. His claim that the internationally-renowned young Baron was in Switzerland attempting to climb the North Wall of the Eiger had spread like wildfire through the press and radio circles of the world. But not everyone had accepted the story as solid fact. Hamburg was sceptical and told Bellman that a similarly reserved attitude was being taken by most of the responsible and authoritative newspapers. Usually reliable sources claimed that the Baron had been seen in Austria, driving south in the direction of Venice. It was thought that Chipperfield had somehow " got his wires crossed."

This much Bellman had learnt on the phone just before lunch, on his return from the uncomfortable interview with *Frau* Albrecht. Far from stealing other men's fishes, with which Chipperfield had bitingly taunted him that morning, Bellman was strongly inclined to question the true nature of the giant fish which his rival claimed to have caught. It was not a task which he anticipated with much pleasure. Though stubborn, he was not vindictive by nature, and on the previous occasion when he had crossed swords with the ruthless journalist it had cost him his job. But he had no choice. His agency wanted the facts, and there was only one way to get them: to tackle Chipperfield head-on.

He branched left and took a path that led towards the Grand Hotel Nordwand. Scattered herds of cows grazed on the soggy, close-cropped ground, the peaceful clonk of their bells adding a touch of charm to an otherwise gloomy scene. The skies were still overcast, but the early morning threat of rain had not developed.

A large cluster of tourists stood on the hotel terrace, and as he climbed the steps he heard the distant buzz of a light aircraft. Men and women around him began pointing excitedly, and a moment later he caught sight of a small red monoplane, reminiscent of the type used for army spotting during the war. Climbing steeply, it settled on course and seemed to head directly for the North Wall of the Eiger. Bellman watched it with puzzled interest, trying to divine its purpose as it buzzed like a small scarlet fly along the mighty girth of the mountain. It was hard to tell with the naked eye if the tiny aircraft was really as close to the grey-black face as it seemed.

He glanced enviously round him at those of the spectators equipped with binoculars. Then he noticed a pretty slim girl in a crisp white blouse and black pencil-skirt standing at the hotel entrance, a pair of field-glasses in her hands. The warm lines of her young face led him to approach and ask if he could borrow the glasses for a moment. She readily assented and he peered with new eyes at the minute red fly as it banked and turned in for a second run along the North Wall.

He focused the glasses on the two tiny figures, roped together one above the other, who were working their way

slowly up a vertical wall of snow or ice about half-way up
the gigantic face. A nearby spectator with the confident
voice of an expert remarked that the two climbers had put
more than half the second icefield behind them and must
have reached a height of over ten thousand feet.

Bellman watched with fascination, then lowered the
glasses. The pretty young girl had turned to a portly
round-faced elderly man at her side and was saying
something in dialect which Bellman failed to understand. He did however catch the phrase " *Herr Direktor*."
Returning the glasses with thanks to the girl, Bellman
said:

" Are they in trouble up there? "

The elderly man shook his head and answered politely:

" No, there's no sign of anything like that. I think the
aircraft is merely taking photographs."

" Taking photos! It seems to be flying dangerously
close."

" Yes: dangerous for the pilot and also for the
climbers."

Bellman looked at him sharply. He had not thought of
the latter aspect.

" You mean from the . . . slipstream? " He could not
think of the German word for slipstream so said it in
English. The young girl answered him, in English with a
charming accent.

" Any kind of distraction could be dangerous, sir. I am
surprised they are allowed to fly so near whilst the men
are climbing."

" Try explaining that to *Herr* Chipperfield," said the
elderly man at her side dryly. " I very much doubt if he
would be interested."

Bellman wheeled, surprised that the realisation had
not dawned on him before.

" Chipperfield? You mean he's in that plane? "

The couple nodded and seemed to look at him with
quickening interest.

" You know him, sir? " said the elderly man, whom he took to be the hotel director.

" Yes, I know him. Very well." Bellman answered grimly. " I actually came to ask him a few questions, but it appears I am too late."

" Did you hear the midday news on the radio? " asked the hotelier.

" No, but if you are referring to Mr. Chipperfield's remarkable theories about the Baron Mandoza, I have already heard them from another source. I am a reporter too."

" You don't think it is true, then . . . his story? "

" I'm not sure. That's what I wanted to talk to him about. Failing him, I'd like to talk to someone who knows the guide Hans Albrecht. His wife is not a very communicative type, I'm afraid."

" Perhaps I can be of service," the hotelier volunteered. " I cannot say I know him well, but I have lived for twenty years on these slopes and——"

" That would be fine, but are you sure you have the time? I have a lot of questions, though I'll try to be brief."

" The subject interests me very much; I will make the time. Would you like to come to my bureau and we can talk there in peace."

" That's very kind of you."

" Good. Claire, would you bring us some coffee when you have a spare moment? "

*   *   *

Twenty minutes later John Bellman was blessing the good fortune that had led him to the hotel. Herr Borgwand was able to tell him much that was valuable not only about Albrecht but also about the Eiger. The shelves behind his desk were lined with books on the subject; it was obviously his hobby-horse. Almost as interesting was the clear impression Bellman received that neither the hotelier nor the charming girl who brought them coffee were totally smitten by the charms of the celebrated Paddy Chipperfield.

"You understand my point of view, Mr. Bellman," Borgwand said. "Perhaps I have spoken too much about our mutual acquaintance and his strange theories. No doubt I am just a rather garrulous old man who ought to have learnt to be more discreet about his guests, but this is an exception. I tell you, I cannot help but feel uneasy about Mr. Chipperfield's methods. My house is open to anyone who wishes to stay here, of course, and business has been bad for a number of years. I shall be grateful for any increase in trade or publicity that comes my way—but I do not want it at *any* price. Mr. Chipperfield appears to think he can turn this hotel into some sort of ghastly carnival."

Bellman nodded. "I think we speak the same language, *Herr* Borgwand." He paused, and then switched back to the theme they had already briefly discussed.

"Tell me more about this mountain; what exactly is the tremendous appeal of the Eiger, why do they keep on trying to climb it? I know the North Wall is difficult, but you've said that other mountains present problems just as big?"

"Perhaps one has to be a mountaineer to understand its fascination," Borgwand answered. "It is not because the Eiger is particularly high. It is only half the height of Everest, and there are peaks higher right here in the Bernese Oberland."

"I wouldn't even say it's especially beautiful, would you? Not like the Matterhorn, or Kilimanjaro, or Fujiyama in Japan."

"Perhaps it is a combination of all the factors which the other mountains have in detail," the hotelier mused. "Thirteen thousand feet is certainly not . . . *winzig*. And it *is* beautiful, in rather a terrifying kind of way. There is

also no doubt about the appalling difficulty of the North
Wall itself. Even Everest does not possess a sheer face of
over six thousand feet in height."

"Yet they keep on trying, knowing full well the
danger they are running into. Why?"

"There you have part of the answer, I think. The pure
danger itself. Why do men want to fly to the moon, cross
the Antarctic by foot, scrape the bottom of the ocean in
submarines? The lure of adventure, the thrill of the unknown, heavily spiced with danger. It is a challenge
which man seems unable to resist. Dangerous though it is,
you cannot stop the young men from trying to scale the
North Wall, any more than you can forbid attempts at
the world's speed record. No matter how many are
killed, there will always be a newcomer who wants to try
—and a lot of onlookers who want to watch him succeed,
or fail."

"And normally you can't watch them, can you?
But you can see them on the north face of this mountain."

"Exactly . . . when the weather is clear. With most
mountains the climber gets lost from sight soon after he
has started. Here, because of the way nature has shaped
the land around us, one can actually follow the climber's
progress from start to finish. Maybe it is that factor that
has turned the North Wall into a kind of legend."

"A legend created by geography, a short but grim
history, and the power of the press. The newspapers
have had a share in it too, I'm inclined to think."

"Ah yes, the press. I am very glad to have made your
acquaintance, Mr. Bellman. Quite frankly, I was
beginning to get rather alarmed at what I believe is
called ' the power of the press,' after my introduction to
Mr. Chipperfield."

"It is a power that can be used for good or evil," said
Bellman simply. "Newspapers have righted a great
many injustices in their time, as well as bringing an in-

expensive form of entertainment and enlightenment to millions. In my experience there are very few reporters indeed like Paddy Chipperfield."

" I am more than relieved to hear it. Now, if I can be of any help please do not hesitate to call on me. I'm afraid I am long overdue in the kitchens. Good-bye, Mr. Bellman."

The two men shook hands and the hotelier politely showed Bellman to the door.

As he passed the reception desk he noticed the girl in the crisp white blouse and black skirt whom Borgwand had addressed as Claire. Without thinking, he surprised himself by saying:

" *Auf Wiedersehen, Fräulein*. Thank you for the coffee. I hope I shall see you again."

She answered him with a direct, friendly smile:

" That would be nice," she said.

Feeling somehow warmed by the slight incident, Bellman stepped briskly out on to the terrace where the small crowd of tourists was still chattering excitedly and jostling one another. The aircraft had flown off, but the two climbers remained an object of magnetic attraction. He heard several times the mention of Baron Mandoza's name; the news from the midday broadcast was spreading rapidly, it seemed.

On the whole the afternoon had begun well, Bellman thought, as he set out at a vigorous pace once more for the chalet of *Frau* Albrecht. He wondered if his luck would continue to hold, or if the pasty-faced woman would slam the door in his face again. Now that he knew the true story of her husband, told him by the hotelier, it might prove easier to engage her in conversation. Borgwand had told him that Albrecht had been expelled from the association of professional mountain guides not on grounds of incompetence—his reputation was in fact exceedingly high—but as a result of his tendency to over-charge for his services. The rules laid down in the *Bergführer-Reglement* were fairly strict on this point, and Albrecht had apparently overstepped the mark too often. Whilst the hotelier had not condoned this malpractice, he had been at pains to point out alleviating circumstances. Two of Albrecht's five children were in TB sanatoria. They had been there for many years, hopeless cases hovering perpetually between life and death, a constant drain on the poor family's resources. It was small wonder, Borgwand said, that the guide had been obsessed by a lust for money.

Armed with this intimate knowledge, and the understanding that came with it, Bellman thought he might be more fortunate in his second attempt to talk to the guide's wife. If she still failed to provide some definite clue as to the identity of the man climbing with her husband, and if Hamburg were unable to trace the licence number of the green sports car, then he would have to go farther back along the trail that had brought Paddy Chipperfield chasing up to Grindelwald. A reporter's job was a lot like a policeman's, he reflected: you knocked on a door, tipped your hat, asked some questions, tipped your hat and knocked on another door. For one minute of drama or revelation there were fifty-nine minutes of fatiguing routine. If you were lucky, one day you asked the right person the right question.

*   *   *

Chipperfield watched with ill-concealed impatience in the almost pitch-black room as the photographic negatives shimmered in the developer-tub, his nerves screwed to a fine point of tension. Each one of these negatives should be worth a small fortune. Reward came to he who took the most chances, to the man with the most initiative and drive. Within twenty-four hours photographs of the climbers would be ten a penny; every balcony and hill-top would be cluttered up with professional and amateur camera-men, some of them equipped with telescopic lenses and all the refinements of their trade. But these first shaky photos snapped from the open window of the Piper Cub at a height of ten thousand feet and a distance from the mountain face of two hundred feet would be unique. He had secured a world scoop and could name his own price.

" How much longer? " he barked impatiently at the dim figure working at the tub with the aid of a ghoulish green light.

" Any moment now, sir," was the composed reply.

" You said that three minutes ago."

There was a silence of several seconds. Time seemed to drag by as in a railway waiting-room. Chipperfield was convinced the photographer was drawing the process out, from a sheer desire to be awkward. Suddenly the man looked up and with a hint of excitement in his voice said:

" They are coming through now, sir."

The journalist jumped forward and watched with feverish interest as the first faint outlines began to evolve on the film. Half-tones of grey began to appear, white dissolved into black, outlines hardened, and then the image of two men roped together on a mountain side became clearly defined.

He had schooled himself not to expect too much, but he was unable to stifle the surge of disappointment that swept over him. Two men on a mountain, their backs to the camera; the leading figure broad and stockily-built, the second man below him taller and thinner: that was all. There was nothing to prove it was not the Baron Mandoza. And there was nothing to prove that it was.

Chipperfield swore bitterly for a few moments.

" I told that damn' fool of a pilot he wasn't flying close enough," he muttered through clenched teeth.

To the photographer he said:

" Is that the best you can do? Can't you get more definition? "

" The prints will be sharper, of course; and we can try blowing them up if you like, but I doubt if it will help a great deal. Actually, the more we enlarge the less definition we shall get."

" Try it, anyway."

" Certainly. They'll have to dry a bit before I can put them under the enlarger, would you like to wait outside? I'll tell you when everything's ready."

" Get a move on, for God's sake. Time is money in my business."

" And in mine, sir," was the smooth reply.

Chipperfield checked an angry retort and went into the office adjoining the developing room. The pilot who had flown him up to the Eiger was waiting. He asked eagerly:

" Any luck? "

" Not sharp enough. The definition's not there. We'll have to try again."

" You mean they are no good at all? "

" I didn't say that. They'll be good enough for the papers. But we were too far away. Next time we must fly in a lot closer to the wall."

" I went as close as I dared. The turbulence at that height amongst mountain valleys is highly dangerous."

" I'm aware of that," said the journalist curtly. " But next trip we fly closer or I get myself a new pilot—one with guts."

The pilot went a deep red and strode angrily to the door. Turning, he said:

" I have been flying for eleven years in the Alps. Apart from Hermann Geiger there isn't a man in the game who knows more or will risk more than I. I've logged thousands of hours, and not a single accident. I've dropped food to trapped climbers, landed many times on glaciers in snow-storms, brought out wounded and dead men. Nobody had ever thought it necessary to question my nerve until now."

"All right, all right, man," said Chipperfield as soothingly as he knew how, " maybe I spoke hastily. But I must insist, as the man who pays, on my right to give the orders. Just take me a few score feet closer to-morrow and I'll be happy. That's all I ask. I'll make it worth your while. If the pictures are sharp to-morrow you'll get a double bonus."

"It's not a question of money," said the Swiss icily.

"No, but it helps, doesn't it?" Chipperfield replied with a cynical smile. "We'll leave at dawn."

"That is too early. You cannot hope for good results in poor light. There's no point in taking off much before nine o'clock."

"Whatever you say, my dear fellow."

*   *   *

The negatives viewed through the enlarger revealed further details about the two mountaineers, but Chipperfield searched in vain for undeniable proof that it was the Baron.

Considerable detail of clothing showed up: both men were wearing grey crash helmets (as a protection against falling rock and ice), a kind of duffle or parka jacket, knee trousers tucked into long thick stockings, and heavy boots. It was even possible to see the spikes of the crampons lashed to their feet. Both men carried rucksacks and coils of rope looped over their shoulders. The lower figure appeared to be securing, whilst the leader was cutting steps with his axe in the sheer wall of ice. The men were roped together in the approved fashion, and there was nothing that the most expert eye could see to suggest that the second figure was an amateur.

Chipperfield peered for a long time through the enlarger. It was not what he had hoped for, but the shots were good all the same, and would fetch a pretty price. He gave careful instructions for the immediate despatch of prints to London and New York, climbed into his car and drove back up the Lütschine valley. At Zweilüt-schinen, where the road forks left for Grindelwald and right for Lauterbrunnen, he paused, then swung right. It would do no harm to establish a reliable contact in that valley; he might have need of a good legman who could be relied upon to watch the " back door " and tell him if anyone of interest came or left by the Wengernalp railway that connected Lauterbrunnen with the Kleine Scheidegg. At Lauterbrunnen station he phoned up to Borgwand and learned that nothing special had occurred during his absence. The climbers were making steady progress, and all seemed well.

His contacts in Lauterbrunnen assured, Chipperfield drove down to Zweilütschinen once more and turned right up the valley to Grindelwald. Here again he enlisted, for a suitable fee, the services of a sharp-witted resident who would act as his eyes in the village whilst he himself was isolated on the slopes near Alpiglen. It was a normal precaution which any general took when planning a cam-paign, though he doubted if such an idea would occur to a second-rater like Bellman.

Grindelwald seemed a lot fuller than on the previous afternoon when he had arrived. People stood in groups gazing towards the huge mountain, a few were watching from balconies and roof-tops with the aid of binoculars, and a small knot of experts crowded round the weather-forecasting barometer in the main street. The skies had remained overcast all day, but still the rain had not come. Chipperfield would have liked to have got a closer look at the small kiosk-shaped structure that housed barometer and other predicting devices, for he had realised that a marked deterioration in the weather could have telling effect on the whole story. But he disliked rubbing shoulders with a bunch of dull-witted tourists. Instead he contented himself with buying a large pile of newspapers at the station newsstand and scanning them eagerly as the train crawled slowly up towards the Scheidegg.

It was of course too early for his own report to have echoed back to the mountain village, but nevertheless he was pleased to note that several European newspapers with a later deadline had carried a mention of it in their midday editions. The demand for the photos he had obtained would be big, and so would their price.

He began composing in his mind the opening lines of the article he would file that evening when Bernie came through at the appointed time. Once that was behind him there was no reason why the rest of the evening should not be devoted to a little gentle dalliance with the desirable Claire who was, he trusted, awaiting him, a second bottle of finely matured bourbon at hand.

On the whole it was not a bad living, a journalist's, once you got to the top. There were few things in life that could rival the sweet taste of professional success and public fame.

*   *   *

Business was fairly brisk in the bar that evening. Chipperfield was unable to get Claire alone for any useful length of time. It was exasperating, but in fact he was himself too busy to have very much time to spare. The article describing the progress made by the two climbers during the day and his own flight alongside the mountain to obtain photographs, took a large part of the evening. There were several technical points which he decided to check with Klaus Borgwand, but the latter was worked off his feet and practically inaccessible. Borgwand however, when he finally succeeded in pinning him down, did tell him something interesting: it was his theory that the two climbers had made such excellent progress not only as a result of their evident skill, but also because a trail had been blazed for them by their pre-decessors of a few days earlier. At many points it might not have been necessary to cut fresh steps in the ice, which would have saved a great deal of time and energy; and there was a chance that the successful German-Austrian team had left behind a few pitons driven in the rock at difficult places. Pitons, he explained, were tough metal spikes which, when hammered into cracks in the rock, enabled a climber to fasten a snap-link and by passing his rope through the link, haul himself up or along sections of sheer or overhanging rock. If, as was sometimes the case, the three men of the previous week had left some of their pitons behind, the two men following up the classic route of ascent would be saved valuable time and ex-penditure of energy. The journalist brightened at the mention of this theory, since it lent weight to his claim that the North Wall was being scaled at a rapid rate by an amateur.

His article at last ready for dictation when the syndicate came through on the phone, he devoted himself to some careful thinking ahead.

As daylight faded the two climbers had last been observed approaching the *Bügeleisen*, a sharp bulge situated on the third icefield at a height of roughly eleven thousand feet. Here, it was thought, they would try to bivouac for the night. It was a spot that had been used for this purpose several times before. That left them with approximately two thousand feet to go; judging by their previous rate of climb it was thought that they might reach the summit, all being well, some time during the following afternoon.

Chipperfield would have given a great deal to be there at that precise moment. It would have been a superb scoop, to have been able to photograph the young Baron at the exact second of triumphal achievement. But the scant time left at his disposal made it impossible. The next best thing would be to try and fly past and photo-

graph the scene from the air. He would keep the pilot on
tap, after the morning's flight, in case this should prove
feasible. Failing that, it would be necessary to watch the
two men descending down the western ridge and judge
the best place to meet them and so secure the first story,
with pictures, before other newspapermen snatched at the
opportunity. Given the right type of persuasion it should
be possible to press the Baron into selling the exclusive
rights of his story—not only his account of *how* he had
scaled the dreaded North Wall but (and this was far more
important from the point of view of sales), *why* he had
done so. Chipperfield shaped in his mind some potential
headlines: " I did it for the queen I love " had a challenging ring about it, and " Rejected lover's daring gesture "
would make a nice-sub-heading. The weeklies and the
Sunday tabloids would lap it up.

Certainly the story was by no means over when the
Baron returned. By use of a little imagination and the
right press backing it could be stretched far longer than the
two or three days which the climb actually involved.
When you had a story as powerful as this it was a pity to
throw it away before all the angles had been exploited.
Chipperfield's only regret was that the climb did not take
longer, and that he had not managed to get word of the
venture during the days when Mandoza was training in
southern Germany. All in all, however, he had a great
many reasons to be satisfied with the way events had gone.

His feeling of well-being suffered a slight shock a few
moments later when, on coming out of Borgwand's office
and making for the bar where several newspaper correspondents were firmly fastened, he met John Bellman. He
ignored him, and, coming up to the bar, asked Claire in a
loud voice:

" Is that fellow staying here? I thought he was nicely
tucked away up on the Scheidegg? "

Claire was saved the necessity of a reply as Bellman, in
a quiet, carrying voice, answered:

" That fellow *is* tucked away on the Scheidegg. I merely dropped by for a drink. As far as I know you don't own this hotel yet, or this particular mountain."

" Keep away from me, Bellman. You're stepping on my toes. That could be dangerous," Chipperfield snarled, without bothering to turn round from his position at the bar.

Bellman advanced to a few paces behind his back, white-faced but cool. A hush had settled amongst the group of drinkers.

" It could be that your feet are too big; it's hard not to trip over them."

" Go blow your horn someplace else, Tittlemouse. And find your own story."

" A news-story belongs to no one man alone, Chipperfield. It belongs to anyone who wishes to report the truth. I'm not sure that includes you."

" What are you fumbling at? You got something you want to say? "

" Yes. An old cliché, one they may have taught you when you were reporting your first church bazaars: check your references."

" Pearls of wisdom from a has-been. You frighten me. Anything else? "

" No, just that. Check your references," Bellman said acidly, and left the room.

Chipperfield swore pithily and said to the silent correspondents:

" Fumbling fool. Give him the sinking of the *Titanic* and he'd be checking his references whilst the ship went down."

An American reporter named Wilson piped up:

" Just the same, Chipperfield, are you sure you got the good word on this wildcat notion of yours? A lot of folks don't reckon it's the Baron up there."

" Who *do* they think it is?—Marilyn Monroe? " he snapped.

The sally brought appreciative chuckles and Chipperfield ordered a round of drinks.

A few moments later Borgwand hurried into the room and murmured to Chipperfield that he was wanted on the phone. The hotelier glanced uneasily at the tough new clientele that had been arriving all afternoon and evening. He had been promised a " bunch of hard-drinking characters " and the prophecy was proving correct. They were certainly good for trade but he did not fancy the task of keeping them content with only one telephone at their disposal. It seemed to him that he heard a few muttered complaints as the famous journalist strode confidently off to take his call on the private line in his bureau.

Chipperfield closed the door of the director's office and picked up the phone.

" That you, Bernie? How's it going? Did you get the pictures? . . . I thought you'd think so . . . How about the price? . . . Not bad, not bad at all; I knew they'd fetch a nice figure. How's the story breaking? "

As he continued to listen the small smile that lingered habitually at the corners of his mouth gradually disappeared.

" That's how the land lies," Bernheim was saying. " They're fighting shy of it, both along the Street and in the States, Paddy boy. Most of 'em want more confirmation before they'll print it the way you want it."

Chipperfield blurted out an expletive. " What the hell do I have to do, lug 'em out here and shove their noses under the blessed mountain? What's holding them back? "

" Well, for one thing, Paddy, the licence number of that car. It doesn't tally. The car's registered down in Bavaria someplace—it's not the one Mandoza usually drives in Bonn."

" All right, so he's bought himself a new car, or hired

one—so what? That doesn't prove it isn't the 'phoney Baron'."

" No, but unfortunately it doesn't prove the opposite, either. Hold your horses, Paddy, things aren't all that bad. Most of the evening papers are running it, but it isn't the five-column lead we hoped for, that's all. They like the story, but no one wants to commit himself to the Baron angle. Listen, here's a sample:

' The mystery concerning the identity of the man who, accompanied by banned Swiss guide Hans Albrecht, is attempting the dangerous climb up the North Wall of the Eiger, still remains unsolved. A well-known journalist writing from the scene of the drama " (that's you, Paddy boy, but of course no credits from that stinking outfit)—" reports that it is the internationally-known socialite Baron Wendelin Mandoza who has suddenly, at this stage of a far from athletic career, turned alpine enthusiast. Authoritative sources however are sceptical. The young Baron was reliably reported a few days ago to be in southern Germany and more recently Vienna. No——' "

" Vienna! " Chipperfield shouted. " They must be mixing him up with Johann Strauss. Who wrote this miserable twaddle, Jane Austen or Thackeray? "

" Paddy boy, I've got to ask you, are you absolutely sure——? "

" Of course I am. The ' phoney Baron ' is up that mountain, believe you me."

" But isn't there any means of identifying him for certain? Can't you get hold of a really powerful telescope——"

" Bernie, you're being dense. The Baron's climbing with his face to the wall, in case you hadn't realised. All we can see is his back. And if we do get a side-view from time to time, that doesn't help much—he's wearing a crash-helmet and snow-goggles. You take it from me, that's Mandoza all right; I *know*, I saw him yesterday in Interlaken."

"I hope you're right. It's a damn' big risk we're taking."

"Who *does* this windbag reckon is up there?"

"Not many papers are willing to chance their arm. One of the press agencies has put out a feeler concerning a fellow named Stringberg. It seems he tried to climb the North Wall a couple of years back, and cracked up. Rescue parties hauled him out in the nick of time, after he'd been nearly frozen to death. When he could talk again, the first thing he said was 'I will return.' Swore he'd one day be back and conquer the mountain that had defeated him. Bit of a theatrical type, it seems. Naturally that didn't make him Number One on the popularity poll with the rescue team that had risked their necks to save him."

"Where do they get this load of bushwack from?"

"I was coming to that. The theory is, it's much more likely to be Stringberg on account of the cool reception he knew he'd get from the local boys if he tried again. Hence all the hush-hush stuff, slipping up to Grindelwald in secret, keeping clear of the hotels, hiring a banned guide, setting out at night, and all the rest of it."

"And would you mind telling me who's floating this cretinous yarn?"

"It came in from Hamburg, one of the agencies— Mondial, I think it is."

"Mondial!" Chipperfield yelled, his face red with anger, "Hell, that's that incompetent relic Bellman! I might have guessed he'd get hold of some cock-and-bull tale. What fool paper is running it?"

"It came in too late for the early issues, but some of the late editions have picked it up. I've heard it on the side that *The Times* plans to run it in the morning."

"Then you can tell old Auntie *Times* from me that they're on a dud story. Now then, fasten your seat belt, here's the real griff and I want you to sell it high, wide and handsome."

He began to dictate:

" Early this afternoon, whilst thousands watched from the valley below, I flew my single-seater plane along the cruel face of Murder Mountain, in an attempt to establish contact with the daring young Society Baron who, at this precise moment, is defying death on a vertical wall of ice more than one mile high . . ."

Five minutes later he had finished dictating. Slamming the phone down he made angrily for the bar. It was going to take a lot of hard liquor and plenty of co-operation from the desirable Claire to restore the good humour with which he had begun the evening.

*   *   *

Light rain was falling and the early morning skies were the colour of pewter as Chipperfield and the pilot made for the Piper Cub on the tarmac.

No word passed between them. From time to time the Swiss glanced anxiously at the heavy clouds drifting amongst the nearby mountains. He was inclined to doubt the wisdom of their flight, but after the sharp scene in the photographer's office of the previous afternoon he was not prepared to risk the journalist's biting scorn once more. It was more than apparent that his client was in sour humour. Sneaking a quick glimpse at his bruised cheek he could not help wondering if an unsuccessful affray with the fair sex did not have some bearing on the matter.

His surmise was in fact very near the truth. But Chipperfield had brushed the irritating debacle with Claire out of his mind. He had always prided himself on his ability swiftly to forget his failures, not nurse them as weaker men did. His thoughts were solely on the task ahead, on the vital necessity of obtaining clear photographs of the Baron, thus vindicating his reputation and destroying Bellman at one and the same time.

As they climbed into the tiny aircraft he tapped the pilot on the shoulder and said:

" Don't forget, I want to get real close to those boys. There'll be plenty in it for you if the pictures are sharp this time."

The pilot nodded coldly, his mouth clamped in a tight line. Fastening his seat belt he checked the instrument panel and gave the thumbs-up sign to the waiting mechanic. A moment later the engine sputtered into life. The chocks were pulled away and he taxied down the perimeter towards the runway, noting from the windsock that a stiff breeze was blowing even at ground level. Things were liable to be a bit bumpy at eleven thousand feet. This would not worry him very much, but it would be interesting to see how his passenger reacted.

He revved-up till he felt the tail start to lift, released the brakes and the machine sped forward. In a few hundred feet they were airborne. Circling the airstrip to gain height, he adjusted the trim tabs and headed up the valley of the Lütschine river, climbing steadily. The Jungfrau was blotted from view, and most of the surrounding great peaks were largely shrouded with cloud. There were sufficient gaps to make it worth while going on, but it was not the sort of weather he would have willingly chosen for such a difficult mission.

They ran into their first heavy turbulence as he banked slowly to starboard within view of Grindelwald. The light machine yawed sharply, lost height and was suddenly plucked upwards once more by some freak of wind. It was a foretaste of things to come, he knew; glancing over his shoulder, he tried to suppress a grim smile as he caught sight of his client's pale face and the small beads of sweat on his forehead.

The smooth green flank of the Scheidegg rose through patchy cloud below, swinging steeply towards Männlichen and the Lauberhorn peak. He eased back the stick to gain more height. The Jungfrau remained hidden, but the Mönch and the Eiger were only partly obscured by shreds of swiftly-moving *Wattebauch*—tufts of cloud that resembled cotton-wool pads. The altimeter needle flickered over the 3,000 metre line and continued to rise steadily. Behind him the heavily-built journalist had crammed his bulky frame into a corner of the cramped cockpit, his face glued to the window. Chipperfield was in the act of adjusting a pair of field-glasses just as the aircraft hit another pocket; a corner of the binoculars hit the Perspex window, jabbing their ends into the journalist's eyes. His stream of curses was drowned by the roar of the engine.

Suddenly Chipperfield pointed excitedly to the glistening black face of the Eiger which was rapidly drawing nearer. The pilot put out his hand for the binoculars, and keeping one hand on the controls, brought them into focus on the North Wall.

In a moment he had picked out the two men, roped together, working their way laboriously eastwards from the bulge of the *Bügeleisen*. They were approaching one of the most dangerous parts of the whole climb: the steep ledge known as the *Rampe*, which led to an exposed and near-vertical icefield called the Spider (on account of its curious web-like structure). Even in the few seconds that he observed them, he saw chutes of water sweeping down one of the Spider's channel-like ruts, drenching the two men with alarming force. He shuddered involuntarily and handed the glasses back to Chipperfield, concentrating on the task of levelling out for the run parallel to the mountain face. It was going to need every bit of his skill, and a portion of luck as well, if he was to fly close enough to the face to satisfy Chipperfield and yet not wreck the plane. He had planned his run up-wind, and so considerably reduced his ground speed, but even so it was going to be a matter of split-second timing if they were to come out alive. And there was not much time to lose; already the Mönch was decked fully by cloud, and of the ground below there was no sight whatsoever. There would only be time for one run.

The same thought had dawned on Chipperfield: there would only be time for one run. It was clear the weather was closing in. In another few minutes the avenues of escape through the bewildering maze of peaks would be sealed off. The first run had to be right.

He gripped his camera and stared intensely at the rapidly approaching mountain. " Closer, man, closer! " he urged in the pilot's ear as the black, ice-covered wall raced up and then parallel to them. A few seconds later the climbers came into view. He aimed his camera. He was shouting, shouting uselessly against the roar of the engine, as if by sheer will-power he could make the two drenched climbers bend to his will.

" Turn round, you phoney, turn and look at the camera! Wave, man, anything, but for God's sake look this way! "

In a flash they had roared past.

He had secured two shots, but a stream of oaths rushed senselessly from his lips. Neither man had turned. The mountain had absorbed their whole attention. It was almost as if they had not even seen the aircraft. Tears of fury and frustration smarted at the corners of his eyes. He lunged forward and grabbed the pilot by the shoulder.

" Once more! " he yelled. " You've got to get closer, they didn't even look at us. Closer, man! "

The pilot shook his head vigorously and pointed at the enveloping cloud. He tried to make his voice heard above the engine's roar:

" I daren't risk it. The cloud's getting too thick, we'll pile up on a mountain side if we don't get out now."

The journalist was shouting like a maniac in his ear, and he caught the words " yellow " and " no guts." A

G

cold fury possessed him. Kicking the rudder hard over he banked steeply to the open north and stood off from the mountain, watching the racing pattern of cloud. There was no hint of the terrain below.

Then suddenly a freak wind parted thick coils of mist, momentarily revealing a gap. The two climbers were visible. It was a gap which only a lunatic would risk, but his gorge was up. The machine bucked and tossed and he fought the controls, then he shouted:

" O.K., you asked for it! "

The wall rushed up to meet them. Foot by foot, inch by inch, he eased the plane nearer, till it seemed that the wing tip must scrape and crash into the gleaming ice-covered rock. One hundred feet, ninety feet, a sudden vicious air pocket and the gap shrank alarmingly.

Dry-mouthed, his fingers damp with nervous tension, Chipperfield crushed his body to the tiny window, oblivious to their danger, oblivious to all else except the driving force of his will, the overpowering desire to capture the second climber on the sensitive film in his 35 mm. camera.

The dim shapes of two men hurtled out of the mist towards them. He pressed the trigger, twisted frantically and pressed again as they came level.

And in that split second the second figure turned and waved.

A huge shout of triumph burst from Chipperfield's lips as he wrenched his body hard round, craning backwards for a last shot.

But he did not press the trigger.

His finger froze on the camera as he saw the jagged chunk of ice fall.

A cry of anguish choked in his throat as the huge lump struck the second climber, catching him for a fraction of a second off his guard. The man's mouth opened in a silent scream, he fought to keep his balance, swayed, and fell to the length of his rope.

The last fragmentary image Chipperfield had was of the injured man dangling in space, shielding his head with one arm and scrabbling with his spiked boots to gain a purchase on the glistening black rock.

CHAPTER VI

No ONE knew.

That was all that mattered. By an appalling stroke of chance no one, except the two climbers themselves, knew of the accident.

The pilot had not seen the man fall. Only he himself, by swivelling in his seat and craning backwards for a last shot, had witnessed the terrible moment. There had been no chance to tell the pilot, even had he wanted to. The light machine had bucked and yawed like a wild animal at a rodeo, and the pilot had had his hands more than full fighting to maintain control.

And no one in the valley could possibly have been witness. The thick clouds had sealed them from view; both plane and climbers had been isolated in a world of their own. He was in sole possession: the drama lay at his fingertips, his to reveal—or withhold.

It was an incredible dilemma for a man of his profession to be in. The headlines of the world were his for the asking. He had to fight back the temptation to rush to the nearest phone and tell what he had seen. But by the time he had reached the photo laboratory he knew what he had to do. It was the pilot who had, unknowingly, clinched the decision for him.

" That's the most damnable piece of folly I have ever permitted myself to carry out in all the years I have been flying," he had said bitterly as they parted at the air-field.

" Why the histrionics? We came out alive, didn't we? "

" I'm not referring to the danger to us, though that was bad enough. I mean the climbers. If they had allowed themselves to be distracted whilst climbing on an exposed place like that, anything might have happened. We were damn' lucky not to start off an avalanche with our slipstream as it was."

Chipperfield had made no reply, and the Swiss had walked away without shaking hands. The journalist watched his retreating figure for a moment, then shrugged his shoulders; doubtless the fellow would sing another tune when he saw the size of the bonus which the syndicate would pay if the pictures were sharp.

The next step was to see what the photos revealed.

With nerves on edge he waited for the negatives to develop. He did not think they would betray him. He had not pressed the shutter-release as the boulder of ice fell on to the Baron. The shock of the dreadful scene and the instinctive realisation that it was his own ruthless folly that had caused it had frozen his hand on the camera. It was just as well, otherwise there would have been the smart-Alec photographic assistant to silence.

He gave an inward sigh of relief. It was as he had thought: there was nothing incriminating on the plates. Two shots were blurred, and one had been taken too soon. But the final shot, taken as they had passed level for the second time, was a beauty. The guide leading the way upward was not in the picture, but the drenched figure at the end of the rope, lodged on a tiny ledge below, was in full view; he had half turned, and was waving cheerfully towards the aircraft.

Chipperfield studied the photo for a long time.

Eventually the assistant said, " That's the man you say is the Baron Mandoza? "

" That *is* the Baron Mandoza."

" A pity he didn't take his goggles off, and his helmet. You could have been sure, then."

" I didn't expect him to do a strip-tease for my benefit,"
said Chipperfield sourly.

" No, I suppose not. Much too cold, at that height."

The journalist shot him a suspicious glance. Was the
smug young fool trying to be funny?

" Anyway, it certainly looks like Mandoza, from all the
pictures I've ever seen," the young man added smoothly.

" It is Mandoza, there's no question about it. Now
then, despatch this last shot the same way as yesterday,
and get a move on. London and New York are waiting."

*   *   *

He drove up to Grindelwald at less than his usual pace.
There was a lot to think about. For the second time in the
extraordinary affair the ball had bounced his way, giving
him a clear field, a perfect world scoop. The photos were
merely a pleasant tit-bit, the natural rewards reaped by
acute journalistic flair; but the snap-glimpse of the Baron
in the Interlaken restaurant, and now the sole knowledge
that the man was injured and had fallen from the mountain, were pure gifts from the gods. He could not exploit
the second priceless gift immediately, for fear of being
charged with the blame for the accident; but foreknow-
ledge of what might be revealed as soon as the cloud lifted
gave him an inestimable advantage over his competitors.
He would make his preparations, have everything ready,
and when the moment was ripe, give Bernheim the word
to release the story sufficiently ahead of the others to
obtain a clean sweep of the market.

Now that he had made his decision he began coolly to
evaluate the advantages of remaining temporarily silent.
If the Baron had only been mildly injured and was able to
rescale the overhanging bluff over which he had fallen,
then the story had hardly changed. But if, as was his
distinct impression, the man had been badly hurt, then
the possibilities were enormous. Chipperfield knew

enough about mountaineering and the Eiger by now to
realise that an injured man stood little chance of climbing
the North Wall—either up or down. Help would have to
be sent, a rescue would be organised as soon as the accident became known, and unless he revealed what he
knew (which he had no intention of doing) no relief
column would be organised until a break in the weather
revealed its necessity. The story would utterly change its
complexion, and gain a new lease of life. At the most
conservative estimate it would be protracted by at least
two days, and possibly more. He had everything to gain,
and nothing to lose, by playing it quietly and cautiously.

*　　　*　　　*

Grindelwald was noticeably fuller, and the train that
crawled up through the mist to Alpiglen was crowded. He
noted with cynical complacence that he was not the only
passenger to alight on the tiny station platform. He had
promised Borgwand an increase in trade, and already the
trickle of new guests was broadening into a steady flow.

As he took the cinder track across the windswept slopes
towards the Nordwand Hotel, someone greeted him by
name. It was McKechnie, a shrewd Scottish reporter for
one of the chief London dailies.

" It's quite a hornet's nest you've been stirring up here,
Paddy," the Scotsman said. " Are you still sticking to
that Baron Mandoza idea of yours? "

" You're dead right I am; it's not an idea, it's hard
fact."

" Have you perhaps seen the piece put out by
Mondial? "

" You mean about some mythical character called
Stringberg? I don't waste much time reading my rivals,
but I had heard about it."

" You don't think there might be something in it? "

" Bellman's flying a kite. Out of pure personal jealousy,

if you want to know. His tale hasn't a leg to stand on."

" What about the fact that Stringberg can't be found? Did you know that? "

" No, but it makes no difference. They probably haven't looked very hard."

" That's not what I heard," McKechnie answered. " The *News* and one or two other papers have started a pretty energetic manhunt, and it seems *Herr* Stringberg is not at home. There have been a few pointers to suggest he was headed secretly for here, bent on tackling that mountain again."

" No doubt Bellman still possesses a few contacts capable of stirring up a useful rumour here and there," said Chipperfield with a supercilious smile. " His tale won't last long, you mark my words."

They walked the remaining distance to the hotel in silence. As they reached the terrace a young man carrying a microphone attached to a long cable bustled forward and planted himself in front of the famous journalist.

" Could we have a few words about your flight this morning, Mr. Chipperfield? " the radio reporter asked.

" Certainly." Chipperfield beamed with pleasure and took the microphone, conscious of the small crowd who were staring at him and whispering to each other. One or two cameras clicked as he gave a modest account of the flight, a brief report of which he had already filed.

" And when do you think the climbers will reach the peak? " asked the radio reporter, speaking into the microphone and handing it swiftly back to Chipperfield.

" It's hard to say, with the cloud as thick as this. But judging from the progress they were making when I last saw them, I should guess they will reach the top sometime this afternoon."

" How did the two men look to you—in good shape? "

The image of the second figure dangling on the end of the rope flashed before his mind, but he answered imperturbably:

" Excellent, I should say—though a bit wet."

" About how far are they from the actual summit? "

Chipperfield hesitated for a second. It was vital at this critical stage not to give any impression that the climbers might be in difficulties.

" Well, let me think . . . I'm no expert, of course, but my guess is they're about a thousand feet or so from the top."

" Then they've reached the Spider? "

" It seemed to me they had."

The figure of a thousand feet was not taken at random. He knew the height they had been flying. It was his swift estimate of where the climbers would have reached at that precise moment, had the accident not occurred. And for all he knew, they might have got that far.

" It must be pretty cold up there," said the reporter. " From what we can see down in the valley, and that's not much on account of the rain-clouds, there seems to be a lot of water spilling off the upper reaches. I should think the climbers are drenched through to the skin; could you confirm that, Mr. Chipperfield? "

" Yes, I did see a great many water chutes. Albrecht and Mandoza must be pretty wet, but they looked in fine fettle to me as we flew past."

" How about stone-fall, and those chunks of ice which has made the North Wall notorious in the past? "

" Those men are tough, they'll fight their way through anything," said Chipperfield impatiently, disliking the turn the interview was taking. " I've been proud—and I use the word with discretion—proud to witness their great battle with the elements, and I want to say in conclusion that my prayers are with them, as I am sure is the case with the thousands of people watching their brave venture. I know they all join me in saying: ' May God grant them a safe and speedy return.' "

He handed the microphone quickly to the reporter and turned into the hotel. He knew from experience that there was no safer way of terminating an interview than by invoking the name of the Deity.

*   *   *

The two men on the mountain remained hidden by cloud all day. Thin rain fell intermittently throughout the afternoon and the barometer sank steadily. There were prophecies from self-appointed weather experts that snow could be expected at high altitudes before long.

Chipperfield spent the hours working at his typewriter, knocking into shape the article describing his flight, and drafting his plans for the instant when the news of the Baron's injury should break.

Scanning his notes once more, he was satisfied that he had prepared for every eventuality. Whether the discovery that an accident had occurred was made by day or night, he was ready. Assuming that the Baron had been unable to go on or go back, the moment they spotted this fact from the valley below, rescue teams would be organised. The relief columns were unlikely to be recruited on the Scheidegg itself, but from the valleys on either side; and he had already placed his leg-men in Grindelwald and Lauterbrunnen; he would be one of the first to receive news of what was being organised. He blessed his foresight in having taken this routine precaution.

If he guessed aright, all would be chaos during the first few hours. It was unlikely that any one man would be put in sole charge of co-ordinating a rescue attempt—at least, not at first. Thus whilst his rivals were wasting time feverishly hunting for the facts in both widely-separated valleys, he himself would be sitting pretty in the middle, at Alpiglen, co-ordinating reports and getting the facts well ahead of anyone else. He would be in a position of unparalleled superiority to report the drama.

But he had thought further ahead than that. His instinct had told him from the very beginning that this would be a big story. Now, by a sudden twist of fate, it stood a chance of mushrooming to a size beyond his wildest dreams. Not just the daily press, but the enormously powerful Sunday papers and the illustrated weeklies from all over the world would be screaming for his reports. The agency could be relied upon to get him good terms, but he had a few ideas which even Bernheim —who had a mind as sharp as a diamond cutter where the exploitation of a news-story was concerned—might not think up.

*   *

At six o'clock in the evening the rain stopped, but thin veils of mist still decked the Eiger from above the second icefield. A few hardy tourists remained clustered round the giant telescope on the terrace, groups of guests lined the windows of the lounge, dining-room and bedrooms, hoping that the clouds would lift. The possibility that the climbers might have reached the summit lent a sharp edge to their watchfulness.

Klaus Borgwand, passing hurriedly through the *Saal*, could scarcely hide his dislike of this crude display of unhealthy curiosity. Not that he had much time in which to indulge his emotions or private thoughts: he was desperately busy, overwhelmed by the demands of his new clientele, and the skeleton staff with which he was forced to work seemed capable only of moving from one crisis to another. Had he been younger he might have relished the challenge, would have controlled the new staff with a firm hand, given encouragement to the old hands who had remained loyal to him, produced wonders from the kitchen and answered tactfully the flood of questions fired at him in several languages by all manner of guests—newspaper reporters, radio technicians, photo-

graphers, and plain ignorant, hungry sensation-seekers.
It was this last aspect of the affair which he detested above
all else. There was scarcely a person staying at his hotel
who had come there because of a love of the mountains
and a joy in the great alpine sport. It was not for this riff-
raff that he had built his house beneath the shadow of the
mighty mountain.

With an uneasy heart he hurried to the reception desk
and conferred with Heinrich about room allocations. It
was beginning to look as though he might have to reopen
the long-disused wing, which presented considerable
problems in terms of bed-linen, towels, chambermaids
and cleaning staff. He looked at his watch and wondered
if he had time to discuss matters with Claire, who was
busy at the bar but might be able to slip away from the
throng of reporters who were besieging her. He himself
would be needed in the kitchens in a short while. Trying
in vain to catch her eye, he decided against calling her,
and took a sheaf of unanswered letters and telegrams
from Heinrich, intending to answer them as quickly as
possible in his bureau.

But the bureau door was locked, from the inside.
Chipperfield must be there, using his phone again. He
stifled a curse and turned round a corner to a small dark
room, little more than a cubby-hole, which housed the
overflow from his bureau—old receipts, *Fremdenbücher*,
past correspondence and old book-keeping files. There
was a small table which could be used as a desk in
emergency. He sat down and quickly leafed through the
telegrams. He was vaguely conscious of Chipperfield's
voice through the thin panel that separated them, but
paid it no attention.

He was half-way through his work, in the midst of
scribbling a reply to an urgent demand from Paris, when
the journalist raised his voice in excitement, penetrating
the thin wall.

The terrible import of what he overheard shocked

Borgwand out of his concentration. Unwillingly he found himself listening.

" . . . I tell you, man, I saw him fall! Yes, of course I'm sure it was the Baron . . . no, they couldn't see from the valley, the cloud was thick as hell . . . no, the rope held . . . not a chance, the man's injured, and they're at least two thousand feet from the top . . . good God, I keep telling you, no one knows about it yet; you've got to hold this till I give you the word . . . all hell will break loose . . . what? . . . yes, it's front-page now, whether Auntie *Times* likes it or not, and yours truly is in on the ground floor; but you can't run it yet—never mind why not, just do as I say. Now, here's what you do as soon as it breaks . . ."

The hotelier started to his feet, his chair crashing to the floor. The room seemed to sway and for a second he thought he was going to faint. He gripped the edge of the table and waited till the ugly feeling had passed and his heart-beating had returned to normal. Perhaps he had misunderstood. He had to find out. He hurried to the bureau door and rapped heavily.

Chipperfield's voice continued in lower tones for a moment, and the old man hammered on the door once more. To his relief he heard the phone disconnect. A moment later the door opened with maddening slowness. He thrust himself inside and slammed it shut behind him.

" Is it true? " he blurted out breathlessly.

The journalist eyed him narrowly and said:

" Is what true? "

" That there's been an accident up there? "

" Accident? That's the first I've heard of it."

" Is it true, for God's sake? "

" Hold on, old man, catch your breath; you'll have a stroke. Why don't you sit down? "

Borgwand shook him off angrily.

" I could not help overhearing what you were saying

on the telephone. You raised your voice—I was next door—I had no intention of eavesdropping, but——"

Chipperfield took hold of him in a grip like a vice and thrust him none too gently into a chair.

"You mustn't get excited and jump to conclusions, you know," he said in a low menacing voice. "Now just what did you imagine you overheard?"

"It was not imagination! I heard you distinctly, that wall is only a thin partition."

"Take it easy, take it easy man, or you'll burst a blood vessel—and then where would your precious hotel be?"

"Never mind about my hotel: has something happened up there on the North Wall? Who did you see fall?"

Chipperfield looked at him steadily for a long moment, then walked deliberately towards the door and turned the lock. Turning, he said softly:

"There may have been a slight accident. I'm not sure. We shall know soon enough, as soon as the clouds lift."

"Good God, it will be dark in another hour or two! By then it may be too late. Those clouds are not going to lift to-day, unless a miracle happens. You *must* tell me, what did you see from that aircraft?"

As he spoke he realised his voice had risen to an unnatural pitch, and his heart had begun to race alarmingly, but the smug little smile on the big man's face made his blood rise in anger.

"I tell you, I am not exactly sure what I saw——"

"You liar! You were sure enough, a moment ago, on the phone."

Chipperfield flushed an unpleasant colour and strode towards the agitated old man, who had half-risen from his chair, trembling with emotion. Seizing his coat lapel in a crushing grip the powerfully-built journalist thrust him back into his seat.

"Watch it! Watch your tongue, Borgwand. I made you, and I can break you, you and your crumbling hotel and your conceited little tart of a barmaid. If it hadn't been for me you'd be out on the grass by now, stony broke. I've plastered the name of this dilapidated barn all over the world, but I can do it the other way too, you know. In twenty-four hours I can make your hotel the laughing-stock of all Switzerland."

" I don't care as much as that about the hotel; and as for your cheap remarks about Claire, I can only assume she slapped your face and sent you packing, for which I am heartily glad."

Chipperfield's eyes dilated with anger and Borgwand sensed a fleeting satisfaction that his shaft had gone home. Reaching for the phone on his desk he said:

" If there has been an accident it must be reported to the proper authorities."

" Aren't you taking rather a lot on yourself? "

" I cannot sit here and do nothing, if men's lives are in danger. Whereabouts did it happen? What height had they reached? "

" How should I know? " said Chipperfield blandly.

" You *do* know. You saw them. And furthermore, I have heard you give two contradictory opinions. Why? You told the radio reporter this morning they were only a thousand feet from the summit. Now you tell your news-paper friend that they have at least two thousand feet to go. Which is correct? "

The journalist gave him an evil smile.

" Take your pick," he said.

Borgwand shot him a look of hatred, then began to dial a number.

Chipperfield watched him through narrowed eyes for a second, then calmly leant forward and with one foot ripped the plug from the wall. The phone hung dead in the old man's trembling grasp. With careful diction the journalist said:

" What's your hurry, man? "

Borgwand gaped at him without comprehension. The

man must be mad, he thought. Or inhuman. The next
moment the journalist's powerful figure towered above
him, and his coat lapel was held in a crushing grip,
tightening viciously round his neck.

"Listen, you fool. You've got everything to gain and
nothing to lose by stretching out this business, and so have
I. The longer it lasts, the better for both of us, don't you
see? Every twenty-four hours we can win spells a fortune
for both of us—but you're such a blind moralising old fool
you can't see it. There's no hurry, man, they'll all find out
sooner or later."

The grip at his throat relaxed, but the old man did not
hear any more. There was a terrible roaring in his head
and then he lost consciousness.

The journalist stood looking down with alarm at the
slumped figure. A wave of panic seized him, and he strove
to master it for several seconds. The old man had passed
out, that was all. He was still breathing. High blood
pressure and a weak heart, probably. A doctor would
soon fix him.

He strode to the door, unlocked it and shouted Claire's
name. She heard him, caught his eye, and realised at
once that something alarming had happened in the
director's bureau. In a moment she was on the scene.

"He's passed out," Chipperfield hastily explained.
"Some kind of stroke, I think. The strain of the past few
days must have been too much for him. Better get him to
bed."

"I'll fetch a doctor first," said Claire decisively.
"There may be one among the guests."

A few moments later she was back with a quiet, be-
spectacled Belgian. The man felt Borgwand's pulse and
made a swift examination.

"He will be all right," he said at length. "Get him to
bed, keep him warm and quiet. I'll give him a sedative
so that he sleeps long."

"What is it, *Monsieur*?" Claire asked anxiously.

" Nothing serious. A slight breakdown, due to nervous strain and overwork, I should imagine."

Claire watched as willing hands carried the pitiful figure out. Chipperfield had left, there was no time to ask him some of the questions that were teeming in her mind. She glanced hurriedly at her watch. Three-quarters of an hour remained till dinner, and there was no one to take charge in the kitchens. It only took her a second to make her decision. She went quickly over to the reception desk and said:

" Heinrich, shut the lights here and take over the bar, will you? I'm going into the kitchen, *Herr* Borgwand is ill. Dinner will be served promptly at the usual time. Tell the service staff to keep their heads—if anyone panics they will have me to reckon with, and I'm not feeling very amiable right now."

*   *   *

Dinner went off without a hitch and very few guests even suspected that the director was absent. If they had done, it would have caused little stir. The minds of all in the hotel were concentrated on the two climbers. Had they reached the summit before daylight expired? Or would they be forced to spend a second night in bivouac on some tiny ledge whilst the cold mists swirled about them and the snow clouds from the west began piling up? It was a matter for tense conjecture. Only dawn and clear weather would provide the answer.

Claire came down from a quick visit to the director's room and bumped into John Bellman in the foyer. Her heart gave a queer little leap as she saw him. It was hard to say why; he was not a romantic figure, she found herself thinking. His hair was flecked with grey at the sides, he must be over forty, probably married and the father of grown-up children—and yet she derived a strange kind of comfort from his presence. Perhaps it was because his quiet, steady manner was in such contrast to the forceful, hardboiled exterior presented by the other members of his profession who were clamouring for her at the bar at that moment.

He asked immediately if it was true that the director was ill.

" Yes," she replied, " he has had a slight breakdown. I don't know how serious it is."

" Serious for you, though. It must leave you terribly short-handed? "

" It is difficult. But we'll manage somehow."

" Is there anything I can do to help? "

Claire gave him an impish smile. " You be careful, or I'll take you at your word and give you a pile of dirty glasses to wash. Anyway, you have your own work to do."

" Things are pretty much at a stalemate at the moment, until the cloud lifts. Unless Stringberg or Mandoza crops up somewhere in Europe, there won't be anything to report till to-morrow morning at the earliest."

" Is there still no confirmation that it is Stringberg? "

" Nothing concrete, I'm afraid."

Further conversation was cut short by a female voice with the penetration of a dentist's drill whining from the bar:

" *Fräulein*, do I get my whisky-sour or have I got to climb over that bar and mix it myself? "

Claire made a grimace, excused herself and hurried off.

Bellman debated a moment. If he went into the bar, there would probably be another irritating clash with Chipperfield. By filing his report about the German climber named Kurt Stringberg, which he had done the previous day after his second interview with *Frau* Albrecht, he had openly declared war on the mighty journalist. From bitter experience he knew what this meant. The self-styled Torchbearer of Truth was an unpleasant enemy to have; he did not suffer public contra-

H

diction gladly. And so far no firm evidence in support of
the Stringberg theory had come in. The German
alpinist was not to be found at his home in Munich, nor
anywhere else. An exciting double manhunt was on,
all over Europe. Rumours flashed like summer lightning,
only to fade as quickly. Public and professional opinion
seemed to be falling into two camps—either pro-Mandoza
or pro-Stringberg.

For the moment there was nothing more he could do.
His interviews that morning in Interlaken with the waitress
and the garage attendant who had apparently inspired
Chipperfield with his fantastic notion had proved in-
conclusive. It had not been difficult to run these vital
witnesses to earth, since the strange behaviour of a
heavily-built foreign journalist on the Sunday morning
was still the talk of the restaurants. But though both the
waitress and the garage hand claimed to have recognised
Baron Mandoza, Bellman could not suppress the strong
suspicion that they were only being wise after the event—
and were quite possibly bribed by Chipperfield to say
what he wanted them to say.

Only *Frau* Albrecht had given him something vital to
go upon. She had never heard of the Baron Mandoza
before the furore had started, but Kurt Stringberg she
knew personally. Her husband had previously guided
the German on tours in the Bernese Alps, the two men
had been good friends, and Stringberg had sworn that
one day he would return and avenge the defeat which
the Eiger had once dealt him. She did not state definitely
that it was him. She had not seen the man who had hired
her husband. But she thought it could only be Stringberg,
no one else. And the idea made sense, whereas Chipperfield's claim was in the realms of fantasy.

He had reported what he had discovered, not as fact,
but as likely fact. The issue remained open, until either
one of the two men was found, or the climbers descended
from the Eiger. There was nothing more he could do,

except wait, and drink, like the others. Or, he thought with a sudden grin, give Claire a hand.

He found his way down to the kitchens and then to an adjoining room labelled OFFICE where a group of tired waiters were listlessly rinsing and polishing a large quantity of dirty glasses. He took off his jacket, found a clean white cloth, and began work, glad to have something to do. After the first glances of blank surprise none of the tired waiters paid him much attention.

*   *   *

Two hours later, when the inexorable flow of dirty glasses coming down the creaking lift from the bar had abated, he laid down his cloth, bade the sleepy staff good-night, and went upstairs and out towards the hotel exit. He glanced in the direction of the bar as he passed but Claire was hidden behind a pall of cigarette smoke and the backs of numerous vociferous clients.

The night air was damp and chilly and Bellman was glad he had brought a coat. He turned the collar up and peered upward at the vast, dim shape of the Eiger above him. Its outline was faintly visible through silvery traces of cloud that seemed to have thinned. If it was chilly down at five thousand feet, he reflected, what must it be like up there, on a naked ice-covered face twelve thousand feet up. He shuddered involuntarily as he thought about it.

He was just about to descend the steps to the terrace when he heard his name called from behind him. Turning he saw Claire coming towards him, blushing prettily.

" You mustn't go without my being allowed to thank you," she said, coming out on to the steps.

" Thank me? Whatever for? "

" One of the waiters has just told me about a mysterious Englishman working like a coolie among the dirty glasses."

Bellman laughed to hide his embarrassment.

" Like a coolie—that's a bit of an exaggeration. I'm sure I broke as many as I cleaned "

" That's not what I heard. Thank you so much, it really was kind of you. Won't you let the hotel stand you a drink, to say thank you for your help? "

He was tempted to stay, and would have done had there been any chance of talking quietly with her alone somewhere. Instead he answered:

" Another time, when you are not so busy. I must be on my way—but I'll hold you to that offer another evening."

" Please do."

" Well . . ." he said reluctantly, wishing after all that he had not said he must get back to his hotel, " Well, I suppose I must toddle along. My small son will be expecting to hear from me."

" Oh," she said, in a weak voice, " is he here? "

" No, he's in America. I meant I must write to him."

" And your wife too."

" No," he answered slowly, " I don't think my wife will be expecting to hear from me."

At the mention of his son it was as though a dry, cold hand had suddenly squeezed her heart. It was absurd, really. It was no possible concern of hers that he was married. She could have kicked herself for the clumsiness of her second question. Trying to cover up, she only made matters worse:

" I'm so sorry, I didn't mean to pry . . . at least, I . . . oh dear, I don't really know what I did mean. You must think me a very rude person."

He looked up at her from the bottom of the steps, the lights from the hotel framing her short, crisp hair, her features hidden by shadow. He said quietly:

" I think you are the nicest person I have met in a long time, *Fräulein*. Good-night."

He turned and walked slowly across the terrace.

She watched him go, then, out of sheer habit, gazed upward at the huge pyramid looming above her. She stiffened, unable to believe her eyes. It was impossible, she must be seeing things. She waited. It came again.

"Mr. Bellman!" she cried out. "One moment, please!"

His footsteps stopped, she heard him returning, but she did not look at him. Her eyes were glued to a point high on the mountain, to a spot where she could have sworn a tiny light had flickered. Her pulse was racing, and every nerve was taut as she screwed her eyes in an endeavour to pierce the gloom. Once more the speck of light flickered.

"Look! On the Eiger. Do you see it?"

Bellman was at her side, peering anxiously upwards. Then he saw it too, a tiny twinkle, infinitesimally small yet miraculously clear.

"What does it mean?" he asked.

"Count it! Count the number of seconds in between," she ordered breathlessly.

He lifted the luminous dial of his watch. They counted.

"Ten seconds."

"Again. Count again. We must be sure!"

Once more they counted. Her fingers pressed lightly on his wrist were trembling. As he reached ten, the tiny pin-point of light glowed again.

"What does it mean?" he asked again, feeling already that he understood.

"The signal. *Das Notsignal!* A light six times in one minute, regularly every ten seconds. They are in distress!"

She turned and ran headlong back into the hotel.

CHAPTER VII

BERNHEIM REPLACED the phone, a smile of satisfaction on his pouchy features. Global Features had certainly pulled it off this time. Not Reuter, nor United Press, none of the mammoth Fleet Street combines and none of the bright American boys, could touch them with a comparable story for hours. It had even come in before the great papers of Fleet Street had been finally put to bed. Paddy Chipperfield's name above his sensational despatch would be on the breakfast table of one in every three homes throughout Great Britain in the morning, and the teleprinters were already clacking out their startling message across the Atlantic. The Torchbearer had his banner headlines at last. Baron or no Baron—and there were still a few niggling sceptics who refused to swallow that angle—a great climb on a treacherous mountain had turned in one dramatic twist into a sensational drama, possibly a tragedy, and Global Features had scooped the world.

As he waited for the lines to come clear to America, Bernheim glanced approvingly through the list of exploitation angles which Chipperfield had dictated after he had phoned telling him to let the story run.

That was one smart boy, one very smart boy indeed, he reflected; there didn't seem to be anything he had forgotten. Some of the items were going to be tricky as far as cutting in on a cash basis was concerned, but viewed from the overall standpoint, each brainchild spawned by Chipperfield would add to the mounting tide of publicity, helping to splash the story across continents by every means of dissemination known to modern man. It was a great pity the TV cameras could not operate on the spot, but the ring of mountains around the Scheidegg made it impractical; nevertheless the big companies would send out their own film units or would fight like cats among themselves for the newsreel rights, and when they came to interview Chipperfield, as they inevitably would now that his famous name was so closely connected in the eyes of the public with the whole drama, it would cost them plenty. Two wide-awake publishers had already been on the phone for the potential book-rights, Hollywood was waiting to come through on the transatlantic telephone, and the biggest French glossy had already made a fabulous bid for exclusive serial rights. They had struck Bonanza Creek.

Bernheim ticked each item off the list, till he came to the scribbled note " query Tin Pan Alley." He could not suppress a smile. The Torchbearer had let his imagination run a little wild there, he thought. He was about to strike the idea out, then he stopped. Was it so crazy? There was money in the song-writing business, big money. Think up a tune, get some hack-writer to knock out a lyric, smear the right band-boys to plug it day and night over the air, and before you knew where you were it was hard to hear the melody above the sweet discord of Charing Cross Road's cash registers.

Come to think of it, why hire a hack-writer? Just for fun he took a fresh sheet of paper and began doodling.

. . . June, moon . . . that was out, the month was August and you couldn't rhyme that, no matter how hard you tried. . . . you, true . . . love, heavens above . . . it wasn't so hard when you got down to it. In a few minutes he had the rough outlines of a lyric. Of course, there would be an outcry from high-brow quarters about bad taste, but that had never prevented a song from being a hit yet, not if the masses liked it and you hired a good tonsil-man to plug it. Chipperfield had coined the phrase " Murder Mountain," and the tabloids had snapped it up. That would make a nice title. He read the lyric through once more:

" *The Man on Murder Mountain*
He makes me think of you:
Why must you be so cold dear?
You know my love is true.
Just think of me this way, dear,
I'll climb to any part,
If only you will promise
A place for me in your heart."

The last line needed brushing up a bit, but on the whole he was fairly satisfied with it, for a first attempt. The indirect reference to the Baron's late forlorn love affair was subtle, the masses would love it. Given the right echoing acoustics, plenty of lush strings, a menacing lead-in on the drums to emphasise the murder-mountain line, it stood a good chance of being a hit. Already he could visualise it, as the cinema lights darkened and the title flashed on the screen, a rich choir and plenty of stereophonic sound to add——

The phone on his desk rang and Hollywood came on the line. He brushed the lyric aside and got down to serious business.

*   *   *

Chipperfield had promised himself a good night's rest. The thought of all his rival journalists scurrying for information whilst his own despatch lay already set up in type warmed him as he climbed into bed. But his head seemed scarcely to have touched the pillow when there was a thundering on his bedroom door. It was not the polite knock of the waiter bringing him his early morning tea. He grunted some sort of answer, groped in the dark for his bedside lamp and, switching it on, swore bitterly. It was scarcely four o'clock in the morning. What the hell did they want from him at that ungodly hour?

Putting on a silk dressing gown he stumbled sleepily to

the door and opened it. It was Heinrich, the ante-
diluvian concierge-cum-hall porter.

"*Bitte um Entschuldigung, Herr* Chipperfield, but it is
very urgent. There has been an accident on the——"

"I know that—surely you didn't wake me up in the
middle of the night just to tell me that?"

"No sir, but the *Obmann* is downstairs, waiting to speak
to you."

"Who the devil is the *Obmann*?"

"The chief guide, the man who is going to lead the
rescue party to the North Wall."

"What the dickens does he want at this hour? Couldn't
it wait till daylight?"

The elderly concierge raised his hands in embarrassment, muttered an apology and pottered off.

Chipperfield cursed loudly and began leisurely to pull
some clothes on. Things were happening quicker than he
had anticipated, and he was not at all sure he liked the
idea of the coming interview.

Fifteen minutes later he took the lift down to the foyer
(someone had at last managed to repair it), and yawning
ostentatiously, strode to meet a group of men who were
awaiting him. One was middle-aged, the other two
considerably younger; they wore thick clothing and heavy
hob-nailed boots, and did not look as though they had
been to bed. Borgwand, he noted with quick relief, was
not present. Only Heinrich loitered in the vicinity,
pretending not to listen.

"Well, gentlemen," the journalist said, "what can I
do for you?"

The oldest of the three men spoke. He was of average
height, burly, ponderous of movement, and had eyes whose
irises, the journalist noted with surprise, were of two
different colours: one was brown, the other deep violet.

"*Grüss Gott.* I am the *Obmann* of the team chosen to
go to the rescue of the men in distress on the Eiger."

His speech was slow, even slower than was usual with

the Bernese. He spoke in careful, unaccustomed High German.

Chipperfield nodded and said nothing.

" We would like to ask you a few questions. We need your help. Before we start out, it is vitally important to know exactly where the two climbers are. On that will depend our choice of route, the equipment we take with us, and even the lives of the men apparently in danger up there."

" I see. And what do you want from me? "

" You are the last person to have seen them—you and the pilot of your aeroplane. We would like you to describe as accurately as you can where Hans Albrecht and his client are."

" Why don't you wait till daylight? It should be possible to see by then."

" It is by no means certain that the cloud will have lifted by then. The weather forecasts are poor. We must start straightaway, every hour counts when men are in peril on the North Wall. They have already been up there two days and three nights—fifty-two hours in the open, at that height and with such weather, is a long time, even for the best of climbers."

" And Albrecht is not one of them, is he? " Chipperfield shot out quickly.

The ponderous guide looked at him from beneath frowning brows.

" *Bitte ?* I don't quite understand."

" Isn't it true that Albrecht was expelled from your *Bergführerverein* several years ago? "

" I don't see what that has to do——" he began.

" It is true, the *Herr* is right. Albrecht was thrown out and forbidden to continue practising as a mountain guide," said the youngest of the three men heatedly.

Chipperfield eyed the young man keenly, and noted that the *Obmann* threw him an uneasy glance.

" That has nothing to do with the matter on hand,"

said the elderly man severely. "Albrecht's ability as a guide was never questioned. Now, *bitte*, we must hurry, there are men in distress and it is our duty to try and help them."

"But you cannot be forced to go, can you?" probed the journalist, feeling his way intuitively towards the soft points that might turn to his advantage.

The *Obmann* paused, scenting trouble but uncertain of what shape it was taking. He answered carefully:

"We are obliged to go. In the rules of the *Bergführerverein* it states clearly that when rescue columns are being formed it is our duty as guides to join them."

"Even on the Eiger North Wall?" the journalist persisted, keeping one eye on the youngest guide. The three men shuffled uneasily, and the youngest, ignoring his companions' warning glances, said:

"You are partly right. The North Wall is an exception. No one can actually force us to take part in this rescue, because of what happened twenty years ago——"

"Yes, I know. The Swiss Government tried to ban all attempts to climb the North Wall, didn't they? They even brought in a law to that effect."

"That is so, but they were forced to withdraw it," said the *Obmann* cautiously.

"Quite. Nevertheless, I have been told that a new clause was inserted in the local regulations, stating that any climber who insisted on risking his neck on the Eiger North Wall did so in the full knowledge that if he got into difficulties he could not expect other men, whether guides or plain volunteers, to endanger their lives on his behalf."

The *Obmann* raised a hand to halt his flow. There was a note of anger in his slow voice when he spoke.

"We are wasting time. All this is past history, and purely theoretical. It does not alter the fact that two human beings are in mortal danger as we stand here spinning words. Seppli, give me——"

" One last question, please. Forgive me, but I am a reporter, I have my living to earn, too," Chipperfield cut in. " Tell me, will you be paid for this dangerous work? "

" A guide receives a daily wage for his services. That is how we earn our bread," said the *Obmann* carefully.

" A big wage? Are you well paid? "

The youngest guide uttered an impetuous laugh.

" We shall never be millionaires! The pay is small, but we love the mountains, it is our vocation."

" Enough of this pointless talk. Seppli, give me the map," commanded the *Obmann*.

A large scale map and several photos of the Eiger were produced and laid out on a table. The *Obmann* pointed out each salient feature of the North Wall—the Hinterstoisser Traverse, the three huge icefields, the *Bügeleisen*, the *Rampe*, the Spider icefield and the summit icefield. He glanced sharply at the journalist to see if the latter was following him.

" Now then, we in the valley last saw them on Monday evening, when they were nearing the *Bügeleisen* at the top of the third icefield. It is very likely that they made their first bivouac there. You reported that you saw them yesterday morning, in the Spider. Can you show me exactly how high they had reached? "

It was the moment Chipperfield had been trying to forestall. He realised that the repercussions of a false statement might be serious, even for a man with his influential connections. There was only one thing to do: affect vagueness.

" It is very hard to say," he answered. " The mountain looks a lot different when you are flying close up to it."

" We realise that."

" Why don't you ask the pilot who flew me? He knows the Alps far better than I ever will do."

" We have in fact tried to reach him, but it seems that he has been called out on a job down in the Valais, searching for some lost climbers on the Matterhorn.

Until he returns, or the cloud lifts and we can see with our own eyes, you are the only person who can help us."

" I see."

He hesitated, then went on:

" You are asking me to take a big responsibility on my shoulders. It is not a burden I am anxious to take. Please remember that."

The guide who had not yet spoken suddenly put in, in excellent English:

" I heard your interview with the radio reporter yesterday morning. You said you had observed them not much farther than a thousand feet from the summit."

Chipperfield glanced at him sharply; but there was no accusation in his eyes; he was only making a statement.

" Yes, that was my rough estimate yesterday."

The elderly guide's finger moved over the largest photograph, stopping half-way up the queer web-like configuration of the Spider. " That should put them roughly near here," he said questioningly.

They stood staring at him, waiting for him to make a decision.

" About there, I should say," he answered at length.

There was a moment's silence, then the men began hurriedly folding up the maps and photographs. The young guide said to the *Obmann*:

" Then we try the *Stahlseilgerät*? "

" Yes, I think so."

" And the route? It will be slow going with heavy equipment like that."

" That is so. I think we will do best to go by train as far as the Jungfraujoch and strike back from there. If the weather is not too bad it will be quicker than climbing the south-west flank."

Deep in conversation the three men hurried out into the night.

Chipperfield yawned, more from nervousness than fatigue, for by now he was wide awake. Heinrich, he noted, was still hovering behind the reception desk. He went over to him.

" Heinrich, what the dickens is a *Stahlseilgerät*? "

" It is a device for rescuing men who . . ." he began gesticulating with his hands, then gave it up and fetched a dictionary from Borgwand's office. At first they could not elucidate the complicated term. Some kind of steel-rope apparatus was obviously indicated, but it was not until the concierge took pencil and paper and drew a rough diagram that Chipperfield was able to understand.

" I think I get it. A kind of winch, with a steel cable wound on a drum, capable of lowering a man over the edge of a cliff. Pretty hefty thing to lug up a mountain thirteen thousand feet high. However, that's what they're paid for, I suppose. Thank you, Heinrich, you've been very useful."

Slipping the old man a handsome tip, he walked through the deserted hotel to Borgwand's office, switched on the light, and fitted a sheet of paper into the typewriter. After a moment's thought he began hammering out the first news to reach the outside world of the relief column that was being organised, the means of rescue envisaged and the route up the mountain that was planned. Once again he had secured a clean scoop. Once again the ball had bounced his way. And that was not all: the unguarded speech of the three simple, unsuspicious men had filled his armoury with some priceless ammunition, should he be forced at any time on to the defensive.

His chores behind him, the story duly filed, Chipperfield climbed once more into bed, a contented mind and an unruffled conscience smoothing the path to deep sleep.

*   *   *

Whilst Chipperfield slept, the valley came alive. The news that disaster of some kind had struck the two men on the Eiger spread like a prairie fire. By daybreak there

were few homes in the wide semi-circle stretching from
Grindelwald to Kleine Scheidegg and down on to Wengen
and Lauterbrunnen that had not received word of the
distress signal.

The weather had improved, and much of the cloud had
shifted, but not all of it. The Eiger was only clear as far as
the third icefield.

A gap appeared once, shortly after dawn. Had they
known that it was the only glimpse they were to obtain of
the trapped men for twenty-four hours, many more
telescopes and binoculars would have been trained on
the north face during those vital two or three minutes.
But most people were in the act of struggling out of bed or
preparing breakfast, and so the chance had passed before
more than a handful of reliable witnesses had seen all
that there was to see.

And it was little enough. A man hung on the end of a
rope. He was alive, apparently injured in one arm, but
hanging securely from the face of the mountain. His
companion was not visible. That was all.

Controversy as to which climber it was, and the exact
spot from which he hung, raged fruitlessly all morning.
No one was absolutely certain. At the time he had been
visible, shifting skeins of white mist had swirled over the
summit, making it impossible to pinpoint with accuracy
his distance from the top. It was thought that he dangled
somewhere on the Spider—the treacherous icefield that
stretched from shortly above the third icefield to a few
hundred metres from the peak. Its configuration was
baffling, and the rest of the mountain was masked by
impenetrable thick mist. The injured man might be one
thousand feet from the summit, and he might be two
thousand: no one was certain.

As to his identity, a larger degree of unity was reached.
Majority opinion decided it was not Hans Albrecht, the
Swiss guide. Even this was hotly disputed by some. It
was possible that many minds were swayed by the con-

viction that if one of the two mountaineers had fallen, it was less likely to be the professional guide.

Meanwhile, as rumours flashed in conflicting variety from one end of the valley to the other, work went feverishly ahead on the formation and organisation of a relief column. Despite the *Obmann's* determined efforts, it was not ready to leave the Kleine Scheidegg until shortly before midday. A large quantity of equipment had to be assembled—ropes, pitons, *Karabiner*, hammers, ice-axes, skis, sledges, the steel winch, Gramminger seats, food, tents, medical supplies, portable radio sets and a host of minor items. Volunteers from both the Grindelwald and Lauterbrunnen valleys reported in by phone, messages flashed from village to village, rendezvous were made, weather forecasts studied, until gradually order resolved itself from apparent chaos and the relief column, composed of over twenty men from three different nations (an Italian guide and two experienced Austrian alpinists holidaying in the vicinity had immediately offered their assistance to the Swiss) was at last ready to start. Light rain began to fall again, the skies remained dull and the heavy banks of cloud showed no signs of lifting.

As word spread of the formation of the relief column, the entire area began to fill with eager-eyed tourists, each armed with binoculars and, futilely enough, cameras, bent on catching the first glimpse of the trapped men as soon as the cloud shifted.

Bellman made his way through the excited throng on Scheidegg Station back to his hotel a hundred yards away and wrote a short, unemotional account of the rescue preparations, then phoned this back to his office in Hamburg.

Something was puzzling him, nagging relentlessly at the back of his brain, something he had learnt by means of a direct phone call which he had received from his head office in London. Chipperfield had swept the headlines in the British national press that morning with his newsflash announcing the accident. His story, complete with a surprising amount of detail, had reached the morning editions and been printed in full.

Bellman could not understand how this had been possible. He himself, peering into the darkness alongside Claire, had been—so far as he could confirm—the first to witness the electrifying distress signal. He had filed a report at once, before going to bed, but it had only been a brief statement of the startling fact, and had only just been in time to catch the stop press column. Yet Chipperfield had caught the front page. It didn't add up.

Bellman was honest enough to admit that some of his feelings were pure sour grapes. But not all of them. He did not understand how it had been possible for the man to have been so astonishingly well-informed at such short notice. It was almost as if he had possessed prior knowledge. But that was unthinkable. Even Paddy Chipperfield, " ace of all ace newshounds," did not possess the gift of second sight, the powers of a prophet.

Pushing the thoughts for the time being to the back of his mind, he decided to go over to the Hotel Nordwand at Alpiglen before lunch, to see if there was anything new. If he also happened to see Claire again, he would not be disappointed.

As he approached the hotel he was astonished to see how full it had become. Fresh waiters were darting to and fro serving hot drinks to the hardy tourists who, clad in hats and raincoats, crowded the terrace, craning their necks upwards at the mist-shrouded mountain that dwarfed them. The giant telescope was constantly in use and curiously enough seemed to be partly fenced-off by a crude kind of wooden cage. He did not pay it much attention but forced his way through the jostling crowd. Claire was not to be seen, though the bar, unrestricted due to the genial Swiss licensing laws, was doing a steady trade. A strange face he had not seen before was serving behind it.

I

The ground floor of the hotel was like a business-men's convention at apéritif time. A confused babble of conversation in many tongues filled the smoke-laden air, glasses and bottles rattled as waiters weaved skilfully through the commotion, and it was almost impossible to find a place to sit down. A group of tense-looking news-papermen stood near the single phone booth, which was apparently permanently occupied.

With difficulty he found a spare seat in the packed lounge and eventually managed to catch a waiter's eye and order coffee. There were several journalists present whom he knew, and before long he was talking " shop " with two of them. One was a German colleague from Berlin, the other an American named Doug Wilson, who was Paris correspondent for an important New York daily.

They exchanged gossip, and were soon arguing the pros and cons of Baron Mandoza versus Stringberg. Because he had been the first reporter to advance a strong alternative to Chipperfield's incredible tale of a Society playboy climbing dangerous mountains, Bellman had come to be regarded by many as the principal leader of " the Stringberg faction." It was not a role he would willingly have chosen for himself, but circumstances had thrust it upon him. Fundamentally he was convinced that he was far nearer the truth than his rival, even if his theory held less glamour in the eyes of the great public.

In the course of the discussion that followed, Doug Wilson the American challenged him:

" What d'you make of the straw-poll two of our boys took this morning, John? "

" I haven't heard about it. What did they discover? "

" That neither side wins. Two bright boys armed themselves with a batch of photos, some of Mandoza and some of Stringberg, and set out, separately, one going after the other. The first guy showed pictures of Mandoza all round the valley and down in Interlaken—you know the routine: ' Excuse me, madam, but have you ever seen this man before? ' Everyone swore black and blue they'd seen him a couple of days back—including some old gal who insisted that the same man had tried to sell her a Hoover. Then the second guy covered exactly the same territory, only he showed pictures of Stringberg."

" What had he been selling—Kleen-e-ze brushes? "

" Nope. They got the same result. There wasn't one of 'em that had any doubt that it was Stringberg they'd seen. Strike one for both sides."

" And what do they reckon they've proved? "

" Damn all. Except that the average human being is plain darned gullible. The cops back home have exactly the same trouble every time they run an identification parade: everyone has seen the criminal, including the blind and those who were looking the other way at the time."

" It makes nice copy, if you happen to be short of material," put in Bellman's colleague from Berlin. " But as you say, they have proved nothing. There is only one way to prove who it is hanging up there from the end of that rope: find Stringberg or the Baron, somewhere in Europe."

" Which is what just about every journalist and amateur sleuth is doing at this moment, I imagine," said Bellman.

" I've tried approaching it from the psychological standpoint, John," said Doug Wilson. " As you know, the States took over where Freud left off."

The other two men chuckled. It was one of Doug Wilson's attractive characteristics that he was capable of pulling his own country's leg. The American went on:

" What I mean is: who is it most likely to be? High Society glamour-boys don't go risking their necks on mountains as a rule, which weights the scales heavily in favour of a man like Kurt Stringberg. But there's something about this North Wall. It seems to attract the crack-pots, the glory-seekers, as well as the steely-eyed mountain-eers themselves. If it was any other mountain than the Eiger I'd go one hundred per cent for Stringberg. But I've met this Mandoza character. That's one hell of a queer type. Climbing the North Wall is just the sort of crazy thing he would do to draw attention to himself."

" You may be right," said Bellman. " Anyway, we shall know soon enough. The answer can't be more than a few hours off."

" What beats me," said Wilson, " is how that goddam Juggernaut Chipperfield gets hold of his information so quick. I had it straight from Paris this morning that he managed to plaster a full story right on the front page. How did he do it, when nobody knew the guys were in a mess till sometime around midnight? Me, I didn't even make the stop press."

" Wait a second," interjected the Berlin reporter, " here comes Wonder-boy himself. We can ask him."

Chipperfield must have been gratified to notice the stir which his entry into the crowded room caused. If he detected an atmosphere of hostility in some of the glances directed at him, it obviously caused him no concern.

" Say, Genius! " Doug Wilson called out in penetrating tones, " just how did you manage to place that story of yours all over the front page? You got a private phone to God or something? "

A hush settled over the room. Even those unconnected with the newspaper business ceased talking, sensing that something dramatic was happening.

The smug little smile that lurked habitually on the handsome journalist's features remained undisturbed by this frontal attack. Spreading his hands as though to ward off an imaginary physical assault, he answered:

" Oh come, now, Dougie, you wouldn't expect me to reveal the sources of my inside information, would you? "

" There's something screwy all the same, Torchbearer. I've been in this game too long not to smell a rat when there's one lying about."

" Call it flair, Dougie, plain reporter's flair. Some go around smelling rats, whilst others smell out the news. You ought to spend more time reading my stuff—it's a good way of keeping up to date."

" You insufferable bounder! " exploded a silver-haired, normally dignified representative of one of London's quiet but influential newspapers. " First you think up a cock-and-bull story about a useless social parasite climbing a mountain—a wild surmise which I assure you my editors are not printing—then you monopolise all the phones, and not content with that you start giving yourself airs as if——"

" Hold it, Saltash," Chipperfield cut in, completely unruffled. " I've got a lot of witnesses here, so don't say anything which you're likely to regret. Your kind of newspaper is practically extinct, so what your dear old fuddy-duddy of an editor decides to print or not to print is of no great interest. I have it on good authority that London and New York are selling an awful lot of newspapers with my Baron story, however much the high-brows may dislike it."

" Mine's running it," admitted a reporter from Chicago.

" Mine too," chimed in another voice.

" For my money the guy on the end of that rope is Stringberg. It makes sense, that's why," said a Canadian writer. " Society playboys don't go for risky angles like climbing the North Wall."

" I hear they're taking odds on it in London."

" Yeah, but the bookies are playing it safe—even money either way."

" D'you hear about the public opinion poll? Forty-seven per cent believes it's the Baron up there, and thirty-something go for the German lad."

"And the rest think it's Prince Rainier of Monaco," wisecracked someone.

"What do I care so long as it sells papers?" put in a fat English journalist named Ferguson.

Chipperfield turned to McKechnie who stood nearby, and smiled broadly.

"As you said, quite a little hornet's nest, isn't it? It can't be half that bad a tale if even the boys on the spot are burned up about it. Well, excuse me, gentlemen, but I must get myself a bite to eat, I missed breakfast."

He strode out of the room, leaving the air charged with explosive conflict.

He went straight to the director's bureau, intending to order a meal and have it served there. But a fussy little clerk whom he had not seen before tried to bar his entry.

"Excuse me, sir," flustered the clerk, "but the *Herr Direktor* has given strict——"

He got no further. Chipperfield reached out with a mighty paw, lifted the clerk one foot from the ground and hissed close to the terrified little man's face:

"Next time give it to me in writing!"

He deposited the clerk on an adjacent stool, swung open the bureau door and marched in.

A complete stranger sat behind Borgwand's desk, filing his nails with assiduous care. He raised thin eyebrows at the surprising intrusion, but said nothing, continuing his careful manicure.

"Who are you?" blurted out Chipperfield insolently.

"My name is Hans-Peter Hügi."

"And what the hell d'you think you're doing here?"

"Forgive me, but I think that is by rights my question." The voice was clipped, succinct, and very assured. "I am the new director. What are you doing in my office?"

Setting aside the nail file he snapped his knuckles with an ugly crackle and stared icily at the huge figure towering above him.

For a brief moment Chipperfield was nonplussed. Then he said:

" I wasn't told about this. Where's Borgwand? "

" In bed, I imagine. He's rather ill. You still have not answered my question. What do you imagine you are doing in my office? "

Chipperfield was unaccustomed to arrogance rivalling his own. But he did not hesitate long in deciding how to handle this upstart. He picked up the house-phone and began ordering himself breakfast. The new director watched him coolly. When the journalist had finished and replaced the phone, a smile of triumph on his face, Hügi leant forward, took up the phone and said simply:

" Here is *Direktor* Hügi. Cancel that order. Meals will be served in the proper place, at the proper time."

He replaced the phone and said:

" Is there anything else? "

The journalist let out an oath and grabbed the desk with both hands, as if he were going to tip it on top of the cool, ascetic figure sitting behind it. He was shaking with anger.

" For two pins I'd throw you out of the window, you . . . God, do you know who you are talking to? "

" I was waiting for an introduction."

" Well then, get this: I'm Paddy Chipperfield. When I write an article it goes in scores of newspapers right round the world. Millions know my name, and people generally find it wiser not to rub me up the wrong way. Furthermore: I started this . . . beehive out there, the whole fanfare and farrago; this is *my* story, do you understand? I made it. I filled this decrepit hotel—you could hear your whispers echoing in it when I came, but I splashed its name around the world."

" I see."

The thin, ascetic hotelier cracked his knuckles again, then folded his hands together in an attitude of prayer and studied them. Then he said:

" And what were you seeking in this room? "

" The telephone. Borgwand gave . . . Borgwand and I had an agreement. He gave me the monopoly of his phone. I also use this as my place of work."

" Why? "

" I need somewhere quiet. It was a gentlemen's understanding we had."

" How very convenient—for you. And what was your contribution to this bargain? "

" I wrote him up."

" I beg your pardon? "

" I've just been telling you. I gave Borgwand publicity. I mentioned his hotel in every article I wrote. You'd have to pay a fortune to buy the advertising space through normal channels."

" I see. I had no idea the old man was so astute. From what I had heard he was rather a dreamer."

" Astute! He was the biggest old fool I've met in a long time. He's sitting on a gold-mine right here and now, and refuses to dig the blasted thing. The arrangement about the telephone was the only instance when I could get him to see reason."

" That is an interesting opinion, Mr. Chipperfield. In what way does this hotel resemble a gold-mine? "

" In hundreds of ways. A blind man with the slightest nose for business could see it."

Struggling to control his temper Chipperfield lit a cigarette and strode to the window which commanded a view of the terrace. His eyes opened wide and he gave a grunt, half surprise and half approval.

" Is that your idea? "

" Which one? I have several," answered Hügi suavely.

Chipperfield indicated the giant telescope on the terrace. It was caged in by a rough wooden fence, with a small gate permitting access to its use. Guarding this gate was a hard-faced elderly woman in black, selling tickets.

" How much are you charging? " he asked.

The director told him. Chipperfield whistled in surprise.

" Half an hour per person, or what? "

" Five minutes. I am not here for my health."

The journalist could not suppress a chuckle.

" Fair enough," he said. " But why the tickets? That tough old crone doesn't look as if she'd let the Archangel Gabriel through without paying."

" That tough old crone—who happens to be an aunt of mine—sells tickets, the first and last numbers of which I note. It is the only way I can prevent her from cheating me."

Chipperfield burst out laughing. He was beginning to form a second opinion of the dapper little man behind Borgwand's desk. At least Hügi did not seem bent on spouting tedious ethics like his predecessor.

" Who *are* you, anyway? " the journalist asked. " You can't kid me you're a bosom friend of old Borgwand? "

" Far from it. I am employed by a certain finance company in Zürich—the exact name need not concern you. We expect to own this hotel within a short while. *Herr* Borgwand was in slight monetary difficulties and found himself compelled to apply for a loan. I very much doubt if he will be in a position to repay on the given date."

" So that's how the land lies. And in the meantime you intend making a little hard cash on the side? "

" Exactly."

" *Herr* Hügi, I think you and I should have a little business talk. It could be that if you play ball with me and I do the same with you, together we could make a nice little pile here. What do you say? "

He offered the dapper little man his hand, and the latter took it. It was like clutching a frog and Chipperfield released it quickly.

" I am always interested to talk business," said Hügi.

" What are your ideas with regard to exploiting this . . . gold-mine? "

" We'll talk it over when I've had a bite to eat. I'm starving."

" Certainly. But not here, if you please. My staff will bring you anything you desire in the dining-room."

" O.K. But I'll be back shortly; and I shall want to use your phone."

" By all means."

Chipperfield turned to leave.

" There's just one small thing," the hotelier said, the faintest glimmer of a smile hovering on his thin features.

" Yes? "

" You will find a small notice in the key-rack amongst your correspondence. Each guest will receive the same note, so I trust you will not be offended."

" What's in it? "

" The price of your room has gone up."

" Yeah? By how much? "

" Double."

The new director snapped his knuckles, murmured " *Auf Wiedersehen*, *Herr* Chipperfield," and devoted himself to a pile of letters on his desk.

CHAPTER VIII

CLAIRE SAT stunned at the sick man's bedside, forgetful of the passage of time. It was late in the afternoon, she had spent the whole of her two hours free time with him, and she almost wished that she had not come. Borgwand lay slumped amongst the pillows, his breathing erratic; his desperate attempt to convince her of the truth had exhausted him.

" I *do* understand, *Herr* Borgwand," she repeated

soothingly, " I understand, and I will do all I can. But you must try not to excite yourself so."

She let go of his limp hand, rose and smoothed the pillows, and wiped his feverish brow with a cool cloth. At her touch the old man's eyes, bright with fever, opened, and he whispered once more:

" Chipperfield *knows*. He is hiding the truth. You must find out what he knows, it's terribly important."

" I'll do all I can. Please rest now, you must get some sleep."

" Promise me you will——"

" I promise."

It was obvious that his last reserves of strength had been drained in telling her of the incredible quarrel with Chipperfield, but he seemed to find some relief now he had at last been able to tell someone. For the first time since his collapse he appeared able to relax. The terrible burden of knowledge had been passed on to her, and suddenly she felt tired, deeply tired and heavy of spirit.

If only she had someone to lean upon, some steadfast friend to whom she could turn. Now that Borgwand's place had been taken by the ruthless, frigid little man from Zürich, there was no one. Unless . . . but no, that was unthinkable, after the foolish way she had behaved on the hotel steps the night before. Was it only the night before? Only Tuesday night, scarcely three days after the whole affair had begun? It seemed like an age.

Grimly she realised that there was no one to fall back on except herself. She would have to challenge Paddy Chipperfield alone. Her mouth set in a firm line, she slipped quietly from the sick man's bedside, and went downstairs.

Heinrich told her that Chipperfield was to be found in the director's bureau.

Mercifully the officious clerk whom the new director had brought with him was not on guard at the door. She knocked once and receiving no answer tapped again and entered. The journalist was alone, his bulky frame hunched over a typewriter. He was working at high speed, and from the manner in which he jabbed at the keys one might have imagined they were personal enemies. He looked up with annoyance at the interruption. Claire suppressed a slight shudder, it was obvious that he was in a foul temper.

" *Herr* Hügi is not here, *Fräulein*, as you can see," he snapped curtly.

" I came to see you, not Hügi."

" Oh? Don't tell me you've come to apologise for your childish behaviour the other night? " he sneered, unconsciously fingering the faint bruise that still lingered on his cheek.

" No, I haven't. If there is any apologising being done, then it ought to come from you."

" Well, well: I had no idea we were so old-fashioned around here."

" I haven't come to discuss morals, *Herr* Chipperfield —at least, not that kind. I want to know what your conversation with *Herr* Borgwand last night consisted of."

The journalist stiffened in his chair. For the first time she noticed that the lurking hint of a smile at the corners of his mouth was not there. He was frowning heavily, and when he spoke his voice, though guarded, had a cold menace in it.

" You want to know rather a lot, don't you, *Fräulein*? I fail to see how it is any business of yours what we discussed. Tell me, what is the latest court bulletin on the old boy? "

" He's very ill. Something seems to have given him a terrible shock. I know his heart has been weak for a long time, but there's more to it than that. I want to know what passed between you to cause an upset as big——"

" What an impertinent young madam you are! How dare you assume that *I* was the cause of his stroke."

" Look, I'll be plain: I'm not just guessing. I've been with him all afternoon and he told me——"

" This is indeed interesting. Are you really going to produce the babblings of a sick old man as some kind of factual statement? "

"He was clear enough in his mind about what he wanted to say. You are withholding something—some-thing vitally important. You know more about the accident up there than you have admitted."

" I assure you I've told all I know."

" That's not true! *Herr* Borgwand is convinced the guides of the rescue team have got the position wrong, and that you know it. For some wicked reason you are holding back. Why? "

" Since you can think up the absurd questions I wonder you don't supply your own ridiculous answers."

" All right, I will. *Herr* Borgwand says it is because you want the story to be dragged out longer. God knows why—it's beyond human belief that anyone should not want those two poor men rescued as soon as possible. But you aren't human. I think you are some kind of fiend, an agent of the devil——"

Chipperfield cut her off with a harsh laugh.

" Now we're entering the realms of fairy stories. You will be telling me about pixies and hob-goblins soon."

He stood up, ripped the page he had been typing from the machine, stuffed it into a brief-case and started for the door. Taking his hat and raincoat from the stand he turned and said:

" You must excuse me, but I have to go and interview a bunch of bumptious Germans who've just arrived. Let me give you a fair warning about our little talk. I presume you are acquainted with the laws of libel and slander—they are no doubt more or less the same in Switzerland as elsewhere: what you have just said be-tween the two of us was foolish and quite unfounded. If you should repeat it to a third person I'll have a lawyer on your neck like a ton of bricks; in no time at all you'll find yourself with a court case for slander on your hands. Watch your tongue, young lady—it could get you into trouble."

He swung out of the room and slammed the door, leaving her standing there, nervous, disturbed, but still grimly determined to find out the truth.

For more than a minute she stood looking at the telephone, trying to summon up her courage. She could think of no one else, and she realised she was powerless un-aided. The clumsy way in which she had learnt that Bell-man was married still sent prickles of shame down her spine, and she would not admit to herself the reason why she had wanted to find out.

Then she thought of the men in distress on the Eiger once more, and, stifling her inhibitions, picked up the phone.

The voice that answered her from the hotel on the Scheidegg was soft and confidential. No, Mr. Bellman was out, his key was in the rack; he had most probably gone with all the other gentlemen of the press to interview the German rescue team. Did the *Fräulein* wish to leave any message?

Claire hesitated, puzzled by this reference to a German rescue team and wondering if it had anything to do with Chipperfield's reference to "a bunch of bumptious Germans." In the end she told the clerk to ask Mr. Bellman to ring the Hotel Nordwand. At this the clerk seemed to prick up his ears.

"Is that by any chance *Fräulein* Claire on the line?" he inquired, his voice purring with friendly discretion.

"Yes it is," she answered, somewhat surprised.

"Oh dear—Mr. Bellman has been trying to reach you on the phone for some time."

So he had wanted to speak to her again. It was re-assuring, though a trifle puzzling.

"No one told me I was wanted on the phone," she

said. Then she thought of the frigid-faced new director
and guessed that he would allow little time to be wasted on
matters of a personal nature.

" I could nip over to the station and see if I can find
Mr. Bellman for you," volunteered the clerk eagerly.

" No, I'm sure he hasn't time now. Thank you all the
same. I'm sure I shall be able to get in touch with him
soon."

" As you wish," said the clerk regretfully. " At any
rate, I'll tell him that you called. I'm sure he'll be glad."

She was forced to smile at the clerk's somewhat over-
evident good will, but all the same she felt considerably
happier when she put down the phone.

Going out into the foyer she whispered to Heinrich
that she was going to be absent for half an hour, and
accepting his offer of an umbrella, set out for the Kleine
Scheidegg. She did not care if her absence was noticed by
Hügi or any of the rather dubious personnel he had
brought with him.

As she made her way through the crowd on the terrace
she noticed that a hasty construction resembling a
newspaper kiosk was nearing completion near the outer
steps. A worker was in the act of nailing a sign, in flaring
red letters on a white ground, that read:

" Trinkets, Andenken, Souvenirs of the Eiger
North Wall
Buy them here—they're cheaper! "

*   *   *

The news that the German *Bergwacht* from Munich was
joining in the rescue attempts did not at first cause very
much surprise. A large crowd of radio reporters, newsreel cameramen, journalists and photographers had
collected on Scheidegg Station to greet them, but few
would have been prepared to prophesy that their arrival
would, inside a matter of hours, add a totally new

conflict to the unfolding drama. The layman might have been momentarily puzzled as to why a German rescue team more than two hundred miles away should hasten with such remarkable speed to offer its assistance in the Swiss Alps. But to those at all versed in matters of mountaineering there was nothing surprising in the incident at all. The climbers from Munich were not only recognised as amongst the best in Germany, but also amongst the finest in all Europe. It was a German-Austrian team that had first succeeded in conquering the Eiger North Wall in 1938. Several members of the rescue team that was on its way had first-hand experience of the perilous north face, and the reputation of the Munich *Bergwacht* for skill and achievement in countless rescues carried out in Germany and Austria was widely recognised. The alacrity with which they had flown to the scene was regarded by nearly everyone as a shining example of co-operation among the nations. Few except the petty-minded even so much as dreamed of questioning their motives. A man hung in mortal peril on the end of a rope eleven or twelve thousand feet in the air, his comrade vanished; no one knew for certain what the nationality of the injured man was, and from the humanitarian standpoint it hardly mattered.

But many believed him to be Kurt Stringberg, famous Munich climber. This was the point that galled Chipperfield. He could only read (and could only imagine the world reading) one interpretation into the arrival of the Germans on the scene: they had come to rescue their colleague and fellow-countryman.

It was like a stinging blow in the face, a finger of derision levelled at him for his Baron Mandoza theories. He was seething with anger as he paced the station platform. He took good care to avoid those whom he knew to be his enemies, but all the same he felt certain he intercepted frequent mocking glances and derisive laughter that could only be at his expense.

Eventually the train from Grindelwald came into sight. Although it had been laid on for their sole use by the Swiss authorities, some delay seemed to have held up the German team down in the valley, and daylight was beginning to fade by the time they arrived. There was a confused scramble towards the carriages, much shouting, popping of flash bulbs and considerable disorder until the leader of the party had been singled out and surrounded by newsreel cameras and a rapid fire of questions.

The leader of the nine-man team was a massive, shy, uneloquent man, clearly ill at ease in the sudden glare of publicity that spotlighted him. He gave his replies to the stream of questions in a low, halting voice that was not always audible above the hubbub.

Chipperfield led the interview in his customary arrogant manner, though Bellman noted the curious fact that the famous journalist lapsed into silence once a hatchet-faced local reporter named Zellwäger began his questions.

" What is your opinion as to the identity of the man hanging on the end of the rope? " Zellwäger asked.

" It is difficult to be certain," the German leader answered, " but we think it quite possible that it is Kurt Stringberg."

" What makes you think that? "

" I know him well, he is a personal friend of mine. This is the mountain where he once failed. A true mountaineer does not give in easily. Kurt always promised himself a second chance at the *Nordwand*."

" Despite the danger he was causing to other men's lives? "

" I am sure the guide Hans Albrecht—— "

" I don't mean Albrecht. No doubt he was well paid to undertake the job. I mean the courageous men who are risking their necks to get Stringberg out alive."

K

The German looked worried at this thrust, and being unskilled in the art of dialectic and cross-questioning, was unable to parry it. McKechnie the shrewd Scot seemed to sense the big man's helplessness, for he snapped across to Zellwäger:

" I don't suppose Stringberg or whoever it is up there took an accident for granted when he was making his plans. After all, disaster is not exactly inevitable when one is climbing a mountain."

" No," sneered Zellwäger, " but that's what happened, isn't it."

" Yes, but you're putting the cart before the horse."

Another reporter asked, " What route are you planning to take? "

" We will climb the south-west flank from *Eigergletscher* Station."

" But the Swiss are coming over the top, from the Jungfraujoch."

" I believe that is so."

" What makes you think you know better than the Swiss? " Zellwäger shot in quickly.

The German paused before answering. Bellman happened to glance at Chipperfield and fancied he caught a queer gleam in the man's eyes.

The German leader answered carefully:

" Please, it is not a question of knowing better than anyone. We made inquiries whilst in Grindelwald, my comrades and I: the weather reports from the Jungfraujoch are very disturbing. I fear the Swiss team may run into difficulties if the forecast proves correct."

" So you think the Swiss team have taken the wrong route? " Zellwäger snapped eagerly.

" I . . . we . . . that is not——"

" Why are you taking the south-west flank? Because it is quicker? "

" Under normal circumstances it is."

" Will you climb during darkness? "

" We must if we are not to lose valuable time."

" Will you put yourselves under the command of the Swiss when you get to the summit first? "

By now the German was becoming more wary. He stood up and answered stiffly:

" I did *not* say we would get there first. We are here to try and save the lives of two trapped mountaineers. That is all that interests us. Please let us get on with the job."

Ignoring further questions he brushed his way through the throng and made for the special train which, loaded with all their transferred equipment, was waiting to take them as far as station *Eiglergletscher* at the foot of the Eiger's south-west flank.

As the crowd hurriedly dispersed Bellman noticed that Chipperfield quietly made his way towards Zellwäger. The two men shook hands and after a few moments' talk left together for the station buffet.

The scene was innocent enough, the natural desire of two newspapermen to get acquainted over a drink: yet he could not help thinking there was something sinister, almost conspiratorial, about their appearance as they disappeared together. It put him in mind of a painting he had once seen of Guy Fawkes and Catesby planning to blow up the Houses of Parliament. Then he laughed at the analogy and tried to put it out of his mind.

Shrugging his shoulders he turned and looked instinctively, as he had done a hundred times in the past few days up at the cloud-hidden massif of the North Wall.

Stringberg, or the society playboy?

And alive, or dead? Could they possibly last out till help came?

A voice over his shoulder seemed to echo his thoughts.

" I sure hope those poor devils can hang out till morning," said Doug Wilson, the American correspondent from Paris.

Bellman nodded and the two men fell into step.

" Our mutual friend the Torchbearer grew kinda quiet, didn't you think? " Wilson said.

" The same thought occurred to me. I rather got the impression he was content to have someone else stir up the mud for a change."

" You mean that ferret-faced bastard Zellwäger? "

" Yes."

" What's eating him? Seemed to me those Munich boys are absolutely on the level."

" *Herr* Zellwäger appears to think otherwise."

" What d'you reckon he's driving at? "

" I'm not at all sure. We shall know soon enough when his paper comes out."

" Yeah, I guess so. Me, I only hope they get those boys down pretty quick, and I don't give two hoots who collars the glory. Man, it must be real cold up there. Cold and wet. Where do you figure the guide Albrecht has got to? "

" Who knows? " Bellman answered. " Possibly he's injured too, somewhere out of sight. Or maybe he's gone on ahead on his own to try and fetch help."

" That's what a lot of people figure. I wonder how long that guy on the rope can hang out."

" A lot depends on how badly he's injured. And on what the weather does between now and to-morrow morning."

" Yeah. Those German boys were hinting at some rugged stuff on the way. I wouldn't like to be up there if snow started coming down."

" I wouldn't like to be up there at all," Bellman commented dryly.

" You and me both, Johnny. Eighteen hours is a hell of a long time to be hanging by a bit of nylon rope to a mountainside."

" Eighteen hours—or more."

The American stopped, his brows furrowed in concern.

" You still chewing over the Torchbearer's scoop? "

" I would like to know how he managed to get his news of the accident so quickly, that's all."

Wilson nodded slowly.

" Me too. You'll let me know if you find out anything? "

" I will."

The two men parted at Bellman's hotel and the latter went up to his room to draft a brief account of the interview with the Munich rescue team.

He had almost finished when the discreet voice of his friend the reception clerk announced on the phone that a young lady was asking to see him in the hall. He hurried down immediately, feeling certain it was Claire and surprised at the elation that seemed suddenly to glow inside him.

Any constraint that might have stood between them was swept away by the tense anxiety written on her face. She said immediately:

" I had to see you—about *Herr* Borgwand. Something terribly urgent has cropped up."

" Has something happened to him? " Bellman asked swiftly.

She shook her head and glanced nervously round for a quiet place where they could talk. With difficulty they found an empty corner in the crowded lounge and she told him of the disturbing accusations which the sick man had made against Chipperfield.

Bellman turned white as he listened, though whether from anger or plain shock Claire was not certain. When she had finished he said:

" And Chipperfield denied it entirely? "

" He didn't even bother. He just sneered at me, and tried to scare me with threats about slander. Actually he does scare me, though I try not to let him know it. Sometimes I have almost the feeling as though he were . . . how do you say . . . *ein bisschen verrückt*."

" The big word for it is megalomania, and you may not

be far wrong. Ambition and lust for power can often make a man deranged. I've wondered the same thing myself about Chipperfield recently. But you say Borgwand's condition is semi-delirious?"

"I know what you're thinking," she answered desperately, "but I tell you, I *know* him—it's not just the wanderings of a sick mind. He was speaking the truth. You've got to do something!"

"I had a feeling all along that there was something queer about the whole business," he said. "What you have told me makes sense. It's the only way Chipperfield could have got his story out so quickly. He must have known that poor devil has been hanging on the end of the rope since yesterday. Somehow or other he saw it happen, when all the rest of the world didn't. God, what a swine the man is!"

"*Herr* Borgwand said the rescue teams must be told. If Chipperfield lied about the position and time of the accident, then Borgwand says the relief columns may have taken the wrong equipment and the wrong route. We must get in touch with them and warn them."

Bellman looked at his watch and stood up.

"Wait here," he said. "Heaven only knows if they'll listen, but the least we can do is try. I'll see if there is any hope of contacting them."

He was gone perhaps ten minutes. When he returned the gloomy expression on his face told her the answer.

"Too late. I phoned up to the Joch, but the Swiss have already set out, with all their equipment."

"What about the Germans? Couldn't we catch them?"

Bellman studied his watch again.

"They should reach *Eigergletscher* Station in a short while. I'll try again then, though I don't know what I have to tell them. It isn't as if we knew exactly where the man is hanging. All we have to go upon is a strong suspicion that the accident happened a lot earlier than people think, and that the two men are probably a good

deal lower on the face than is generally imagined. That's
pretty slender evidence. I doubt if they'll bother to listen
to me."

"Wouldn't they listen to the pilot?"

"I was just thinking of that. I must find him and talk
to him. His word should count. The question is, how to
get hold of him. And before that I must have a word with
Borgwand, if possible. I ought to learn from him first-
hand what he heard Chipperfield say on the phone."

Taking her arm they left the lounge together, followed,
Claire was quite sure, by the beaming approval of the
reception clerk.

*　　　　*　　　　*

At almost the same moment Chipperfield came out of
the railway restaurant, his good humour restored.

Zellwäger would play ball. Indeed the man had needed
very little prompting. He appeared to nurse an almost
pathological hatred of the entire German nation. Chipperfield had not bothered to probe into its causes; sufficient
for his purpose was the obvious fact that Zellwäger hated.
The man could be relied upon to conduct a subsidiary
and highly useful campaign of his own.

He himself had his hands more than full with the disquieting realisation that Borgwand had talked. For the
hundredth time he cursed himself for his own carelessness
in speaking so loudly on the phone. But he had locked the
door, and the idea that he might be overheard through a
thin wall had never entered his head.

Somehow the old man's mouth had to be sealed. He
had at least to be prevented from further dangerous
gossiping until the trapped climbers had been rescued and
the story had faded from the glare of public notice.

Then he saw Claire and Bellman, leaving the hotel
near the station together. They struck out hurriedly in
the direction of Alpiglen and the Hotel Nordwand. In a

flash it was clear to him what had happened. Despite his warning, the girl had repeated what Borgwand had told her. And repeated it, of all people, to Bellman. Though he despised the latter, Chipperfield knew that Bellman was a man of high principles and stubborn character, a man not to be dismissed lightly.

The situation was serious. He knew he had to get to Borgwand before they did.

There was a second path connecting the two hotels; although it was longer, he might get there first if he ran all the way. He just was about to set off when he saw a bicycle leaning against one of the railway sheds.

He strolled casually up to it. No owner appeared to be in sight, no one was looking. Leisurely he mounted the saddle and pedalled away. Not until he was safely out of view behind a dip in the land did he begin to pedal furiously.

The track was bumpy, a mere cow-path, and a cold wind was blowing with steadily increasing strength, but his route lay downhill, and he arrived with plenty of time in hand. Hiding the bicycle behind a clump of wind-swept trees he walked the last hundred yards and entered the congested hotel unnoticed.

Borgwand's room was on the third floor, he knew. He had visited him there before the old man had been taken ill. Using the staff staircase he approached the room via the back way. The corridor was empty. If anyone should question his right to be there, he had his answer ready: he was merely paying the sick man a friendly visit.

He tiptoed to the room and noiselessly opened the door.

Borgwand lay on his back, his breathing congested and irregular. He seemed to be in some kind of a coma. Small beads of sweat glistened on his forehead and his face was an unhealthy colour. On a bedside table stood a tray laden with uneaten foodstuffs. There were also several bottles of medicine and boxes of pills. Chipper-field examined these for a moment without touching them, then decided against the notion. He had no wish to be caught for murder by the use of some such stupid device as switching pills, and knew that he lacked the necessary medical knowledge to carry out such a foolhardy scheme.

He circled the bed and drew back the thin curtain a fraction of an inch. His heart missed a beat. Bellman and Claire were just mounting the outer steps to the terrace. They had been quicker than he had thought possible.

He was on the point of slipping out of the room when he saw the giant wardrobe in a dark corner. He opened it quickly. The old man's lack of prosperity in recent years was clearly indicated by the small amount of clothing inside. There was ample room, even for a big man. For a second he hesitated. It was risky, but it might pay off: he would give a lot to find out just what Bellman and the girl were hatching together. He heard a faint murmur of voices along the corridor; stepping swiftly inside the wardrobe he closed the door. He could not lock it from the inside, but he was able to keep it firmly closed by gripping the reverse part of the handle.

A moment later Bellman and Claire entered the room. They spoke in low tones but he was able to understand what they said. He could hear someone fussing about near the bed, smoothing sheets. Then Claire said:

" He doesn't look too good. I don't think we ought to disturb him, do you? "

" No, I'm afraid not. Is the doctor due again soon? "

" He promised to come directly after dinner."

" Maybe I can come up then, and try to get a few words with Borgwand whilst he's treating him. Meantime I can get on with the job of chasing up that other fellow."

" Right. I'll just see that he's well covered-up. If he caught a chill in this condition it could be very serious," Claire said.

Chipperfield heard her movements at the bedside. For what seemed an eternity he waited for the sound of their footsteps going towards the door. They did not come. Instead, to his horror, he heard the girl say:

"Just a second, we are terribly short of clean kitchen aprons, I'll just see if he has any in his wardrobe."

Panic surged in waves through him as he heard her coming towards his hiding-place. Grimly he tightened his grip on the reverse half of the handle. A second later he felt the pressure of the girl's efforts to turn it. Then the pressure relaxed.

"Oh dear, it appears to be locked," came her words from only a few inches away. He did not dare to breathe.

"The kitchen staff are complaining all the time about having to use dirty *Schürze*—never mind, I don't suppose he kept many for himself."

Chipperfield's heart continued to beat wildly as he heard them go towards the bedroom door. He heard it open, and then close softly behind them.

For some time after the sound of their footsteps had faded along the corridor he remained in the cramped dark space, sweating with fear. He wished he knew who "that other fellow" was whom Bellman was intent on chasing up.

Then he let himself quietly out, tiptoed to the door, listened carefully and, reassured by the utter quiet, returned to the sick man's bedside, a foolproof plan which the girl had unwittingly given him forming at the back of his mind.

*　　　　*　　　　*

Later that evening Hügi looked up from the newspaper he had been studying and gave Chipperfield a glance of cool appraisal.

"You certainly know your business," he said, tapping with a thin, carefully manicured finger at the huge headlines which, under Chipperfield's name and a date-line mentioning the Grand Hotel Nordwand, accompanied a vast photograph of the unknown climber waving cheerfully from the mountainside.

" Thank you. A certain amount of credit must go of course to the lay-out editor. It's not enough to have a good story, you must know how to display it too."

Hügi raised his eyebrows at this unusual evidence of modesty, but contented himself with remarking, as he indicated the huge photograph:

" That must have sold a lot of copies? "

" It did. It most certainly did."

" And supposing your theory is not true? "

Chipperfield bared his teeth in a grin. " It still sold a lot of copies."

" That doesn't answer my question. Supposing it is Kurt Stringberg and not your socialite Baron up there? "

" It's the Baron all right, never fear. I could probably prove it beyond dispute here and now."

" Then why don't you? "

" It wouldn't be smart. Keep 'em guessing, like the thriller writers do, right till they haul his frozen carcass off the Eiger. The funny thing is, it wouldn't even matter if I were wrong—which I am not, I assure you. The Baron served his purpose as far as I'm concerned by focusing attention on this benighted spot. Look who's turned up: *Time*, *Life*, *Paris-Match*, *Oggi*, *Revue*, *Quick*—all the glossies that count. And all the big daily boys are here, and the Sunday tabloids; newsreel men, radio reporters, the whole works except for TV, and they'd have been on the scene but for those blasted mountains. And why are they all here? Because it's a fundamentally important story? Not a bit of it. Simply because it has glamour. You can thank pretty-boy Mandoza for that. And you can thank him again, when he slipped off that mountain. He couldn't have done anyone a greater service if he'd thought about it all night."

"It increased the scope of your story?"

"Exactly. Inside a matter of minutes he turned a mere climbing stunt into a great rescue-drama. The public loves them. They can't have too many of 'em, especially if there's only one or two men at the most who need to be rescued."

"Ah, yes, you mentioned something about that earlier to-day. One man in danger is . . . how did you put it? . . . a hundred times better than a horde of people. An interesting theory, though I'm not sure I understand it."

"It's easy enough. The public is one single reader, a man or woman sitting in a comfortable chair before the fire after a dull routine day: empty, gullible, hungry and bored. It's no good feeding him with sweet little tales about harmony and high ethics and gentle happiness, that only sends him to sleep. He wants drama, the cruel hand of fate, a bit of bloodshed; that keeps him awake."

"Schiller and Shakespeare knew that."

"Quite, only they wrote for a smaller public than mine, of course."

The remark was made without a trace of irony, Hügi realised. Through half-closed lids the Swiss surveyed Chipperfield as the latter enlarged on his theme. Not for the first time it occurred to him to wonder if the journalist was entirely sane. There was a queer, fanatical light in the man's eyes as he talked, and the gestures which he made with his powerful hands were little short of grandilo-quent. He was a brilliant reporter, of that there was no doubt; but lust for money, lust for fame, and above all lust for power—power over lesser rivals, power over the minds of millions of readers—seemed almost to be driving him towards the fringe of megalomania.

"But that's by the way," Chipperfield went on. "Here's the point about numbers: your single reader by the fireside can't grasp the drama if it's on too large a scale. You can't reach him with famines in India or whole native villages being wiped out by plague. He simply can't identify himself with so many nameless individuals. But give him a lone woman having a baby on a beleaguered lighthouse, a trapped miner down a wrecked shaft, a single sailor adrift on a raft in the Atlantic, or a pilot fighting for his life in a damaged plane when all the rest of the crew have jumped to safety —*that's* the kind of news his imagination can grasp."

The journalist began pacing the room, warming to his theme, as Hügi listened with a thin smile of cynical interest.

" They call it ' reader identification.' Your single reader *becomes* the man or woman in distress, lives all the panic and struggle and heroic desperation from the comfort of his arm-chair, enjoys the whole gamut of human emotion from A to Z without running a bit of risk himself."

" You don't seem to have a very high opinion of the average reader's intelligence," said Hügi.

" I don't have to. It doesn't concern me. I'm a newspaperman, not a teacher or a moral uplifter. I take people as I find them. The public is empty: we fill them. It's as simple as that. Just like you fill the stomachs of your hungry guests."

" Ah, but my guests have paid to be well fed and looked after, they are entitled——"

" So have mine paid! For a few coins the newsboy sells them pages and pages of entertainment. Nobody made them buy it. Nobody stood there with a gun and forced them to read any particular paper or newsstory. It's a free world, this side of the Curtain, and a free press. The public can take my stuff or leave it. I don't owe them anything."

" Yes, but the intellectuals argue that the press has a certain responsibility towards the public——"

" That kind of twaddle makes me weep. Our only responsibility is to give them what they want. And our only crime would be to force them to take what they don't want. A newspaper-owner is a business man, like any other. He's there for his shareholder's profit, not for his health. He's got to show a reasonable dividend at the end of the year, and he can only do this by feeding the masses what they want, not by preaching and moralising or pretending the world is a garden inhabited by fairies. And we reporters are simply the commercial travellers and reps., the middlemen stationed between owner and public. We get a lot of mud thrown at us but in actual fact we're a pretty harmless bunch, no more wicked than any other middleman or retail agent who earns his daily bread by seeing the masses get what they want."

The hotelier was about to answer when the internal phone on his desk rang. He picked up the receiver.

" *Ja* ? "

He listened for a moment, quoted a price, said something in swift dialect about rooms and baths, then hung up.

Chipperfield said bluntly:

" What's that about a room with a bath? Mine's been taken away from me. You don't mean to tell me you're letting someone else——"

" Don't jump to conclusions, Mr. Chipperfield. That was a guest complaining to one of my staff about the price he had to pay to sleep *on* a bath! I've had them all boarded up with planks. We are running out of bedrooms."

Chipperfield relaxed his belligerent attitude.

" You don't miss a trick, do you? "

" I try not to."

" How much are you charging? "

The hotelier told him, and even the hardboiled journalist was forced to chuckle.

" And if they refuse to pay? "

" They are at liberty to go elsewhere. I'm quite safe, the law of supply and demand is on my side; everywhere else is packed out. You see, Mr. Chipperfield, my business at the moment rather resembles yours—no one is actually forcing the guests at the point of a gun to come here."

He snapped his knuckles, allowed himself a bleak, fleeting smile, and then began ticking off some items on a list. After a moment he drew an adding-machine towards him and began totalling a column of figures with unbelievable dexterity. He had evidently counted money before.

When he had finished he gave a grunt of approval, circled the total in red and passed the torn-off slip of paper to Chipperfield.

" Receipts from the souvenir kiosk. Not bad for the first day, eh? "

The journalist glanced at the figure and nodded.

" They'll be better to-morrow, when we get into our stride."

" Now let us get down to work on this postcard idea. What do you think, black and white, or coloured? "

He passed a rough artist's layout over the desk to Chipperfield. The latter studied it carefully. It showed a photograph of the North Wall, and superimposed on one corner was a sketch of a mountaineer hanging from the end of a rope in space.

" Coloured," said Chipperfield emphatically. " Make the mountain silver and black, with a hint of purple here and there. Vivid white at the snowline. Purple gentians at the foot. The sky must be tinged pink—*Alpenglühen* and all that rot; pink skies always suggest drama. Maybe the climber could have a yellow shirt and brown trousers, just for colour contrast."

Hügi picked up the phone and said:

" Then we must get the printers moving right away."

A discreet knock came at his door.

" *Herein.* "

Hügi's private secretary, the fussy young man who had fallen foul of Chipperfield earlier that day, paddled in on flat feet, glancing warily at the big journalist as he circled past. He deposited a sum of money and some ticket stubs on the desk. Without looking up Hügi, who by then had begun talking on the phone, pulled out a drawer, tossed a roll of tickets to the clerk, ordered " Check them," and carried on speaking as the clerk left the room.

". . . I know it's asking a lot, but the price is right, I think? . . . well then, let me have a few hundred cards on sale in my kiosk to-morrow morning and the rest can follow later . . . I don't care if it does mean working all night, that's what I'm paying you for . . . *uf Wiederluege.*"

" O.K.? " asked Chipperfield.

" They'll be ready."

The journalist was about to speak when the external phone rang. Hügi picked it up. There was the sound of atmospherics over the wire. Above the crackling Chipperfield heard his name mentioned.

" It's for you," said Hügi, handing him the receiver.

The journalist listened intently for a moment and suddenly broke into a broad smile.

" Splendid . . . is she alone? . . . perfect. Now, hang on to her until I get down there. Whatever you do, don't let anyone else get a glimpse of her, even if it means locking her up till I get there. Keep her under cover, d'you understand? That girl's worth a gold-mine."

He slammed down the phone, a look of triumph illuminating his face.

" Hell, that line is bad. Fellow was only calling from Lauterbrunnen, but he might have been continents away."

" I think there must be a storm on the way," Hügi offered. " Who was that, the wealthy girl-friend just turned up? "

" Yes. But not mine, though. Someone else's."

He began collecting his personal possessions from the desk and stuffing them into his brief-case.

" Will she be requiring a room at the hotel? "

" Yes. But not a boarded-up bath, if you don't mind."

" Of course. Any friend of yours . . . What name shall I reserve the room in? "

Chipperfield gave him a piercing look as he took his coat and hat from the rack.

" You want to know everything, don't you? All right, I'll trust you as far as I can throw you, and that's the length of this room. If you ever double-cross me . . ."

" My dear fellow, we are partners, remember? "

" I'll remember. The girl's name is Jasmine. At least that's the silly pet-name she trades under. She's a model, one of the top mannequins in Paris. I think her real name is Bertha Blott or some such horror. She's the last flame the Baron's supposed to have had before he took up alpine gymnastics: the one he consoled himself with after the royal romance fizzled out."

" What on earth is she doing here? "

" Don't you get it? Why, man, it's a natural. Palpitating beauty down in valley watches heroic struggle as rescue teams fight to save lover-boy on mountain."

Hügi nearly smiled.

" Between us we really think of everything, don't we? " he said.

Chipperfield grunted and swung out of the room.

Hügi sat looking for a long time at the phone, and once his hand stretched out towards it. Finally he decided against it. Although he knew he could sell the piece of news for a good figure, it would perhaps be unwise to cross a man as ruthless as Chipperfield.

He comforted himself by examining his list once again, ticking off each item carefully as he went through it. Telescope, deck-chairs, coloured cards, binoculars, price list in the bar, rooms, souvenir kiosk. . . . It was a good list, comprehensive, business-like, and highly profitable. After about five minutes of undivided concentration he laid down his pencil and relaxed. He really did not think that between them they had forgotten anything.

Except, he thought, with a snigger at his own wit, the man hanging from the face of the mountain.

CHAPTER IX

THE STORM that broke that Wednesday night was not merely unprecedented for that time of the year; in fury and malignancy it rivalled the worst which people in the valley could remember even in winter.

Its effect on all concerned directly or indirectly with the drama on the Eiger North Wall was far-reaching. For some it proved fatal, the last and most terrible night of their lives. For others, it was a queer kind of turning-point. In one instance it even saved a life.

As the cold wind that had keened miserably up the valley all day grew in force and took on the proportions of an impending gale, Claire went through the hotel fastening windows and securing shutters in the bedrooms. It was a routine measure, to prevent rain from sweeping in and to obviate the irritating clatter of loose shutters which would keep the guests awake when they retired to bed an hour or so later.

In a passage on the third floor she bumped into the doctor who was attending *Herr* Borgwand. She asked immediately how the old man was.

" I have not been to see him yet, I am just going now," he answered. " I was held up with a maternity case at Grund."

Claire felt an unaccountable spasm of misgiving run through her as she turned to accompany the doctor to Borgwand's room. Despite the heavy pressure of work on the floors below, she would have found time to come up and confirm for her own peace of mind that all was well, but the doctor had promised to come directly after dinner and she had relied on him.

The sight that met their eyes as they opened the door and switched on the light caused them to gasp with dismay. The old man lay on his side, uncovered, his sheets strewn all over the bed, the blankets on the floor. The window was wide open, the room icy cold.

The doctor muttered an exclamation and sprang to shut the window. Claire snatched the bedclothing together and hastily covered the prone body. For a moment she thought he was dead. The doctor bent over him and made a swift examination.

" My God, I wonder how long he's been like that! "

" I should have come up . . ." Claire stammered, beside herself with anxiety and self-reproach. " I was so busy, and I was sure you had been to see him hours ago."

" When did you last come up? "

Claire looked at her watch. " About four hours ago. How bad is it? "

" Very serious. If he's been uncovered all that time . . . pneumonia at least. We must get him to hospital at once, it's his only chance. I'll do what I can now if you will get on the phone and make the necessary arrangements."

The girl nodded and slipped from the room.

*   *   *

They brought him down to the valley with all possible speed, and then by fast car to Interlaken hospital. He was given penicillin and placed immediately in an oxygen tent. For several hours he hovered on the razor's edge between life and death. By dawn his breathing had become lighter and more regular. The crisis had passed. The doctors made it clear, however, that it would be many weeks before he could even be allowed out of bed.

As she waited at the hospital through the long weary

hours of the night and morning, Claire punished herself with self-accusation. The old man had nearly died through her neglect. It was true that she had been desperately busy. And it was true that she had felt certain she could rely on the doctor to come at the promised time. But if only she had found time to slip up once and see how he was, she would have seen that he had kicked the bed-clothes away in his delirious coma, and would have made sure that the windows were properly fastened before the storm came. There was no one to blame but herself.

Weary and sick at heart she set out shortly after dawn on the return journey to Alpiglen.

The trains were crowded. The whole of Central Switzerland and the Oberland seemed to be heading for the slopes facing the Eiger. Tourists of every nationality discussed with heated excitement and considerable in-accuracy the two climbers' chances of rescue.

As the train trundled slowly up the Lütschine valley, she stared unseeingly out of the window at the familiar scene of blackened chalets and apple orchards heavy with fruit, at children playing along the stony banks of the silver river, at the steady flow of charabancs and private cars making for the head of the valley. Her thoughts moved from the tired old man who had nearly died to the two climbers facing possible death on the North Wall. She wondered what news John Bellman would bring when he returned from his overnight trip to contact the pilot.

She did not know that by the time she had returned to Alpiglen, Bellman's journey would have been rendered almost pointless by the swiftness with which events had piled one on top of the other during the hours of the terrible storm.

*   *   *

The storm that had thus, paradoxically saved a life at

the foot of the Eiger, claimed two lives on the ridge approaching its summit.

Battling their way in pitch darkness at nearly twelve thousand feet along the Mönch Joch against winds of sixty to seventy miles an hour, the three-nation rescue team led by the Swiss guides met the full fury of the tempest head-on. Stinging hail born on the howling wind lashed at them like the blows of a whip. Then came blinding snow, cutting down visibility to a few feet. The sleds laden with over eight hundredweight of equipment assumed monumental weight, and it became clear before they had skirted the Mönch that they would never reach the Eiger summit.

And then it happened. Somewhere in the impenetrable darkness, as the blizzard struck them with full force, a man stumbled and fell whilst the column was reforming for the weary journey back to the Jungfrau. The men were roped together in teams of two. A sledge slewed dangerously out of control on an unseen stretch of ice, two men fought it, lost their balance and were plucked from the ridge by a sudden burst of wind. Sledge and bodies were hurled into the black void before anyone could grasp what was happening. It was beyond human power to save them, and pointless to search for them until the tempest had abated. The desperate column had only one object left: to reach shelter alive, with all their vital equipment intact, and plan a second route when the storm had subsided.

News of the tragedy, and of the failure of the column to reach the Eiger, filtered down to the Scheidegg during the small hours of the morning. Its effect was stunning. In addition no word had been heard from the German rescue team which had set out to climb the south-west flank as darkness fell.

As dawn broke the true plight of the trapped climbers who were spending their fourth night on the Wall became clear to all. Cold rain had swept the valley from end to end throughout the hours of darkness, and the temperature had sunk, at its lowest point, to below twenty degrees Fahrenheit. Men and women who knew the mountains well, stood silent, calculating the merciless cold which a human being would have had to endure on the exposed face of the thirteen thousand foot mountain.

They knew a man could survive an incredible degree of cold provided he were fit, dry and well-fed. Albrecht and his client were none of these things. They had spent a large part of their strength in two days of exhausting vertical climb; their food supplies after three days and four nights would be running low; any form of shelter on the naked face was unthinkable. One man was injured, the fate of the other totally unknown. Both had spent four nights in the open, without proper sleep, standing or at the most squatting in bivouac on ledges no wider than a builder's plank, their clothing drenched from constant chutes of icy water, their lives in perpetual danger from a hail of dislodged stones and chunks of ice. Now they faced a new peril, that of avalanches from the freshly-fallen snow. The last shreds of doubt as to the appalling seriousness of their situation had been swept away by the storm. Few dared voice their thoughts aloud, but those who knew the mountains, above all those who knew the North Wall, held out scant hope for their chances of survival.

As daylight came on the Thursday morning the wind gradually dropped. Huddled groups of tourists swathed in warm clothing peered through binoculars and telescopes, searching for some sign of the trapped men or their rescuers. The cloud was no longer thick. It had more the appearance of early-morning mist, holding out promise of lifting as the sun rose.

The defeated Swiss relief column had descended by rail to *Eigergletscher* Station at the foot of the west flank before daybreak. No time was lost. They clambered wearily from the train, hoisted their heavy equipment and set out once more, this time by foot up the south-west ridge over the same route that the Germans had taken during the night. On their faces could only be read grim determination, exhaustion, and bitterness at the loss which their team had suffered. Even the few journalists who had risen early enough to see the men arrive and set out again, were awed into silence by what they saw.

And then the cloud lifted.

With sudden, theatrical swiftness the gigantic pyramid that had been hidden from view for three days emerged from behind its veil and inside a matter of minutes was clear from top to bottom.

Near-pandemonium broke out. Windows were packed, doorways jammed, every single pair of field-glasses and every telescope swept into use. At the Hotel Nordwand the guests were taking a leisurely breakfast when the Eiger swam clear. In less than a minute the tables in the vast dining-room were practically deserted. A seething mass lined the window-panes.

Piercing the hubbub, a voice from the group crammed round the giant telescope on the terrace screamed:

" I've seen them! Up there, right at the top! "

In the total confusion that followed it was thought that the Baron had been spotted.

" At the top! Where? How did they manage it? "

Then came gradually the sobering realisation that it was neither Albrecht nor his client, but the German rescue team whom they could see, encamped on the summit.

So the Germans had got there first. The news spread with the speed of a bush-fire. It could be no one else, for the Swiss team had only been under way since shortly before daybreak. Four or five tiny black specks moving about on the snow-white peak could be counted, and from time to time other heads were seen bobbing above the cornice.

Feverishly the spectators swept the face of the mountain for any sign of the beleaguered climbers. At first they could discover nothing. The fresh snow that had clung in many places to the sheer mountain face had covered the trapped men as well, rendering them almost invisible even to the most powerful lens.

Chipperfield was one of the first to spot them.

People had been searching too high. He trained his binoculars on the second icefield, moved slowly up to the third, traversed towards the *Bügeleisen* and over towards the foot of the *Rampe*. And there he detected a slight movement.

The Baron was still hanging there. And he was alive. He appeared to be waving one arm, perhaps in an effort to signal, or to restore circulation in his frozen body. He was alive. The slender nylon rope by which he clung to life had survived the wild fury of the night.

Chipperfield's hand was trembling like a leaf as he lowered his glasses, and a wave of relief swept over him. The Baron was no use to him dead.

Vaguely he realised from the excited confusion around him that other eyes had focused on the *Bügeleisen* and had spotted the man on the end of the rope. Someone within earshot, evidently one who knew the topography of the Eiger well, said loudly:

" That's damn' strange. He's nowhere near the Spider. He must be hundreds of feet below. They'll never be able to reach him from there."

A spasm of fear coursed through the journalist's veins. Already one pair of eyes had been sharp enough to realise that there was something unexpected about the position of the injured climber. How long would it be before more eyes, more tongues, weightier voices, joined in the chorus? How long before a body of solemn-faced men called to see him and began asking awkward questions? He tried to shrug the ominous thought away. He had survived quite a few " inquiries " and petulant outcries from rival newspapers during his highly-successful career; it was unlikely that a bunch of cheese-making peasants would present him with difficulties too formidable for him to overcome. By the time attention had begun to focus uncomfortably on himself, the story would be over and he would be half a world away.

Grinding out the last vestige of fear from his mind, he focused his glasses once more on the mountain, this time on the black bobbing figures of the German rescue party at the summit. It was clear they were setting about the task of mounting their rescue operation, but the puzzling thing was that they did not seem to be positioned directly above the hanging man. Could that mean they had discovered the whereabouts of the guide Hans Albrecht? Perhaps they could see him and were concentrating their efforts on him first. From the standpoint of his newspaper story, nothing could have suited Chipperfield better. The longer the delay in rescuing Mandoza, the greater the build-up in the press.

Slowly he trained his glasses in a direct vertical line downwards from the men on the summit. At first he could discover nothing. He tried again, focusing with infinite care, panning slowly down inch by inch. And this time he fancied he saw a tiny figure, huddled beneath a huge ledge in the right-hand corner of the Spider icefield. It must be Albrecht.

So the guide had gone on alone, until exhaustion, injury or some impassable barrier on the face had defeated him. Was he alive? It was impossible to guess. Why had he gone on alone, instead of remaining with his injured companion? That too could not be answered by conjecture. The slow perilous work of the rescue had begun, and the answers to each enigmatic problem would not be available for a matter of hours.

Chipperfield turned and strode towards the director's bureau, his trained journalist's brain already shaping the dramatic events into sentences of eye-catching appeal.

Hügi was in deep conversation with his new chef when Chipperfield walked in. He heard Hügi say:

". . . use much more salt; I want *thirsty* guests at my tables, d'you understand? "

Paying the two men little attention he sat down at the typewriter and began drafting his article. In a moment he had three good headings; Global Features could choose which angle they wanted to play up the most:

" MURDER MOUNTAIN CLAIMS TWO MORE "
" GERMAN RESCUE COLUMN GETS THERE FIRST "
" TRAPPED CLIMBERS SEEN AT LAST "

Then he began to write at speed:

" Last night Murder Mountain struck again. Lashing out with greedy clutching claws it claimed two more victims and added them to its already gruesome bag. As Swiss rescuers fought a weary, fruitless battle in the teeth of a howling blizzard to reach the mountain on which Baron Mandoza and banned guide Hans Albrecht lie trapped, two men in the relief column lost their footing and were hurled into the screaming white hell below. Their bodies have not yet been found, though men were out searching the glacier under appalling conditions all night."

He did not know if the last statement were true, but it sounded effective and would hardly be challenged. He began a second paragraph:

" This morning at dawn came the stunning news that the German rescue team which flew in from Munich yesterday had succeeded in winning the race to the summit. As far as one can judge from here, the Swiss have not yet arrived. That is the news which confronts the grim-faced people of this valley to-day as they switch on their radios to follow the drama on the North Wall. It is a heavy blow to Swiss national prestige. They did not expect outsiders to steal their thunder. But those are the sober facts—the Germans have got there first."

He paused for a moment, wondering whether Zellwäger had produced an article along the lines he had promised. This would be the place to work it in. He left a blank space at the end of his second paragraph, then continued:

" The dramatic lifting of the cloud, for the first time in twenty-four hours, shortly after breakfast this morning revealed the exact position of injured Baron Mandoza. He is alive, and apparently securely lashed to an over-hanging bulge of rock some hundreds of feet below the summit. Tension at the moment centres round the figure of Hans Albrecht, expelled professional guide; he lies farther up the cruel North Wall, it would appear on some tiny ledge in the Spider icefield, much higher up than his comrade and client. It is not known if he is alive or dead. Rescue attempts being mounted by the victorious Germans seem to be concentrated on him, first. Though by no means all is clear to the spectator down below, it seems evident that Albrecht went on, climbed farther on his own after his companion fell. The burning question in all our minds is: why did he go on? And I think I have the answer. Because he could not go back. That is the inexorable law of this terrible, murderous mountain—it is a mountain of no return. There is no going back, once you have started. You can only go on, on and upward. No climber yet has ever failed to reach the top and lived to tell the tale. You cannot descend."

Chipperfield reached the end of his third paragraph

and paused, aware that Hügi had dismissed the chef and was standing at his shoulder, reading what he had just typed.

" Very effective, even if it is incorrect," he said.

" What the hell d'you mean? " Chipperfield barked.

" The Eiger is not a mountain of no return."

" Why not? "

" Men have turned back before reaching the top and still come out alive."

" I don't believe it. Who? When? "

" Offhand I cannot quote chapter and verse, but," he said, taking a book from Borgwand's shelf and turning to the index, " I think this should help us. Yes, here we are, Rebitsch and Vörg in 1937, then again a pair of Swiss in 1946—they got as far as the *Rampe*——"

" All right, but save your breath. No one will know the difference and it's a good line. It can stand."

Hügi shrugged his shoulders. " As you wish. Tell me, have you seen the article by Zellwäger in this morning's paper? "

" No, where is it? " asked Chipperfield eagerly.

Hügi handed him a newspaper from a pile on his desk. Chipperfield turned hungrily to a leading article which ran under a modest headline:

" THE BRAVADO BOYS ARE HERE AGAIN."

As Chipperfield scanned the lines swiftly, his face creased in a contented grin. Zellwäger had indeed kept his promise. He'd pulled all the stops out, with a vengeance. The account of the interview with the German rescue team on Scheidegg station had been written, of course, without prior knowledge that they would be the first to reach the summit. But viewed in this light the article had an uncanny flavour of foresight. Chipperfield read it out loud:

" Speaking in a brusque manner, which the world has come to recognise as typically Teutonic, the leader of the Munich party made no attempt to hide his intention of seeking fame and glory by winning the race to the Eiger Summit. ' The Swiss team have taken the wrong route ' he commented scornfully, referring to the brave men who left early this afternoon (with a notable absence of bombast and bravado) for the overhead route along the Jungfrau and Mönch Joch. Bluntly avoiding the issue of whether they would co-operate with the Swiss in the rescue action—which one could only interpret as meaning they would *not*—the Bravado Boys who have come here to ' show the Swiss how ' made it all too clear that they intend to race to the summit first and so win all laurels by rescuing their fellow-countryman Kurt Stringberg (whom they insist is the man hanging from the face of the Eiger)."

Chipperfield glanced at Hügi and whistled softly.
" Hot stuff, eh? This lad is good. He ought to be writing for something bigger than this wretched local rag. Listen to this bit:

" Once again scores of lives will be risked in an attempt to pluck a foolhardy foreigner from the jaws of death in the Swiss Alps. As the world already knows, Kurt Stringberg failed to conquer the Eiger once before, and swore with melodramatic emphasis that he would return one day for a second attempt. Twice in only a few years the lives of brave men will be risked in conditions of spine-chilling danger, simply because of the vainglorious folly of one man. Is this right? Is it not time for some plain thinking and some equally plain speaking on the part of the local authorities? Should not Berne be called upon to intervene to prevent further recklessness of this kind? This paper thinks . . ."

What Zellwäger's insignificant country paper thought would normally have been only of interest to its limited local circle. But the circumstances were not normal, Chipperfield reflected. A vast audience was watching the drama on the Swiss mountains, with the aid of all the highly-developed means of news-dissemination known to modern man. If the local journalist could find an outlet, a pipeline that would tap that vast audience, his comments were no longer insignificant. And he, the Torchbearer of Truth, was more than ready to provide the pipeline.

He pulled the typewriter towards him again and threaded the sheet containing his article as far back as the blank space he had left at the end of the second paragraph. He tapped steadily at the keys for a minute, then sat back and re-read what he had added:

". . . But those are the sober facts—the Germans have got there first. There are already indications in the local press that the Swiss regard this as an insult to their nation. Far be it from this writer to stir up trouble, when regrettably there is trouble enough, but it does look from my perch on the slopes at the foot of the Eiger as if a bitter little storm is brewing up between the two nations."

With a complacent smile he ripped the sheet from the machine and handed it over to Hügi, indicating the piece he had just added.

" By courtesy of *Herr* Zellwäger," he said with a chuckle.

The hotelier read it without any sign of emotion, then passed the page back to the journalist.

" You know your business better than I do, Mr. Chipperfield, though I must tell you the thought of being insulted had never even occurred to me. However, perhaps I am not a fair specimen. Perhaps the average Swiss citizen——"

" *Will* feel insulted, by the time the papers have told him often enough that he is. Just wait till the German press get hold of this! They'll be absolutely howling for Zellwäger's blood."

" Forgive my simplicity," Hügi said, " but what do you hope to achieve by stirring up this particular wasp's nest? "

Chipperfield stood up, and the habitual quirk puckering the corners of his mouth was clearly evident. He said, choosing his words with care:

" Harmony is not news, *Herr* Hügi. Discord is."

Hügi considered this for a second, then nodded.

" I see. In other words, if you are making a rich cake, don't just throw all the ingredients together and hope for the best. Keep stirring."

The journalist laughed appreciatively.

" You've got it. Keep stirring. Just keep stirring."

He picked up the phone and said:

" Now, if you'll excuse me, I must have a chat with London, and after that you will have the pleasure of meeting Miss Bertha Blott, better known in couturier's circles as Jasmine from Paris. I'm sure you can hardly wait."

*   *   *

The attempt to rescue Hans Albrecht was just beginning as John Bellman arrived at Kleine Scheidegg station.

As he stepped out of the packed train he caught sight of Doug Wilson, who had generously offered to cover for him whilst he drove south by hired car to find the pilot. The two reporters exchanged greetings and forcing a path through the milling throng of sightseers made their way to a quiet point of vantage from which they could observe the operation in progress. As they turned powerful glasses on the snow-capped mountain, the American described the storm during the night and gave a brief account of what had happened during his colleague's absence.

" I wired an interim report to your office a couple of hours back," said Wilson in conclusion. " The only fresh bit of news is that the Swiss boys have just about reached the top as well. Look, you can see them, up on the west flank, right near the peak."

Bellman followed the line of his outstretched hand and brought his glasses into focus. Just short of the arrow-head peak a long thin column of figures could be seen slowly moving towards the final ridge on which the Germans were encamped.

" Good," he said. " I'm glad they got there. I wonder if they'll be in time to help? "

" Not this round," Wilson answered. " Those guys were nearly all in by the time they got down from the Joch in the storm. I reckon they'll be clean washed out by the time they make the Eiger summit. They're bound to rest and let the Munich boys have a go first."

" I expect you're right."

" Did you manage to contact Chipperfield's pilot? " Doug Wilson asked after a pause in which they studied the mountain.

" Yes. But it wasn't very fruitful, I'm afraid. He says he doesn't understand how a fellow in the same plane as him could have seen anything he didn't see."

" Then how the hell did the guy get his news so darn quick? "

" That's still the puzzle, and I don't have the answer. I tried to pin this pilot down on the question of height. He said he couldn't be certain what altitude they were flying on Tuesday morning. Seems the kite was pitching all over the sky. All he would say was that he was sure it was nearer eleven thousand feet than twelve."

" Well that's something, anyway."

" Not very conclusive, I'm afraid. Master Paddy will

only look apologetic and say he must have made a mistake,
if we try throwing it at him."

"A thousand feet is a hell of a mistake to make, all the
same," growled the American. "Especially when a man's
life may depend on it. What about the phone call that
Borgwand is supposed to have overheard—surely we've
got him there, haven't we?"

"He'll wriggle out of it. He always does. All he's got
to do is deny the whole thing. It's his word against that
of a sick old man."

"He's more than sick. From what I've heard this
morning, the old fella nearly passed out in the night.
They rushed him off to hospital with double pneumonia
and the heck knows what complications."

Bellman jerked round and faced his companion.

"How on earth did that happen? Things didn't look
that bad when I——"

"Hey, hold everything!" Wilson cut in. He was
peering eagerly through his binoculars at the north face,
and his body had suddenly stiffened.

"Fasten your seat belts, bud. If I'm not mistaken,
there goes the first guy over the edge."

Bellman swiftly trained his glasses once more on the
shining white peak, lit for the first time in days by the
indirect rays of a watery sun. Wilson was right. A man
was being slowly lowered over the edge of the mountain,
by means of the *Stahlseilgerät*. The rescue had begun.

They watched spellbound, as did thousands of others in
a great arc from Grindelwald to the Scheidegg, whilst a
tiny black speck, visible only to powerful binoculars or
telescopes, was lowered on a thin steel cable inch by inch
down the sheer slopes of the summit icefield. The vast
crowd that had gossiped and circulated with nervous
excitement a moment before became strangely still,
hypnotised by the unique drama unfolding before their
eyes.

With agonising slowness the thin black wire—at times

M

there appeared to be two—increased in length as the minute figure of the German rescuer sank farther and farther away from the men on the peak controlling his rate of descent. Minutes that seemed like hours ticked by as the gap closed between the huddled form of the guide and the tense, bent figure of his approaching deliverer. When he had been lowered perhaps a third of the way, the operation came to a halt.

" Go on, boy, go on," muttered Wilson in a tense voice, " what the heck are you stopping for? "

" I think they have to link up another length of cable," Bellman at his side quietly said. " Look, he's started again."

The tortuous descent continued. Bellman was aware of no sound except the beating of his heart. His mouth was dry with anxiety and the glasses in his hands seemed unbearably heavy and moist in his grip. The uppermost thought in his mind was not that, within an hour, they might possibly have definite proof from the guide as to the identity of the man who had hired him. Bellman's thoughts and hopes and fears were concentrated solely on the trapped men, on their chances of survival, and on the appalling risks which the German volunteer on the cable was taking. As if echoing his unspoken thoughts the American at his side murmured:

" God, I hope he makes it. That boy has sure got guts."

Bellman answered, " I wonder what ' ferret ' Zellwäger is thinking now." Wilson had described to him briefly the tone of Zellwäger's article in the papers that morning.

" He's probably praying with all his mean soul that the cable will break," was the American's bitter reply.

" Small chance of that," Bellman said. " It's 5.2 millimetres thick and has a breaking point of sixteen hundred kilos—that's about the weight of sixteen really heavy men."

" Where did you get the technicalities from? "

" The pilot, yesterday. He was pretty well versed in alpine technique, explained the whole *Stahlseilgerät* to me; it's the most up-to-date thing they have in mountain rescue."

" I'm glad to hear it. They'll need everything they've got to haul those two guys out. How do you think it must feel, to be the other guy, watching and waiting from his bit of rope? "

Bellman shook his head, words failing him.

Once more came a pause as fresh cable was fed on to the drum by the Germans out of sight behind the cornice. Then the operation continued, at the same agonisingly slow pace. The two reporters watched in silence as the tiny figure like a black fly descended laboriously down the glistening snow-flecked face. His progress was snail-like, but they forced themselves to realise that each scarcely perceptible movement of descent as witnessed from the valley represented a drop of scores of feet on a mountain that soared over a mile above the pastures of Alpiglen.

The tension mounted unbearably as the gap shortened. Soon it seemed as though the rescuer on the cable had only to stretch out his hand in order to touch the huddled shape of the guide. And then he seemed to stop, only a few feet away.

Nothing happened, as the minutes ticked past. He remained dangling in the air, without having made contact with Albrecht.

Doug Wilson could suddenly stand the strain no longer.

" For Pete's sake, what's holding him up? He's only got a few feet to go."

For several minutes the small black figure hovered a short distance from the ledge on which Albrecht lay. From where they stood it was impossible to judge the exact distance of the gap that separated rescuer and guide. It seemed insignificant, a matter of twenty feet or less. But the gap refused to close. Something had gone wrong.

" Maybe Albrecht's dead," muttered the American.

" Alive or dead, they'll bring him out now they're that close."

" Then what the hell d'you suppose has happened? "

" Perhaps he can't see exactly where Albrecht is lying. It's hard to tell, we've really got a side view from here."

" I reckon he ought to be able to see him. Maybe the cable's not long enough to get down that far, or perhaps it's got stuck on the winding winch."

" I think he's down far enough," said Bellman after a long and careful scrutiny. " I believe they can get up to a thousand foot on the drum. I'm inclined to think he's too far over to the left. It doesn't look as if he's been lowered in a direct line above Albrecht."

Wilson peered through his glasses again and said after a few moments:

" You could be right. But don't those boys have radio? Surely that's a set he's got strapped on his back? "

" Yes, I believe they've got walkie-talkie sets of some kind. But what good would that do if he's been lowered in the wrong place? "

" Hell, he's only got to tell them to swing him over a bit so as he can reach——"

" That's a steel winch they've got up there, not a crane," Bellman put in. " The man hooked on to the cable can only be lowered in one direct line. He can swing a bit to the left or right, but not much; it's far too dangerous. And even if he could swing over as far as the ledge, he's always got to get back again, with a man on his back, we hope. If the fellows working the winch have misjudged the position—and it must be pretty tricky to calculate with dead accuracy when you're peering over the edge of a mountain like that—then they'll probably have to rewind the cable and set the whole complicated apparatus up farther along the cornice."

" But that'll take ages," Wilson almost groaned.

" Yes, it'll take time. Look! There he goes, up again.

He's had to give it up. God, just imagine how it feels to be those two poor devils now. So near, and yet . . ."

They watched in silence as the rescuer was withdrawn. Eventually Bellman said:

" Maybe we should follow the next attempt from the Hotel Nordwand. It's got the best frontal view, with no side-angle distortion."

" I was just thinking the same. Have we got time to get over there, d'you think? "

" I should guess so. It'll take them some while to put another man over the side. I wonder how long Stringberg or whoever it is can hang out."

" He's been over eighty hours on the mountain, and maybe thirty or forty on the end of that rope. If he has to spend a fifth night out in the open . . ."

He left the thought unfinished.

Unwilling to drag themselves from the scene they watched the rescuer being laboriously hauled towards the summit. His arms were entwined above his head, gripping the cable for support, his legs thrust hard out at the vertical rock face, one foot advancing slowly above the other in a queer kind of crab-like climb as he slowly gained height. On the final ridge of the west flank the tail end of the Swiss team could be seen, looking to the naked eye like a handful of black ants crawling up the gleaming snow. Bellman realised they must have witnessed from close quarters the abortive rescue attempt; now they would have a chance themselves. He remembered the portable radio sets they had taken with them, and said to his companion:

" Before we go over to Alpiglen how about seeing if we can pick up any news at the Swiss headquarters? There's a chance they may be in radio touch with the team that's just arrived—maybe we can learn what went wrong."

" O.K. Let's go."

As they descended from the hillock from which they had been watching, a tiny aircraft from the Swiss

Mountain Air Rescue roared overhead and climbed steadily, apparently bent on a reconnaissance flight along the north face. They watched it fly past, until drifting cloud swallowed it from sight.

*   *   *

The scene in the temporary headquarters which the Swiss authorities had set up on the Kleine Scheidegg resembled a battle command post. Only by showing their press cards were the two journalists able to force an entry through the ring of excited spectators that jostled one another round the door.

Inside there was an atmosphere of electric tension. Groups of drawn-faced men stood or sat hunched around a complicated mass of radio equipment, and the crackle of atmospherics and occasional disjointed sentences in Swiss dialect could be heard on the receiver. A large number of reporters from newspapers all over the world filled the room and the babble of conflicting tongues was incomprehensible. The air was heavily laden with cigarette smoke and smelt strongly of human sweat and coffee. Steaming white mugs seemed to flow on an unending band from the kitchens of the nearby Scheidegg hotel.

Bellman saw one or two faces he knew, and then caught sight of McKechnie and signalled to him. The Scottish journalist came over to where they were standing. They exchanged greetings and Bellman said:

" Did you follow it from here? "

" Aye, I did."

" What went wrong, d'you know? "

" It seems he was too far to the left, couldn't reach the poor chap. They are in touch here with the Swiss team that's just reached the top. The Germans had to haul their man up again and now they'll be remounting the *Stahlseilgerät* farther along the cornice."

" Forgive my ignorance but what exactly is the cornice? " Doug Wilson asked. " Johnny here uses the technical terms like a native, but me, I'm just a hick from the big city . . ."

" It's the overhanging mass of snow and ice that gets piled up by the wind on top of a mountain," McKechnie explained. " The men up there have to be quite certain their apparatus is driven into solid rock and not just anchored in loose or frozen snow, otherwise it won't take the strain of a man being lowered on a cable. That's why it takes so long to get things organised."

" How long do they reckon before they can try again? "

" Nobody seems to know for certain. Some considerable time, anyway."

" Any news about Albrecht? Is he alive? "

" They don't know. The German that went down on the cable shouted to him but got no reply. He could see him quite clearly but there was no sign of movement. It's clearly touch and go."

" Then we still don't know——"

" Aye, we still don't know if the other one is Mandoza or Stringberg."

" And still no word from the outside. You'd have thought someone would have succeeded in digging up either one of them by now."

" There's a man-hunt spread over half Europe."

" If you ask me," Doug Wilson said, " the Torchbearer's lousy agency has got hold of one of 'em and put him under lock and key—just to keep the public guessing."

McKechnie looked at him incredulously.

" That's a wee bit far-fetched, don't you think? "

" I wouldn't put anything past Chipperfield," Bellman said tersely.

" Well . . ." said the Scotsman dubiously. " Anyway, whoever the second man is, he's alive, that's certain. You can see him moving about from time to time on his rope."

" Alive, but for how long? He can't hold out for ever. If the next attempt is on Albrecht again, how many hours will it be before they can get at Stringberg? "

McKechnie said, " It's not only a question of how long, where he's concerned, but *how*? He's a good deal farther down the mountain than anyone imagined. Even with the *Stahlseilgerät* I don't see how they hope to get at him. It doesn't reach that far."

The words that Borgwand had uttered with such deadly earnestness to Claire came flashing into Bellman's mind. " They've taken the wrong route and the wrong equipment " the sick old man had feverishly whispered. Borgwand knew the mountain like few others. His words seemed pregnant with menacing prophecy. Bellman asked:

" What do the Swiss say? Can they get at him? "

" Nobody's in a hurry to commit himself to that one. They've got their hands full with the guide for the time being—and with the German trouble."

" What trouble's that? "

" Have you not seen Zellwäger's anti-German article? "

" Doug was telling me about it. Sounds a filthy piece —but surely no one's taking it very seriously, are they? "

" You know how it is: maybe one swallow does not make a summer, but it only needs one dirty newspaper article sometimes to make a first-class storm. Do you see those chaps in the corner over there? " He indicated with a nod of his head a group of newspapermen talking in heated High German.

" That's most of the German press contingent. I tried to talk with them a while ago, but they're as prickly as a bunch of hedgehogs. Zellwäger's nasty little piece has made them a wee bit hot under the collar."

" That's understandable enough. I don't suppose they enjoyed the description of ' Bravado Boys ' very much, especially after that fantastic climb their men made up the west flank in the storm last night. That was some achievement."

"You can say that again," Wilson chimed in.

"But Zellwäger's local rag doesn't count for much, outside its own small circle. It will all blow over if no one else joins in the chorus."

"Aye, I hope you're right. There's enough trouble here without people getting hurt feelings and imagining their national honour has been slighted."

"I fancy our friend the Torchbearer would disagree with you," Wilson put in. "For him there's never too much trouble. I heard the great man pronouncing in his usual lofty manner the other night at the bar. One of his pet epigrams is: ' Discord is news, harmony isn't '."

"But you don't think he's behind this little runt Zellwäger, do you? " asked McKechnie, clearly troubled.

"I don't know," said Bellman pensively. He thought of the strangely conspiratorial impression the two men had made as they entered the railway buffet on the previous afternoon. He went on:

"That's one of the things I'd like to find out about our mutual friend. Listen, Mac, Doug and I are planning to cover the next rescue attempt from Alpiglen. Would you——"

"Surely. I'll follow it from here and we can club together afterwards."

"Fine. Be seeing you."

Bellman and the American left the Swiss headquarters and set out at a sharp pace for the Hotel Nordwand.

CHAPTER X

CLAIRE WAS making a swift tour of supervision through the *Saal* when she glanced out of the window and saw Bellman arrive with Wilson at the terrace steps. She went to meet them in the foyer and Doug Wilson made for the bar, leaving her alone with the quiet, strangely attractive Englishman. She asked him at once:

" Did you find the pilot? "

" Yes. But I was unable to extract anything very conclusive out of him."

He told her briefly what he had already recounted to Doug Wilson. Then he asked about Borgwand, and she described the ordeal of the previous night.

He cut short her self-accusations by saying:

" You did all that was humanly possible. You have nothing whatsoever to blame yourself with."

" I wish I could believe that. The only consolation is that the doctors assure me he will be all right. Though even when he does recover, he won't want to come back to the hotel, after the circus Hügi and his bunch of *Gauner* have made of it. We've got people sleeping on boarded-up baths, in arm-chairs in the lounge, and one even spent the night on the billiard table. The prices they are paying are mad."

" Where is Chipperfield? "

" Counting the shekels somewhere, I expect," she replied bitterly. " He should appear soon, he's holding a cocktail party at twelve o'clock."

" A cocktail party? At a time like this! "

" He and the new director are cooking up something, I'm not quite sure what. There's been a mysterious new guest arrived, but nobody has been allowed to see her yet."

At that moment Doug Wilson came from the bar. The expression on his face was a curious mixture of disbelief and anger.

" Now I've seen everything! Come and look at what that bastard has pinned up in the bar."

They followed him into the packed bar, where a group of newspapermen and women was crushed round a small green baize notice-board. On it was pinned a slip of paper, its message typed in three languages:

" The ladies and gentlemen of the press are invited to take cocktails with P. Chipperfield at 12 a.m. in the coffee lounge, where an important personality will be introduced."

Doug Wilson said, " I've always wanted to go to a royal audience. Do we curtsy or just bow? "

Someone slapped Bellman on the back as he was about to make an equally acid comment.

" Hiya, John. What's the news on Stringberg? You found him yet? "

It was Ferguson, the fat reporter from one of England's huge Sunday tabloids.

" No," he answered curtly, " have you? "

" Haven't been looking, old man. It's all the same to me who's hanging up there, though of course Mandoza's better for circulation. You going to Chipperfield's clambake? "

" I hardly think so."

" Why not? The drinks are free."

" Say, who's this important personality he's got tucked up his sleeve? " asked Doug Wilson.

" I've heard it from a little bird that he's salted the Baron's latest bit of fluff away some place. God knows how he's managed it, but I'm interested to find out."

" He really thinks of everything, doesn't he? " said Bellman thinly.

" Yes sir," agreed Ferguson heartily, missing the irony. " There's no dust and cobwebs on that boy."

" What's the point of this little get-together? "

" You'll see. Come on, at least it'll kill time till the next rescue attempt."

There was a general surge from the bar in the direction of the coffee lounge and Bellman found himself being swept along with it.

Chipperfield received his guests from behind a table laden with glasses, a bowl of ice, silver shakers and a large array of bottles. As each person entered he greeted them by name and dispensed drinks. Even his bitterest enemies were forced to admit afterwards that it was a brilliant performance of the role of genial host. It did not entirely escape notice that almost all the representatives of the more sober, thoughtful press boycotted the party, and that not a few present had clearly come only to heckle. But Chipperfield parried any sardonic remarks with skill, exuded charm at his admirers and, calculating the moment of curiosity to a nicety, opened a side-door leading to a small ante-room, disappeared, and returned a moment later with a striking flame-haired girl on his arm.

" Ladies and gentlemen," he called out, a broad smile beaming over his face, " I want you all to meet Jasmine."

The words were scarcely out of his mouth before cries of surprise and recognition and a stream of questions filled the air. Photographers dropped on one knee or climbed on chairs to obtain striking camera angles, and the room soon smelt of the slightly acrid odour of exploding flash bulbs.

" Reminds me of Jayne Mansfield's last press conference," said Doug Wilson ironically.

" A slight difference in vital statistics, wouldn't you say, old man? " Ferguson chimed in.

Wilson eyed the thin figure which the girl's profession demanded and said, " Yeah, you've got a point there."

" What I don't understand," said Bellman, " is the exact purpose of this vaudeville act? "

Ferguson looked at him pityingly.

" You may be a good reporter, John——"

" Strictly old school."

" As you wish; but you certainly don't know much about exploitation. The Torchbearer's a positive genius when it comes to working all the angles. Don't you get it? This Jasmine creature is the last girl Mandoza was seen going around with, before he disappeared on his mysterious journey into Southern Germany."

" And? "

" Well, it's obvious, isn't it ? The great public loves to see pictures of horror-stricken wives waiting at the doomed pit-head, and if you can get the wife of a test pilot in your camera sights whilst hubby is doing slow rolls at nought feet in an experimental jet, then boy, you're on to a really good thing."

" I'm learning all the time."

" Actually," Ferguson went on, " I had the same idea myself, only I was thinking along the lines of using Frau Albrecht. At least we are certain that it's him up there. Snag is, she's left home. Seems she got tired of answering questions for the papers and skipped off when no one was looking. Probably hiding out with relatives somewhere."

" I don't blame her," said Wilson.

Bellman said, " Now I understand. We shall be treated to the spectacle of a man hanging on to grim life by a piece of rope whilst a titian-haired beauty makes the necessary facial expressions in the valley below."

" That's the rough idea. You catch on slow, but when——"

" What, no clowns? No acrobats, no cootch-dancers? Nothing else in the act ? "

Ferguson shook his head and ignored the sarcasm.

Questions continued to flow, but it soon became clear that the striking young mannequin was not going to be allowed by her impresario to answer many herself. Chipperfield intercepted practically everything that was fired at her, apparently oblivious to the fact that his guests were growing restless. Then Ferguson cut through with a direct question during a momentary lull.

" *Mademoiselle* Jasmine, what made you come all the way from Paris to this spot in the Swiss mountains? "

The girl shot Chipperfield a quick look, and the famous journalist nodded almost imperceptibly.

The mannequin answered in a low voice with a convincing Parisian accent:

" Because I know it is the man I love who is in great danger on the Eiger."

" What makes you so sure? " challenged a Canadian feature writer.

Chipperfield was quick to intercept:

" That will have to be all for now, folks. *Mademoiselle* Jasmine is terribly tired after her long journey and the strain of the past few days. I'm sure you will excuse us."

Before anyone could protest he had taken the girl by the arm and swept her from the room. There was a stampede for the telephone and in a moment the room was deserted.

John Bellman might never have known the true facts concerning Chipperfield's protégée, had Claire not overheard a short while later, a conversation in the corridor leading to the mannequin's room:

" . . . but I keep telling you, I hated the spoilt brat," a girl's voice with no trace of Parisian accent had protested, " I never want to see him again."

" SShh! you little fool, do you want to ruin everything?" had come a reply in a voice she recognised immediately as Chipperfield's. " The public wants a lover for the man in distress, can't you get that in to your head? "

" What public? That rabble of hungry sightseers out there? "

" Oh, my God, how can you be so dense! Your public is the great wide world now. I keep on telling you, play it smart and you'll have your picture in every paper from Fiji to Istanbul."

" What good will that do me? They don't buy Paris gowns in the Fiji Isles."

" For heaven's sake stop thinking about clothes. You don't want to be a mannequin all your life, do you? This thing is bigger than fashion shows and idiotic posing. This way you may get your picture seen by an Indian maharaja or a Chicago meat-packer, or even an Arabian oil magnate. Mark my words, the offers of marriage will come flooding in. You'll never look back. Now put that idle body of yours to rest, don't answer the door to anyone but me, and be ready for when I call you. And for Pete's sake when the newsreel cameras start grinding, keep your profile turned sideways to the mountain— that's the shot the public wants to see."

*   *   *

Lunch was nearly at an end when word filtered through via the Kleine Scheidegg that a second endeavour to rescue Hans Albrecht was about to be made.

In a moment the windows of the dining-room were jammed, the terrace filled with a seething mass, and an ungainly struggle for use of the giant telescope was taking place.

Bellman and Doug Wilson found a position on the hotel steps and a moment later Claire joined them. She slipped her hand into the Englishman's and they watched in tense silence as the operation began.

From a balcony directly above them a quiet-voiced British radio reporter was transmitting a description of the scene. Bellman found himself listening to the unemotional voice and soon realised that it belonged to an expert, a man qualified to analyse and interpret what was happening on the mountain. His descriptions were careful and factual, and the very reserve with which he spoke seemed to heighten the drama unfolding before them.

". . . must be about thirty or forty men from several

nations grouped on the summit. The tip of the Eiger is notoriously sharp—it is no more than a thin razor-like edge; one wonders how they all find room to stand and to work there. The weather has improved considerably, though the skies are by no means completely clear. Over the spine of the Scheidegg towards Lauterbrunnen a pile of broken cloud seems to be building up rather than diminishing. If the pessimistic forecasts are accurate, this may be the only day in which the two men in distress stand a chance of being rescued.

" But there are large patches of blue sky, and a watery sun keeps breaking through from time to time. The people in front of me crowding the hotel terrace and the slopes around are dressed for the most part in bright holiday clothing—if you did not know the deadly earnestness of what is happening, you might imagine some kind of sporting event was taking place. Everything seems weighted to make a bitter contrast between our safety and comfort down here and the cold peril which the men on the North Wall, and their rescuers, are facing. Fat cows are grazing placidly on the adjoining slopes like a scene from a box of Swiss cheese—perhaps you can hear the gentle clangour of their bells every now and then. One feels ashamed of one's safety, ashamed at being unable to do anything to help. But there is nothing we here at Alpiglen can do, except wait, spellbound, watching, and praying too."

He paused for a brief moment, then went on, his voice charged with an edge of subdued excitement:

" Things seem to be getting under way on the summit. The combined rescue teams have moved their camp farther along the cornice, and this time hopes are high that they will be able to lower a man with greater accuracy down to the narrow ledge on which Hans Albrecht, the Swiss guide, lies. Though all eyes are fastened for the moment on him, there is not one of us here who forgets for more than a second the other climber, the man who has been hanging on the end of a rope for at least two nights and a day. It is impossible to imagine his feelings as he realises that he must wait his turn to be rescued.

" Aircraft of the Swiss Mountain Air Rescue flew close by his precarious perch this morning, examining the best method to try and save him. The Swiss pilot reported that he is clearly injured but appears to be in astonishingly good spirits, despite what he has been through. Mystery still surrounds his identity, despite energetic efforts to find out. He still wears his climber's helmet and goggles, no doubt as protection against falling rock and ice, and his back is naturally turned to us, so that it is impossible to say—wait—I think—yes, there goes a tiny figure on the end of steel cable over the side of the mountain. The second attempt to save Hans Albrecht has begun."

A rustle of excitement like a gust of wind rippled through the crowd packed tight on the terrace. The trade at Hügi's kiosk, which had been brisk all morning, slackened perceptibly, as all eyes strained upward at the massive mountain. The reporter on the balcony continued talking quietly and unemotionally into his microphone, though his tempo had quickened slightly.

". . . it looks simple, and possibly even sounds simple, to fasten a wire on to a belt around your waist and lower yourself over the edge of a mountain. Yet none of us are under any illusions about this semblance of simplicity. The man going down on that cable—be he German or Swiss or any one of the international team assembled there—is taking his life into his hands every foot of the way as he swings down for one thousand feet or more into space. It was dangerous this morning, when the first endeavour had to be abandoned. It is more dangerous now. This morning he had a hail of stones and slabs of dislodged ice to contend with, apart from the grim possibility of something going amiss with the apparatus itself.

N

He wears a crash-helmet like a motor-bike racer to protect himself against stone-fall. But now it is not just stones, rock and ice he has to fear. As the afternoon sun begins its work of softening up the fresh snow that fell last night, as the natural warmth of the mid-afternoon hours begins to melt the ice and steal beneath loose boulders that the ice has hitherto held fast, a bigger danger looms over him— the danger of avalanches. Only a few years ago two young men, one of them a Swiss and the other a German, were killed by an avalanche on the summit icefield, the very same spot over which the rescuer is now being tortuously lowered.

" He is going down very slowly, very carefully. No matter what the outcome, the world will not forget quickly the bravery of these men who have volunteered for such a formidable undertaking. Some of them are professional guides, and some are amateurs, members of climbing clubs who earn their livings in offices and factories and farms. All are volunteers. They will not be paid a reward for what they are trying to achieve. It is not money, or fame, that has drawn them from all over Europe to this strange meeting-place in the Bernese Oberland. Only one motive has brought them together— the instinct of common humanity."

A second later the reporter's voice was lost as a loud murmur, punctuated by cries of anguish, surged through the crowd. A flurry of white like a horse's tail swept suddenly from the summit icefield and blotted the slowly descending rescuer from sight. For several seconds his fate was unknown. Then the crowd gasped with relief as the white plume poured downwards into the funnel of the Spider and the tiny black figure emerged once more into view. The full force of the avalanche could not have struck him, Bellman realised, though for the long-drawn-out seconds of its duration he must have been blinded and unable to breath.

The steady voice of the announcer came again:

". . . survived this sudden, frightening onslaught. He is about half-way now between the trapped guide below and the men working the winch above. I very much doubt if he can see either. Can we, here, possibly imagine what it is like, to be on the end of that cable? Above him stretches the smooth treacherous icefield and the sharp ridge of the Eiger's peak; below him, nothing but a sheer drop of one mile to the rocky slopes above Alpiglen. His life hangs, literally on a thread, dependent on the men operating the winch, and on a piece of wire 5.2 millimetres thick. I have just measured the width of my smallest finger nail: it is *twice* as thick as that wire. He swings in a silent world of his own. The demands upon his courage and endurance at this moment must be at their highest. Slowly, inch by inch, foot by foot, he is going down—as far as we can tell, in a direct line to the beleaguered guide. If he succeeds, this rescue will find its place in history as a miracle of modern technique, as well as human bravery. Only a few years ago, before such equipment as the *Stahlseilgerät* had been invented, such an operation as this would have been impossible. No number of average climbing ropes knotted together could possibly have stood the strain or reached so far. Now they are trying out this new invention they call the *Stahlseilgerät*, for almost the first time, not as a practice exercise but in conditions of grim reality. It is a harsh test."

Though he was careful to avoid melodrama, the radio reporter was clearly not blind to the gripping suspense in the scene which he was describing. He endeavoured to keep his voice steady, but it grew increasingly tense, charged with suppressed emotion.

" I would say that the man on the cable has only a few score feet to go. Within a matter of minutes, if all goes well, he will have reached the narrow ledge—it can scarcely be as wide as a coffee table—on which Hans Albrecht lies. Slowly he goes down . . . slowly . . . with infinite caution . . . he dare not hurry; one careless movement and he would dislodge an avalanche of snow or stones whose sheer weight and speed of descent would prove fatal to the man it is hoped to save.

" There are only a few more feet to go . . . he seems practically level but of course distances are hopelessly deceptive from our viewpoint beneath this massive mountain. Down he goes . . . slowly . . . down . . . down . . . now he has stopped . . . I'm not sure . . . yes, I think I can definitely say he has reached the trapped guide. He appears to have got a foothold on the narrow ledge . . . I think the cable is slack, giving him freedom to move . . . he is bending over the huddled body . . . already, if the radio strapped to his back is in good order, he will have signalled to the men waiting anxiously on the summit the news for which the world is waiting—is the guide alive? He may even know a second answer, the answer to the mystery which has caused so much dispute in the world's press—the name of the man who climbed with Hans Albrecht. But that can wait. It is not of the same importance as—wait, I think I can . . . yes, the rescuer appears to be struggling with the guide's body, I think he is trying to slip the *Grammingersitz* under him; it must be an incredibly difficult thing to do in that confined space . . ."

Doug Wilson, who had also been able to hear the quiet commentary coming from the balcony above, said to Bellman:

" What the heck is a *Grammingersitz*? "

As if in answer, realising that few of his listeners would understand the term, the reporter continued:

". . . a kind of sling, one might describe it as a bucket-seat made of strong canvas or leather, into which a rescuer tries to place the body of a man being rescued. Then he must hoist the man on to his back . . . that must be what is happening now . . . yes, there he goes, struggling to his feet . . . one slip, one inaccurate movement of the foot and the narrow ledge will not hold them . . . the risk

is appalling, but he is on his feet, the full weight of the
guide on his back . . . this a moment of acute danger . . .
and as far as I can judge, there is no help coming from the
man in that canvas seat; his arms are hanging limply at
his sides, his head is sagging . . . I don't know if that
means . . . I cannot say, he may only be suffering from
utter exhaustion. Now they are waiting for the signal to
be hauled up the face of the mountain again—a distance
of one thousand feet—it will be a long, dangerous,
exhausting journey, twice as dangerous as the descent, for
this time the rescuer has a helpless man on his back—
alive or dead, we here at Alpiglen do not know.

"Now they have started . . . the rescuer is thrusting hard
at the icy wall with his crampons—the steel spikes
lashed to his climbing boots—and taking some of the strain
of the cable. Up they go, slowly, incredibly slowly, with
tremendous caution . . . like a father carrying his son
piggy-back. It is a long, hard climb, a terrible strain on
the heart when one considers the burden the man is
carrying and the thin air he has to breathe at that
altitude . . . I don't think many of us here can have any
conception of how tough a struggle that must be."

In a pause that followed, Claire said to Bellman in a
taut, low voice:

" What do you think? Is Albrecht alive? "

Bellman lowered his glasses after a long scrutiny of the
slumped figure.

" It looks doubtful. He's not even gripping with his
arms—that would be the natural thing to do to keep his
balance on the other fellow's back. And his head is lolling
to one side. At the very least he's clearly unconscious."

" Listen John," Doug Wilson said urgently, " I'm going
to cut over to the Scheidegg and see what Mac's got on the
guide. Maybe he's picked up something over the Swiss
short-wave sets. You take over from here and I'll see what
I can find out. If Albrecht had enough breath left in him
he may have told the name of the other poor devil hang-

ing on that rope. Just for once I'd like to beat Chipperfield to it."

"You could try phoning from here."

"Chancy. The lines will probably be jammed already."

Bellman nodded and the American slipped swiftly
through the tense, silent crowd.

He was not proud of the emotion, but he had to admit
that the same thought was pressing uppermost in his
mind. It was of secondary importance, compared to
whether the two men could be saved or not; but he had to
be honest with himself and admit his burning desire to
know, once and for all, if it was Stringberg or the Baron
Mandoza.

As he continued to gaze at the laborious ascent up the
Spider icefield towards the glistening white peak, Claire
nudged him and said quietly:

"Now where do you suppose *he's* going?"

He followed her glance and saw Chipperfield roughly
thrusting a passage through the packed hotel doorway into
the foyer.

Bellman knew at once what his rival had in mind. On
a sudden impulse he turned and followed in the journalist's wake.

He was in time to see the door of Hügi's bureau close.
In a few seconds he had reached it. Anger at the arrogant
way in which Chipperfield had monopolised a telephone
for his own permanent use overcame any scruples he
might have had. He tried the door handle, and it
opened; Chipperfield had been in too much of a hurry
this time to bother to lock it.

He pushed the door gently open.

The journalist had his back turned towards him. He
was bent over the desk, speaking with frantic urgency into
the phone.

"... died a few moments later? Did he say anything on
the ledge? ... what the hell d'you mean, it doesn't make
sense ... for God's sake, *what did he say*?"

His powerful body suddenly stiffened, as though he had suffered a swift electric shock. He straightened up slowly and repeated, as in a daze, the message that had crackled over the wire, the message uttered by the dying guide.

" *Das Flugzeug war schuld . . . Sie haben es gesehen.*"

Like a man in a dream he replaced the receiver, and slowly turned. It was as though he did not see Bellman standing at the door. His face was as white as a sheet.

Gradually the shock receded and his eyes swam into normal focus. The realisation that Bellman, of all people, had overheard what he had said, did not appear to stir him. He seemed past the point where he could be shocked again.

" You heard? " he said, in a low, choked voice. " He's dead . . . without naming the man on the rope. All he said was——"

Bellman nodded grimly and finished the sentence for him:

" *Das Flugzeug war schuld. Sie haben es gesehen,*" he repeated slowly. " The aircraft was responsible. They have seen it."

CHAPTER XI

By NIGHTFALL the man on the end of the rope was still alive.

They knew this for certain, for his voice had been heard. He had shouted an answer to the Italian volunteer who had descended later that afternoon in a vain effort to try and reach him.

The cable of the *Stahlseilgerät*, even when coupled in three-hundred-foot lengths, was not long enough to reach him. A gap of many hundreds of feet stretched between the spot where he hung, lashed to a rock at the base of the *Rampe*, and the farthest point to which a rescuer could be lowered.

" Can you hold on? " the Italian had shouted. " Help is coming. Are you all right? "

The answer that had floated up, tossed by the fickle wind and nearly drowned by the whine of loose stones smashing to the slopes below, had sounded like two words:

" Hungry . . . cold."

It seemed like proof at last. Not only that he was alive—there had been no doubts about that, for he had clearly been seen moving of his own accord from time to time—but who he was. It must be Mandoza. From the wealth of detail which energetic research had succeeded in unearthing about Kurt Stringberg, it was known that the Munich climber knew no English. Doubt vanished— until someone pointed out that the words were almost identical when spoken in German:

" *Hungrig . . . kalt.*"

It could have been either language; either man. No one was any longer certain. They only knew he was still alive, though obviously weakening. And they knew that he could not be saved in the same fashion that Albrecht had nearly been saved. Modern technique had performed wonders, and there was little doubt that the *Stahlseilgerät* would have saved Albrecht had there been more than a flicker of life in his exhausted, wounded body by the time the Swiss rescuer had reached him.

But the bitter words the guide had whispered on the ledge had been uttered with his last ounce of strength. He had died during the long, laborious haul up to the summit. It was not cold that had killed him, nor hunger, though both had drained him of the reserves of strength with which he might have fought his injuries. It was clear that he had fallen, and that it had been a severe fall. One leg was broken, and there were cuts and ugly bruises all over his body, but it was loss of blood from a terrible gash on the side of his head that had finally killed him.

Exactly where he had slipped, and how, as well as why he had become separated from his companion, nobody knew.

Chipperfield dwelt on this in his article, perceiving the chance to add a new twist to the story. Under a heading of " MURDER MOUNTAIN SNATCHES THIRD VICTIM," he wrote:

" We may never know the answer to the mystery of what made Hans Albrecht go on alone. Rumour has produced the startling theory that he might have quarrelled with his illustrious client. Is this so impossible? Stranger things than that have happened on the cruel face of the Eiger. Men in acute danger do not always act heroically, whatever the wishful thinkers would have us believe."

It was pure speculation on his part, merely another brand tossed into the fire; but someone had to start a rumour—they didn't start themselves. Fearing that perhaps he had gone too far, he added:

" Or was he not merely trying to save himself, was it in fact a gesture of the purest heroism, a gallant attempt to reach the outside world and so bring succour to his doomed companion? The clouds that shrouded the Eiger all Wednesday, the fearful storm that raged throughout that night, and the heavy snow-fall that blotted out all traces of the guide's movements, may well for ever keep their fateful secret."

As he neared the end of his article describing the dramatic events of the fifth day, Chipperfield could not suppress a rich inward glow of triumph at the way fortune had played along with him. The whole story had far

exceeded his earliest expectations. It had already lasted
five days and showed promise of lasting for at least one
or two more. Seven days: no isolated item of news could
possibly hope for a longer life than that. Each single facet
of the story, each strategic move he had planned, had
proved a scintillating success.

Jasmine had performed with commendable skill
during the day's final rescue attempt. Without doubt her
face would be on the newsreels projected in cinemas and
on TV screens all over the world by the following day.
Already Bernheim had sent him a handsome offer from a
Sunday newspaper for her life story, which he would in
due course write for her under her name, and two
German and one French illustrated weekly with huge
circulations had made handsome bids for her picture (in
full colour, with the Eiger as background) for their next
cover-photo.

The flank attack which he had launched on the German
relief column through Zellwäger's paper was showing all
the signs of developing into a bitter controversy. As he had
anticipated, sections of the German press had hit back
with violence; an acid dispute was building up between
the two nations, much to the delight of those members of
the public who enjoyed a slanging match of this nature.

Another source of satisfaction to Chipperfield was
Bernheim's exploitation of the financial angles in London
and America. These, when added to the pleasant, if
purely subsidiary arrangements he had made with Hügi
at the hotel, would make him a very rich man by the time
it was all over. Rich and famous. A public larger than
any he had every dreamed of had come to recognise his
name, played up by shrewd editors in thick type above
his sensational despatches. He was even toying with the
idea of altering his self-attributed title—the Torchbearer
of Truth. It had a slightly pedestrian air about it, he was
beginning to think. He rather fancied something like
" Ace of all ace newshounds," or " the world's greatest

columnist." Editors wouldn't like it, but they would have to swallow it; from now on, he was the one that called the tune.

All in all the future was incredibly rosy. It had only one small dark cloud: the words spoken by the dying guide.

This was trouble indeed. But he had ridden worse storms than that in his career. He would ride this one out too.

At first he had been stunned by the news of what Albrecht had said. Fate seemed suddenly to have turned on him, dealing him a vicious, back-handed blow. There was no chance of hushing it up. Every man of the combined rescue teams on the summit must have learnt of it. Before long it would probably filter throughout the valley. He would have to find some method of countering it.

First, he set himself the task of analysing the threat, in all coolness. The guide had uttered two sentences. Were these sentences, however, so formidable? Taken out of context, they were almost meaningless. *Das Flugzeug war schuld*. What aeroplane? His was not the only one that had flown alongside the climbers in search of sensational pictures. " Was guilty, responsible "—for what? The guide had not said. And the second sentence, *Sie haben es gesehen*: they have seen it. Who were " they "? And what were they supposed to have seen?

Enemies like Bellman would no doubt try to make capital out of it. A highly-successful man grew accustomed to the snapping of jealous curs at his heels. There would be trouble. But he was convinced he could handle it. No one could possibly place great weight on the muttered words of a dying man, a man who had gone through the nightmare of four days and nights on the North Wall of the Eiger, culminating in a terrible storm and grievous bodily injury. Albrecht had died, before he could say more. The dead could not bear witness. He had nothing to fear. And one aspect of the matter was firmly on his side: everyone connected with the rescue operation would have his hands more than full on the following day, when an all-out effort to reach the remaining man in distress would be launched.

As he put the finishing touches to his article preparatory to phoning it through to London, the telephone on his desk rang.

It was Zellwäger, reporting from the Swiss rescue headquarters on the Scheidegg. His voice was taut with suppressed excitement.

"Listen, the air's thick with news down here. They can't agree on the best method to try to get at the man on the rope. Everyone seems to have his own pet theory."

"Excellent," replied Chipperfield suavely, "a little bit of dissension never did a story any harm. What have they decided to do? "

"Well, as far as I can judge, there are going to be no less than three separate columns working independently to-morrow."

"Three! Then it's not just Germany versus Switzerland? "

"Nothing so simple. A whole new batch of volunteers have joined in, each with his own ideas. The three plans are as follows: some of those on the summit are going to stay there, and try once again lowering a man down the *Stahlseilgerät* as soon——"

"But they've tried that. He can't get down far enough, a blind man could see that this afternoon."

"Yes, but the idea is, to lower him as far as possible on to the Spider icefield, and let him work his way out from there and then downwards towards the *Rampe* where Mandoza is hanging."

"Do they all admit it's Mandoza, now? " Chipperfield butted in eagerly.

"No, I can't say that they do. The Germans and a good many others are still sticking to Stringberg—they say it must be him because he called out ' *hungrig . . . kalt* ' in German."

" That doesn't prove a thing," snapped the journalist irritably, " it could just as easily have been ' hungry . . . cold,' the words are almost identical."

" Quite so. Anyway, attempt Number One comes from the summit, as I said. But a lot of experts argue that it's impossible, a crazy scheme. Even if the rescuer succeeded in working his way out of the Spider, which is frightfully dangerous, and then down the *Rampe*, they don't see what he could do to get at the Baron, to extract him. It's clear he's pretty badly injured in one arm, he'll hardly have much strength left to help himself. It'll take more than one man to haul him out, at the very least."

" The same argument holds for any method of approach, I should have thought."

" Perhaps. Anyway, theory Number Two is, it's no use trying to get at him with only one man. So a team is going to climb up from below, and hopes to get at him that way."

" That will take hours—the whole day at least. The Baron's hanging at eleven thousand feet, they'll never reach him to-morrow."

" By the normal route, they wouldn't. Here's the interesting item: they plan to take the train—the *Jungfraubahn*—as far as a spot called the *Stollenloch*, mid-way between stations *Eigergletscher* and *Eigerwand*. The railway runs through the heart of the mountain, via a huge tunnel——"

" I know, I know," said Chipperfield testily. " The *Stollenloch* is a gallery, or a series of galleries, cut like windows into the face of the mountain."

" Exactly. Well, the rescue column will come out on to the North Wall through one of these galleries, and start their climb from there. That means they will already have a height of roughly nine thousand feet before they start."

" I see. Not a bad scheme, though it sounds risky. And the next? "

" The third column is going up the north-east flank, via the Lauper route, on to the *Mittellegigrat*. There's even a rumour that Swiss Air Rescue planes may fly them up there and try to land on the Mittellegi ridge, in order to save time."

" Splendid. ' Swiss birdmen dicing with death '—it'll sell a lot of newspapers. And what then? "

" It's something that's never been done before, so far as I can gather: they are going to try and enter the wall from the north-east, via the *Rampe*, and get at him that way."

" Why has it never been done before? "

" I don't know—technical difficulties from the climbing aspect, I think. A Swiss guide I've been talking to told me no one has yet succeeded in finding a route out from the *Rampe* on to the Mittellegi ridge, so I presume the reverse holds true. So there you have it, three teams with up-wards of fifty men in all, trying to rescue a single man."

" Excellent. Call it sixty. Sixty for the sake of one. It's very impressive. Any idea what nationalities are involved? "

" Some Belgians have joined in, and a couple of French guides from Chamonix, as well as a famous Japanese amateur climber who appears to be holidaying in the district. There must be about six or seven different nationalities in all, counting the original four."

" Call it eight. ' Eight-nation team ' scans better. Find out more about the scheme to fly the third party on to the north-east ridge—that's got a lot of potential glamour. Hasn't anyone thought of using a helicopter? "

" A helicopter? It's impractical. Someone raised the idea during a conference at headquarters this evening, but it seems the average machine isn't capable of operating much higher than eight thousand feet; that's their . . . how do you say it? . . . maximum ceiling."

" There's a machine in the States that can get up to fourteen thousand, I believe," said Chipperfield.

" Yes, but America is a long way off. Take my word for it, it will be one of those three groups that will get Mandoza out."

" O.K. Is that everything from your end? "

" Not quite."

Zellwäger paused, and then went on:

" There's one more item of news circulating around here."

Chipperfield was not certain but he fancied he detected a touch of malice in the other man's tone. The last sentence had been spoken almost with relish, as if it were the juicy titbit which he had been saving for the end of his report.

" What might that be? " Chipperfield demanded sharply.

" There's talk of a board of inquiry."

Chipperfield's heart missed a beat.

" Into what? "

" The conduct of the rescue operation."

There was a silence on the phone for several seconds. Chipperfield thought rapidly. With a man of Zellwäger's calibre he had to be careful. His type changed sides very easily. Eventually he said:

" What is there to inquire into? "

" A lot of things, apparently. People are criticising the conduct——"

" What people? Who are these people? "

" The Germans, to start with. And a good many Swiss, too. They say the first rescue attempt on Albrecht was full of blunders. The Germans are only hitting back on account of the criticism which their arrogant attitude aroused, of course——"

" Not unnaturally, when one considers the venom with which you wrote about them," Chipperfield put in smoothly. It was time to start trimming this local upstart down to size. He smiled thinly as he imagined Zellwäger gulping with annoyance at the other end of the wire.

" But you yourself suggested——" Zellwäger began, his voice pitched on a high note of protest.

" Do go on. You were telling me about the board of inquiry. Who else is joining in the chorus? "

" The Swiss," answered Zellwäger in a sullen voice, " it seems that getting to the top after the Germans did has upset their national pride a bit; and then their failure to bring out Albrecht alive."

" A very gallant failure, I should have said."

" Yes. But a failure all the same. The critics of the Swiss rescue team say that Albrecht might not have died if they had reached him earlier. The latter are hitting back, of course. It appears to be the idea that an inquiry tribunal might clear the air. Your name has been mentioned. I thought I ought to warn you."

" My name! Where the devil do I come in? "

It was only what he had anticipated, but he had to appear surprised and suitably irate.

" I'm not at all sure. It seems the *Obmann* who led the first relief column intends calling you for questioning if there is to be an inquiry. Something to do with those curious words Albrecht spoke before he died. And, I gather, something about the height you gave them."

There was a further pause, during which Chipperfield could imagine the other man furtively licking his lips.

Then Zellwäger said lightly:

" I just thought you'd like to be in the picture. I'll let you know if anything further develops."

With a cheerful greeting he hung off.

Chipperfield was annoyed to find that his hand was shaking slightly as he put down the phone.

*   *   *

He had of course expected it, but not quite so soon. He had braced himself for trouble from one source or another, but he had not counted on matters coming to a head quite so swiftly. But as yet, nothing definite had been fixed, no date or place or list of names which would confirm the actual formation of a board of inquiry. They could not possibly begin any kind of probe until Mandoza had been saved. That gave him a certain amount of time—at least twenty-four hours—in which to prepare his defence. And he was rock certain of one thing: the best defence was attack.

It was not, as he had thought most likely, Bellman whom he had to fear, not an alliance of professional rivals snapping jealously at his heels as he stole trick after trick from under their noses. It was a ponderous Bernese peasant, an elderly slow-witted mountain guide, who was threatening him.

The fact that, a moment before, he had used the phrase " a very gallant failure " to describe the work of the *Obmann* and his companions, troubled him not in the least. He wrenched the typewriter across the desk and fed paper into it. He would destroy the guide and his two companions, destroy them with their own words. He searched his shorthand notes for the interview when they had dragged him out of bed at four o'clock in the morning. It was as he had thought: hardly a word need be altered. They had been putty in his hands.

After a few moments thought he began savagely typing.

*   *   *

When he had finished he put a call through to London, then ordered Hügi's frightened little clerk, who was hovering outside the office, to bring him a drink from the bar. He sipped the double whisky thoughtfully, and chain-smoked until the phone rang and Bernheim's voice sounded on the line. He said:

" I've got two big stories for you, Bernie: a report on the abortive rescue to-day, and a follow-up. They're both hot, so get that secretary off your knee and start listening. Are you ready? . . ."

He dictated at speed. When he had finished the first piece of copy he said:

" And now for the follow-up: ' Rumours have reached me late this evening, as the one-time society playboy prepares himself for the gruelling ordeal of his fifth consecutive night on Murder Mountain, that an independent committee of inquiry is being formed, to probe into the organisation and general conduct of the rescue operations on the North Wall.

" ' Frankly, I am not surprised. I am in a position to reveal certain disquieting facts about the men who formed the first relief column—men whom public opinion has been apt, a little too readily, it seems, to regard as picture-book heroes and the greatest experts of their kind in the world.

" ' The principal criticism being levelled at these men, I understand, is their choice of route, which appears to have been the direct cause of their failure to rescue Hans Albrecht alive. It was certainly a baffling choice. By their decision to go by train up to the Jungfraujoch and then set out along the laborious " overhead " route via the Mönchjoch to the Eiger summit, instead of climbing in a few hours the west flank of the Eiger (as did the German team half a day later), much valuable time was lost and valuable energy expended. It did not help matters or explain their curious decision by afterwards subjecting the Munich climbers to a number of cheap jibes and sneers. It was no doubt very galling for them not to have reached the summit first, but there is an old saying in sporting circles: " may the best man win."

" ' However, I doubt if there is much point in mentioning sporting codes or morals. Mountaineering has been held proudly before our eyes as one of the very few sports untainted by commercialism. It is very painful for me (as I am sure it is to my readers) to have to reveal the words of one of the guides who formed the nucleus of the first rescue team. He said: " *We shall never become millionaires, the pay of a guide is niggardly.*" I leave it for my readers to judge whether this remark, in the light of the heroic lives at stake, was untainted by commercialism or not.

" ' The issue of whether one should expect to be paid for saving a man's life, in this sorry day and age, is perhaps an open question. What will, however, come as a distinct shock to my readers (and again, I quote verbatim), is the remark made by one of the men in whose hands the rescue of fellow-guide Hans Albrecht was entrusted. It will be remembered that Albrecht was expelled some years ago from the local mountain-guides association. The bitter words that assailed my startled ears were: "*Albrecht deserved to be thrown out and forbidden to work as a mountain guide.*" Add to this the astonishing reply to my question as to whether they were going to organise a rescue party: " *We are obliged to go,*" which was qualified a short while later with the even more disillusioning comment: " *No one can actually force us to take part in this rescue*"; add all that together and you will feel, perhaps, as I do, that there are good grounds for disquiet.

" ' But I pass no judgment. That is not a reporter's job. I simply leave it for my readers themselves to decide what chance the pitiful, doomed men on the face of Murder Mountain had, when their chances of rescue were in the hands of men moved by such dubious motives as personal animosity, international rivalry and sordid misgivings concerning the ultimate financial rewards.' "

Bernheim's voice came, after a long silence.

" Paddy boy, that stuff's dynamite. Are you sure you know what you're doing? "

" You can rely on me, Bernie. Have I ever let you down yet? "

" Yes. Frequently. But that's beside the point. Tell me,

why are you suddenly gunning for the Swiss team? The
word here is that they put up a pretty good show. Wasn't
it a Swiss who finally pulled the dead guide out? "

" I believe so. But there's no need to mention it. My
reasons are strategic, Bernie; I'll tell you all about it
when the story's dead."

" I'll have to check your tale for libel before I try
selling it along the Street."

" Don't bother, it's watertight. Practically every word
is in my notebook, and my shorthand is very legible."

" Nevertheless, there is such a thing as ' misinter-
pretation,' to give it a polite name."

" And there's still such a thing as ' fair comment,' too.
Now get those stories out, and get 'em out fast, for Pete's
sake. I've never given you any better. Here's the next
titbit: it's not confirmed yet, but I think there are going
to be no less than three different attempts to save the
Baron to-morrow. There'll be anything up to sixty men
from about eight nations crawling all over that mountain."

" Sounds big stuff. Sixty for one, eh? "

" That's it. The public will go for it. Three teams of
intrepid death-or-glory seekers. And yours truly has had
a bright idea. Why not make it four? "

" You climbing up there yourself, Paddy? " came the
sarcastic reply. " If so, I'll order a wreath right now."

" Not me, boy. Nothing so foolhardy. Paddy Chipperfield has never climbed a mountain by any other means
than an upholstered railway seat in his life, and he isn't
going to fool around with ropes and crampons at this late
stage in his illustrious career."

" I'm glad to hear it."

" Here's the scheme, Bernie, and make sure you're
sitting down, it's a stunner . . ."

When he had finished speaking, Bernheim had to admit
that it was.

CHAPTER XII

ZELLWÄGER'S information was correct. Three relief columns, comprising a total of over fifty men from seven different nations, set out in the small hours of Friday morning in an all-out effort to save the life of the man hanging on the end of the rope. The hopes of millions of decent people throughout the world went with them.

When dawn broke on the Friday morning two of the teams were in position. Column Number One, on the summit, was ready, waiting for the early morning mist to disappear. The same report came in to the Swiss headquarters from the second column waiting at the *Stollenloch* —the open gallery inside the mountain. The third party, which had the greatest distance to cover, reported by short-wave radio that they hoped to reach the Mittellegi ridge by midday. It had proved impossible to fly them in. Everything stood in readiness. Only the thick mist masking the North Wall held them up. They could not start until it shifted.

But the mist showed no signs of moving.

As full daylight came, nothing was visible of the giant pyramid except its massive base. It was impossible to start the operation.

The morning wore on and the mist became dense cloud. Not a single peak in the whole mighty range of the Oberland was free. And the wind that had moaned uneasily sometimes in fitful gusts and sometimes with gale force, during the previous week, the wind that alone could shift the cloud, eased gradually into a gentle breeze, and then died. Weather forecasts were studied, experts who knew the valley well were questioned, but no one dared make a clear-cut prediction as to how long the period of sullen calm might last.

Amongst the vast crowds that waited in the great natural amphitheatre below, speculation ran rife over the chances of the surviving man. Had he endured his fifth night in the open? How much longer could he last?

There were some who said they had caught a glimpse of him, in a momentary gap in the clouds. There were others who claimed they had been able to pin-point the spot where he had been hanging on the previous day, but had caught no sight of a human figure. These latter were sure the man on the rope had lost his slender hold on life and had fallen. Rumour cancelled rumour, imagination ran wild, and the truth lay hidden behind banks of impenetrable white cloud.

There was nothing anyone could do. There was nothing to do, except wait.

For some this was the most intolerable part of the whole tragedy, even to men like John Bellman and Doug Wilson, McKechnie and Saltash—hardboiled newspapermen, supposedly inured by long experience to every aspect of human sorrow and tragedy.

For others, equally moved by pity and deep concern, there was at least the safety-valve of hard work. Claire was one of these, along with scores of others whose duties as staff in the hotels, restaurants, shops and on the railways meant long hours of exhausting work.

For others, the delay meant only one thing: pure profit. These were the disciples of Paddy Chipperfield; men like Ferguson and Zellwäger, who viewed each stage of the drama solely in the light of its ability to make news and to grip the attention of the masses. And for men like Hügi; each extra day that the story lasted meant a day of astonishing financial profit for him. It was true that the telescope stood practically neglected, but the trade at his kiosk on the terrace, the custom at his bar and in his restaurant, the number of guests crammed into his rooms, was formidable. There had never been a time quite like it, in all his wide business experience.

Nervous tension, Hügi discovered, makes itself felt in a number of ways. In bad tempers and unreasonableness, but also in thirst and hunger. The constant demand for food was incredible. The fact struck him forcibly that no one seemed to have time or patience in which to enjoy long meals prepared with skill. What was required, he saw instantly, was snacks. Quick to seize the change in the wind, he removed the many small tables that normally filled the large dining-room and lined them along the wall. Emergency stoves and portable hot-plates were hastily assembled, and in a short while a brisk trade in sand-wiches, coffee, hot-dogs and every conceivable kind of short-order food took place, regardless of the hour of the day. The once elegant *Saal* became a gigantic, noisy snack-bar, and there were none of Borgwand's gentle old-world guests left to resent the transformation; they had all left as soon as the hotel began to appear in the world's headlines.

If the prices which Hügi demanded were the cause of a few complaints, none could deny that the food itself was good. The right man had met the right hour. There was nothing to do during the long wait except eat, drink and talk.

As if by common consent, most of the journalists had collected at one end of the *Saal*, and were sitting or sprawling in the chairs which waiters had provided for them. When John Bellman came over from the Scheidegg, a dry, normally taciturn reporter from Amsterdam was speaking heatedly. Chipperfield, he noticed, was not present.

". . . you can say what you like," the Dutchman, named Schenk, was saying, " I think the whole affair is a scandal. Fifty men risking their necks to save the life of one foolhardy citizen. It just doesn't make sense."

" No, but it makes news," put in Ferguson cynically as he swallowed the best part of a hot-dog at one gulp.

Schenk ignored him and went on, " I don't care who

it is who is hanging up there, whether it's a spineless society playboy or a glory-hunting German from Munich, it is still a criminal folly that one man should endanger the lives of so many. The general public is incensed by the whole thing."

" Your public may be," interjected Ferguson again. " But mine isn't. They're lapping it up."

" They ought to ban all climbing attempts on the North Wall," said a French woman reporter from one of Paris's leading illustrateds.

" They tried that years ago, Jacqueline," Doug Wilson pointed out. " It just didn't work. The climbers themselves weren't having any, nor were most of the professional guides."

" How would you set about banning it, anyway? " said Bellman. " Short of ringing the Eiger round with barbed wire and mounting guards day and night——"

" Even that wouldn't keep 'em out," put in McKechnie thoughtfully. " Your alpine enthusiast is a queer bird, if you ask me. There seems to be some strange force in him, compelling him to risk his life for no apparent purpose other than the sheer joy of taking risks. One either understands that urge, in which case the sport becomes not only intelligible but even admirable—after all, they don't do it for money; or else one doesn't understand, and the whole business is practically incomprehensible."

" The only guys who could tell us what it's all about are the climbing boys themselves, but as far as I know they don't have the gift of the gab as a rule," said Doug Wilson.

" I could actually quote you a dozen names that have written well about mountaineering——" Bellman began.

" That's just a pose—the stern, silent hero with the inevitable piercing blue eyes and jaw as long as his lantern," scoffed Ferguson. " If you ask me they're just a bunch of hypocrites, out for glory and their faces in the papers."

"Not hypocrites: madmen. Madmen who ought to be locked up," Schenk retorted.

"Mountaineers *are* mad—if it is mad to be possessed by a passion," McKechnie put in reasonably. "But which one of us is not a fanatic about some sport or hobby? I happen to be devoted to chess, at any time of the day or night. Doug, there, spends every available hour of his spare time on the golf course, isn't that so, Doug?"

"Sure thing."

"No one has ever been killed by playing chess or golf," snapped Schenk.

"Maybe not, but an awful lot of people climb mountains without getting killed, too. Students, doctors, professors, young girls and old ladies. Except for the rare occasions when they get into difficulties, I don't think it is often that they risk anybody else's lives except their own. If you are going to ban sports that endanger other people's lives, it seems to me there are a good many targets you should fire at first—how about motor racing, to start with? Remember that ghastly pile-up at Le Mans in 1955? Over eighty spectators were killed inside a few seconds. But motor racing continues to flourish, and millions would be furious if it were banned."

"All the same, I tell you that in this case the public is incensed——"

"The public is very fickle," McKechnie interrupted him. "When Hillary and Tensing succeeded in getting to the top of Everest, nobody was very incensed, were they? Nobody suggested that they were madmen who ought to be locked up."

"Perhaps because they *got* there," suggested Bellman. "No lives were lost, no one got into distress, no rescue teams were needed. Perhaps the verdict of the public differs according to whether you succeed or fail."

"You may have a point there, John. That makes it a pretty harsh system: if you get to the top and back in one piece, the public falls over your neck and calls you a national hero. If you fail and break your neck, then you're an irresponsible fool. No greys in the picture at all, only white and black."

Bellman was about to reply when he caught sight of Claire beckoning to him from the doorway of the *Saal*. He made his way over to her.

" Have you seen the Great Man anywhere? " she asked.

" Chipperfield? No, I was wondering why he wasn't in there, telling us how to write. Why? "

" One of the guides has come with a message for him. It's a message from the *Obmann*."

" Has something happened? Are they able to start? " he asked quickly.

" No, I don't believe so. The guide says there is no chance of the cloud lifting yet. He seems to want to see Chipperfield personally. I'll go up to his room and see if he's there."

" Shall I come with you? "

" I'm always glad of a bodyguard when his wandering hands are near," she said with a smile.

They took the lift up to the second floor. Claire led the way to Chipperfield's room. She knocked and receiving no answer, opened the door. The room was empty.

" Perhaps he's with that mannequin creature somewhere," Bellman said.

Claire cast a practised eye round the room and shook her head.

" He's not just out. He's gone."

" Gone! You mean he's left? "

Then he saw it for himself. There was no luggage visible anywhere in the room, no array of toilet articles above the washstand. He opened a wardrobe. It was empty.

" Well, I'll be damned. The bird has flown, before the story's over. I don't get it."

" Perhaps this will help," said Claire, picking up a

small note she had discovered on the bedside table. It was addressed to Hügi, the director. She read it out loud:

" Regret sudden departure necessary. Forward bill to Global Features Agency, London, E.C.4. Regarding private arrangements, will contact you in due course. P.C."

Claire said, " What do you make of that? "

" Not very much, I'm afraid. I suppose you have heard the rumours about a pending inquiry? "

" Yes. Maybe that's what the guide has come from the *Obmann* for."

" And Chipperfield knew it was coming, so he skipped out before they could ask him a few awkward questions. It could be. What I don't get is that bit about ' private arrangements '."

" Matters concerning hard cash, if you ask me," Claire replied. " He was very close with Hügi, they were always in the bureau together, with the door locked. Each time they finished one of their little chats the price of something in the hotel went up."

" Perhaps he had a share in that ghastly kiosk, or those revolting coloured postcards which the tourists have been buying. Anyway, that's beside the point. I wonder where he's gone. It's not like him to run out on an unfinished piece of business, no matter how hot things have become for him."

" There'll be no tears from me, I assure you," said Claire. " Whenever he was anywhere near me I got gooseflesh, I don't really know why."

Bellman answered dryly, " He's not one of my favourite people, I have to admit."

Claire suddenly took his hand and looked him squarely in the eyes.

" John, may I ask you something? I know it's none of my business, but——"

" Go ahead."

" What happened between the two of you, that time in New York? "

" Who told you——? "

" Mr. Wilson. In the bar the other night. He's your friend, so I did not think it wrong that we should talk about you when you were not there. He said you had a ' raw deal,' whatever that may mean."

" It's quite simple, really. Chipperfield got me sacked from my job."

" How? Why? "

" Because I failed to report a piece of news."

" In New York? "

" Yes. I was a correspondent there at the time."

" What news? "

" A friend of mine, a well-known British actor—a decent, clean-living man with a nice family—got involved in a minor scandal. I tried to hush it up. Because he was my friend, you understand? "

The girl nodded and waited for him to continue.

" It was a bad car smash, and there were a few evil tongues around who tried to maintain that Guy was drunk. That's a serious charge—drunk at the wheel in an accident, but it wasn't true. Guy wasn't drunk, only over-tired. I tried to suppress the story. I didn't bribe any-body, there was no need. It was just a road accident, two people were injured, and for me there was no doubt about the matter at all, the other party had been at fault. Road accidents happen every hour somewhere in New York, the whole thing would have passed off without any publicity at all if Chipperfield hadn't been in New York at the time."

" Did he know this friend of yours, the one called Guy? "

" Yes, knew him and hated him. Guy was rather out-spoken and had called him a paid digger of dirt, once, at a cocktail party. Chipperfield never forgave him, which perhaps isn't very surprising. By bad luck he got wind of the story about the car-smash, and saw his chance to get his own back. The public likes to build up idols, and Guy had been one of these; but it likes to tear them down too. Chipperfield filed a sensational story back to London, Guy was ruined, and I lost my job for failing to report it."

Claire was silent for a moment. Then she said:

" I see. Perhaps I should not have asked, but I'm glad now I did. It seems very harsh, to dismiss a man because he tries to protect a friend."

" Unfortunately friendship doesn't have much place in the world of business. A reporter's job is to send news. I failed to do this, and so got the sack. It's as simple as that. I've survived, as you see."

He smiled, and changed the subject.

" Come on, we must go down to Hügi and deliver this note. I'm looking forward to the sight of his face when he learns that Chipperfield has left without paying his bill."

" Especially if it includes the telephone calls," Claire answered gaily and they both laughed.

*   *   *

The hours dragged by. Time hung as heavy as the cloud that enveloped the Oberland. The afternoon came, and still there was no news from the Eiger, beyond the fact that the third relief column, climbing the eastern ridge under conditions of considerable danger, had arrived in position on the *Mittellegigrat*.

Chipperfield's unexpected departure became known, and caused a mild stir, then was forgotten. Controversy in the *Saal* revolved endlessly around the identity of the man on the rope. A heated discussion had been caused by a double-page feature in a famous American magazine, in which the characters of the two men, Stringberg and Mandoza, were analysed by an extraordinarily confident psychologist. Stringberg's photo occupied most of the left-hand page, with arrows pointing out a stubborn jaw, thoughtful brow, strong eyes and a host of technical details apparently deducible from his features. Alongside were listed the known facts about him: unmarried, age thirty-six, by profession accountant, by vocation mountaineer; other hobbies, sailing and poetry (his own). The right-hand page was devoted to the Baron, again accompanied by the well-known details of his private life. In many ways the two photos were rather similar. Both men were blond, and of approximately the same height and build. But Mandoza was considerably younger, and his character as laid bare by the analyst's all-seeing eye was markedly different. Arrows pointed out a weak chin, sensuous mouth, aristocratic nose and a vainglorious set to the eyes. The text that followed listed the known facts of the mystery —the German filter cigarettes, the hired car, the conflicting eye-witness reports from the Salzburg mountains and from Interlaken. With astute care the analyst left the issue open; the reader himself was invited to act as his own psychologist, to deduce from the given information the true identity of the man on the rope. The cover of the magazine was devoted to a tinted enlargement of Chipperfield's dramatic aerial photograph, showing the unknown climber in helmet and snow-goggles with his back to the camera, half-turned and waving cheerfully. The caption to the title-photo was printed in flaring red script on a white ground: " WHO IS HE? "

They chewed the mystery over, all afternoon, as they had done since the story began.

" I'll tell you what beats me," said Doug Wilson. " Why haven't relatives or close friends of either Stringberg or the Baron come up with a lead? "

" Stringberg appears to be a quiet type of fellow," mused Saltash. " Despite the attempts to make him out as bombastic and vainglorious, I don't think that's his true character. Poetry, sailing, mountaineering—those are all the pursuits of a lonely, thoughtful, one might almost claim, spiritual man. I would say that he is not the type to have told friends or relatives of his private plans."

" I'm with you there. Whereas the Baron could no more have hatched a beauty like this and kept quiet about it——"

" How do you know? " put in McKechnie. " I have it on good authority that they've tried getting something out of his relatives, without the slightest success. It seems the Mandozas belong to the stiff upper lip tradition: ' We prefer not to talk about the black sheep of the family '."

" Nevertheless, it's quite impossible that a man of Mandoza's calibre would take up a dangerous sport like mountaineering," Saltash persisted.

" Why? He's crazy enough, to start with. And courage, or recklessness, isn't limited to those without blue blood in their veins. There were a good many titles and noble names in the Commando brigades during the war."

" All right, supposing for one moment that it might be the Baron, why all the secrecy? Why creep up to Grindelwald like royalty travelling incognito? "

" Perhaps because he thought the authorities might try and prevent him from carrying out such a stunt."

" Or because he was using the Greta Garbo technique."

" And what might that be? "

" The more mysterious you are, the more people are interested in you. In other words, the gentle art of keeping in the limelight by pretending to take elaborate pains to avoid it."

And so it went on, the seemingly endless controversy about a man's identity. When they grew tired of the theme, the conversation swung to the bitter dispute aroused in Swiss-German climbing circles by Zellwäger's article. Several German newspapers had reacted in vitriolic terms, and a long line of past affronts and long-buried vendettas was being disinterred. It would be months before the bad blood stirred up by a few malicious lines was forgotten.

Late in the afternoon Bellman and Wilson walked over to the Swiss headquarters on the Scheidegg.

The atmosphere of acute tension which had dominated the radio-room on the previous day had given place to one of frustration and near-despair. The two reporters were told of the attempt by three Frenchmen from the third relief column to strike into the Wall in the direction of the *Rampe* and establish vocal contact with the surviving man. They had been defeated by the complete lack of visibility. To have gone on would have been suicidal; the three volunteers had been forced to turn back. Weather reports that came in as the evening approached gave some promise of better conditions on the morrow, but no one was willing to hold out much hope of the injured man's chances of surviving a sixth night on the mountain. It was true that men had endured an ordeal as long as that and still come out alive—but only with the aid of warm food, adequate clothing and the chance of shelter and some sleep. The talk was of previous tragedies, of Sedlmayer and Mehringer, of Toni Kurz, of Corti and Stephano Longhi; and of the great triumphs, led by men such as Harrar, Heckmair, Buhl and Terray. Bellman listened and realised that there were few mountains in the world with a history as awe-inspiring as the Eiger North Wall.

He was almost relieved when Doug Wilson suggested they leave the radio-room. Both men walked in silence for some time, weighed down by the air of depression which had unconsciously affected all at the Swiss headquarters.

Eventually the American said:

" They reckon they could have got him, if the cloud hadn't clamped down? "

" Possibly. But I don't think they hold out much hope now."

" Five days and six nights. What do you think . . . will he even be alive to-morrow? "

" God knows. Depends on how tough he is, and how much he wants to live, maybe. If it's Stringberg up there, my guess is he won't give in easily. They say a true climber goes on hoping and fighting long after reason tells him to pack up."

" And if it's the Baron? "

" I don't see how it can be; you know that. But if by some weird freak Chipperfield hasn't made it all up . . . I don't know. Again, it depends on how tough he is, and how much he wants to live."

" Mandoza's not tough. None of those degenerate middle-European aristocrats are. They're all rotten from intermarriage."

" Maybe. But the Baron's a very complex character. Did you read, for example, in that double-page spread, that judo, as well as fast driving and hitting night-club waiters, is one of his favourite pastimes? I was surprised, I don't mind telling you. He's probably tougher, both physically and mentally, than we think. I wonder how strong his will to live is, too? "

" We'll know, as soon as the cloud lifts. I say it's Stringberg up there, with odds-on chances of his being alive. If it should be Mandoza, then I don't reckon he'll make it."

*　　　*　　　*

Opinion amongst those journalists who had not already committed themselves to either faction seemed to crystallise along those lines. If the man on the end of the rope had survived a sixth night, then his name was most likely to be Kurt Stringberg. Ferguson even tried to take bets on the issue, but angry opposition from many sides crushed the idea stillborn.

" There's been enough vulgarity about this whole business without your adding further monstrosities to it," said the silver-haired correspondent Saltash acidly. " I speak for a good many of us here when I say that decent people have been revolted by the manner in which you and your kind—led by that odious fellow Chipperfield—have exploited this story. You have gone beyond the bounds of human decency with one cheap sales-trick after another——"

" I'd keep quiet about sales if I were you," Ferguson retorted, quite unabashed by the vehemence of Saltash's attack. " Your precious paper, along with a few others that put themselves on such a lofty pedestal, is bought by precisely three per cent of the great British public."

" Are there *no* other values in your life except percentages? " Saltash snapped in a thin voice.

Ferguson flushed.

" A newspaper can't afford to ignore sales. You have a circulation no bigger than a county newspaper, and you're losing ground every year. I have an audience of millions to keep happy, not just a few hundred highbrows and club-intellectuals. I give my readers what they want. So do the illustrateds, and the radio and TV boys. You're out of touch with the times, Saltash. In another decade or two you'll be as extinct as the dodo."

The argument might have become even more bitter, had not someone switched on a portable radio and drowned the conversation.

A commentator's voice, delivering a breathy, sensational review of the Eiger drama, momentarily held their attention. The account ended with the words:

" And don't forget, folks, there are big prizes—a TV set, a luxurious refrigerator and a custom-built Superjet (the finest car on the road to-day, folks)—just waiting to be won in our competition. It's not too late: join in the manhunt to-day! The world is still searching for these two men: Kurt Stringberg, crack alpinist, and Baron Wendelin Mandoza, one-time suitor for a royal hand. One of these two men hangs——"

" For God's sake find something else! " Saltash barked.

The owner of the radio turned the knobs and found some music. It was Brahms, and for a while the superb voice of Kathleen Ferrier singing the Alto Rhapsody softly held the room in its spell. But an impatient hand twiddled the dial again and found a dance band. A popular number came to an end and the fruity voice of an announcer eulogised the preceding tune and went on to describe the next:

" Now here's Jake and his boys bringing you the very latest hit straight from London. The vocalist is that glamorous star of stage, screen and television, Miss ——"

The name of the strident-voiced singer who followed was happily lost in a surge of lush strings with which the number began. The strings faded and the steady beat of drums echoing fatefully in a carefully-designed studio led up to the opening refrain:

> " *The Man on Murder Mountain*
> *He makes me think of yew,*
> *Why must you be so cold, dear,*
> *You know my love is trew.*
> *Just think of*——"

With an oath Saltash lunged at the radio and switched it off. Glancing across at Ferguson, who was in the act of devouring a ham-roll the size of a 3-inch naval shell, the elderly journalist said:

" I suppose you didn't write that charming little ditty, by any chance? "

Ferguson shook his head, swallowed and replied:

" No—wish I had, though. Should make a pot of cash."

A woman reporter from a powerful ladies' magazine interjected:

" I think the whole thing's disgusting. Is there absolutely nothing sacred to-day? "

" Sometimes I'm ashamed merely to be living in this sorry century," Saltash said, his head between his hands.

" I don't agree," said McKechnie.

Saltash looked up sharply. The Scottish journalist was a man whom he respected, even though they wrote for rival newspapers.

" You think that song was in good taste, Mac? " said Saltash in surprise.

" No, of course not. I think it was regrettable. But there's nothing new in making up little ditties about public events, however grim they may be. Don't forget, they sang bawdy songs about Napoleon's threatened invasion of England, and they've sung songs about every conceivable event in history right up to and including the atom bomb. You know your history as well as I do, Salt. There's nothing new in vulgarity. It's been with us since Cain and Abel, and it'll last till the end of time."

" That doesn't mean one has to defend it."

" I'm not. I'm just trying to come to terms with it. A sort of co-existence policy, if you like."

" But you would hardly claim that we live in an age of elegance or good taste, would you? " Saltash challenged him.

" There never has been one if you put them all under the microscope. I simply say, there's nothing new about vulgarity—except one thing: the means of disseminating it have grown. There's probably the same amount of respect for morals and standards now as there ever has been; the bad seems to outweigh the good because it's more evident. The snag is, to-day, that we learn about the bad, the vulgar, more swiftly and more surely than ever before. A song like the one we've just been treated to reaches the ears of millions in a few minutes; before, it wouldn't have got farther than the nearest pub for months. A cheap article written in to-day's yellow press would have been no more than a coffee-house pamphlet in earlier times, but now it gets dolled up with exciting pictures—another means of mass-dissemination—and shoved under the noses of millions of readers whose forbears a century ago couldn't even read. There's probably not much more vulgarity abroad to-day, but simply with the aid of newspapers, the cinema, radio, TV and the illustrated magazines it becomes just that much more evident."

" So who's to blame? " said Schenk.

" To blame for what? That we are what we are? That human nature isn't perfect? I side with Saltash wholeheartedly in deploring some of the tricks which have been used to publicise this story in the Alps. But even Paddy Chipperfield and men of his ilk didn't invent human curiosity."

" Why not call it by its proper name: plain sadism? " Schenk retorted.

" It's both, isn't it? " Bellman put in. " Think of the crowd at a circus, gazing up at the man on the trapeze or the high wire: some of them are filled with wonder and curiosity, and some with a sadistic desire to see the man fall and be killed. Both attributes are human, the wonder and the sadism. That's what has brought these droves of people here now, staring up at that poor devil swinging on a bit of rope: part sadism, and part wonder and hope and prayer. Some hope he'll get out alive, and some hope he'll die. The one thing we all have in common is our curiosity."

*   *   *

On the following day, the seventh and final of the strange story, that curiosity was to be fully satisfied.

CHAPTER XIII

No ONE will ever forget that final Saturday.

It made all that had happened before seem pale in comparison. Event followed event so swiftly, each interlacing and crossing with the other, that many reporters were hard-pressed to keep track of the various incidents and sort them out in the proper sequence.

Unknown to them all at the time, the first act in the day's drama took place before dawn in the mountain village of Lauterbrunnen—the "back door" to the Kleine Scheidegg.

Just before daybreak a huge transport lorry drove up the valley from Interlaken and stopped at the Lauterbrunnen terminus of the Jungfrau railway. Three men, stiff with hours of driving, clambered down from the huge vehicle and began unloading a strange variety of equipment. Several wooden crates were transported to the waiting goods wagons, and work began on the main cargo—large drums that appeared to contain either oil or petrol. They were labelled, in three languages: "Danger. Highly inflammable."

The railwaymen looked at the unusual freight with mild curiosity, scratched their heads and went about their task of loading it on to the special train which had been ordered in advance. The few farmers and other folk whose day began at that early hour vaguely noted the scene, found it incomprehensible and, after a moment's scrutiny, not very interesting. It could not possibly have any bearing on the burning topic of the Eiger rescue, which was the sole thought dominating their minds.

Only Chipperfield's leg-man was stirred to sharp curiosity. The scene grew more intriguing when the weary terse-lipped men unloading the lorry refused to answer his questions. Eagerly he fastened himself on to the Swiss railwaymen, but they knew nothing beyond the fact that the destination of the freight was Kleine Scheidegg. The reporter made a careful note of what he saw and hurried to the nearest telephone. It came as a sharp disappointment to learn that his employer was no longer staying at the Hotel Nordwand. He felt sure that what he had to report would have been of interest to Chipperfield, and it was intensely frustrating to find that the famous journalist had departed without a word to anyone.

There was nothing for him to do except watch as the train crawled slowly up towards Wengen and disappeared from sight. The three men who had arrived in the huge lorry travelled with their cargo, he noted.

Whilst this curious incident was taking place several miles from the Eiger, daylight was slowly breaking on the Kleine Scheidegg. And with daylight came the realisation that the cloud had gone. The whole of the gigantic pyramid from base to peak was clear. The skies were a soft mother-of-pearl, imperceptibly turning to powder-blue as the sun rose. It was going to be a beautiful day— a day for picnics, for tramping over the spongy green alps, a day for swimming and tennis and excursions, a day for idling and laughing and loving. But the vast crowd that collected beneath the shadow of the Eiger had neither time nor thought for any of these light-hearted recreations. All eyes were fastened as though hypnotised on the lonely figure swaying gently on the end of the rope.

Could he possibly be alive? Was it Stringberg, or the young Baron?

Excitement at Hügi's giant telescope mounted to a fever pitch. Not a square inch of the terrace was free. Men and women, boys and girls, speaking innumerable tongues, jostled each other in search of a better view. The hotel balconies were packed to danger point, and every window facing the wall was lined with seething humanity.

Bellman lowered his binoculars after a long and careful scrutiny and said quietly to Claire:

" I don't think he's still alive."

Her face drawn with anxiety, she silently took the glasses from him and studied the mountain.

" One can't be sure, of course," he added. " The light's bad. We shall know more when the sun gets up. But he's not making the slightest movement."

Claire brought the glasses into focus. It was true, he was not making the slightest movement. His head was slumped on his chest, his arms hung limply at his side.

" The poor man . . . what agony he must have been through," she said at last. " How long has it been . . .? "

The Englishman at her side thought for a moment, then replied, " Something like ninety hours. It would be nothing short of a miracle if he were alive."

" A miracle. That is all there is to hope for," she said quietly, and handed him back the binoculars.

A moment later Doug Wilson forced a way through the throng and joined them on the hotel steps. He looked flushed and excited.

" They've started! " he announced. " I just heard it on the intercom."

" Which team? "

" The one from the galleries in the mountain."

Swiftly they trained their glasses on the shadow-dark heart of the mountain. Nothing could be seen clearly. It was not even possible to pick out the galleries.

But signs of activity were visible from the first team. Tiny black dots could be observed bobbing over the cornice from time to time. Suddenly a piercing cry came from the tourist who happened to be in possession of the giant telescope at that instant.

" There he goes! I can see him. He's just going over the edge."

The attempt from the summit had begun. Once more a man was being lowered on the *Stahlseilgerät* cable slowly down the summit icefield towards the Spider. With bated breath the crowd watched his almost imperceptible progress. It was evident that the men controlling the winch were taking the utmost caution. The experience they had gained during the previous days in no way tempted them into heedless confidence. A man's life hung on the careful paying-out of the cable, as much as it had done two days earlier. When, with infinite care, the man had been lowered some three hundred feet, there came the same pause as before, as a fresh length of wire was added. By now even the laymen had begun to understand what the delay signified.

Heavy slanting shadows thrown by the climbing sun baffled all efforts to pick out the party climbing from the galleries. But sharp eyes that had been watching the north-eastern ridge detected movement from the third team on the *Mittellegigrat*. The second independent operation had also been launched.

It was on this team that the greatest hope was being placed. Undeterred by the fact that no one had ever succeeded in finding a way out of the *Rampe* on to the north-eastern ridge, a group of daring climbers led by three Frenchmen was endeavouring to descend by this route. Some said they had undertaken to accomplish the impossible. But one factor was on their side. It was the shortest route. If speed and distance alone could decide the issue, they stood the best chance. Everything depended on their skill in overcoming the obstacles which barred their perilous descent. From the slopes at Alpiglen it was impossible to estimate their progress. For long stretches at a time they appeared to remain completely stationary. The route was evidently every bit as difficult as the experts had prophesied.

Seconds ticked by, dissolved into minutes, merged into quarters of an hour, until almost a full hour had gone by without anyone noticing the passage of time. The sun rose steadily from behind the Wetterhorn and flooded the green slopes with warmth and colour. Only the Eiger remained black with shadow, its north face untouched by the direct rays of the sun.

But the light grew steadily better and at last the third column striking upwards from the galleries became faintly visible. They had reached the base of the impassable *Rote Fluh*, and were preparing for the dangerous 140-foot traverse east along the Hinterstoisser *Quergang*. The leader of the six-man team went on ahead and began driving his first piton into the glistening black wall.

Attention switched a moment later to the group on the summit. They had lowered their man down the mountain as far as the combined cables would allow. Through powerful glasses it was possible to watch him as he too hammered a piton into the rock and secured himself. His feet must have found purchase on some tiny ledge, but at the distance from which they were watching it looked as though he clung with his bare hands to the sheer, naked face. Eventually he gave the signal and the cable on which he had descended was slowly wound up. He remained alone in the heart of the treacherous Spider icefield, some twelve thousand feet above sea level.

No one had forgotten what this meant. The deadly plume of white that had swept over the rescuer two days earlier was still vivid in the memory. The Spider was like a funnel, drawing chutes of icy water, loose stones, slabs of ice and avalanches of snow towards its centre as a funnel collects water into a bottle's neck. Against stones and ice the rescuer was protected to some extent by a steel helmet. But his position, without the security of a companion to whom he would normally have been roped, was perilous indeed if he did not succeed in working his way out of the deadly icefield and along the notorious *Götterquergang*—the traverse of the gods—before the warmth of the rising sun loosened the snow above him.

Tension amongst the watching crowds, and amongst

the millions who were listening by radio, rose to an unbearable point. From three parts of the mountain help was on the way to the lone figure swaying listlessly at the foot of the *Rampe*. Within a short while at least two relief columns might be within shouting distance. The enigma of his identity, and the more terrible question as to whether some spark of life lingered in the limp body, might shortly be answered.

Doug Wilson said to Bellman, in a low voice taut with nervousness:

" I'm going to try phoning Mac over at H.Q. Some of those boys should be within hailing distance soon."

Bellman nodded and the American left his side. At least one benefit, he reflected, had been derived from Chipperfield's sudden departure: the phone in Hügi's bureau should be free.

As the light improved it became clear that the column advancing from the *Stollenloch* was making rapid progress. The six-man team, roped together, was already approaching the first major icefield, and a moment later the leader began cutting the first steps. Of the French party attempting the descent via the *Rampe* there was no sign; projecting rock appeared to be hiding them from view, or even barring their way entirely.

Bellman could see no signs of Jasmine the mannequin. He wondered if she had left at the same time as Chipperfield. He asked Claire if she knew where the girl was.

" No, but I know she hasn't left the hotel. Someone told me she's keeping near the newsreel cameras. Mr. Wilson described her as ' the coolest cookie ' he had met in a long time."

" Yes, she's certainly been well briefed by her impresario. I would give a lot to know where he is. It just isn't logical that he should have left before the story's finished."

" Perhaps we were right, and he really did get scared by talk about an inquiry."

Bellman shook his head. " I'll say this for him, I don't think he knows the meaning of fear."

A moment later Doug Wilson rejoined them.

" Mac says the Frenchmen have been held up," he said. " They can't make it down the *Rampe*. Had to turn back and try it another way."

" Damnation take it," Bellman swore softly.

Claire turned white. " That was supposed to be the best chance, wasn't it? "

Both men nodded.

" What do they say about the man in the Spider? "

" The odds are pretty thin," the American answered. " Even if he gets there in one piece, it's difficult to see what one man on his own can do."

" Has anyone got within shouting distance of Stringberg? "

" I don't think so. The guy in the Spider is not in radio contact with the summit. Seems he had too much gear to take with him, without strapping a bulky radio set on his back. They seem to think the column coming up the wall has the best chance."

Bellman trained his glasses on the six men straddling the first icefield.

" They've got a hell of a way to go. I shouldn't think they can reach him before midday."

" That's roughly what they reckon at H.Q., Mac was telling me. There's something new over there, though. Rumours are buzzing around about putting a plane in. One of the Swiss Air Rescue boys, I suppose."

" What can they do with an aircraft? You can't land on a vertical mountain face."

" Don't ask me. The Swiss are world-beaters when it comes to that stuff, but . . . anyway, there's something in the wind. A whole heap of petrol drums and spare parts came up by train early this morning from Lauterbrunnen, it seems. Nobody knows what for, and the zombies in charge are as tight as clams, you can't get a word——"

His voice faltered as they all heard the buzz of an aircraft engine at the same moment. The crowd stirred restlessly and heads craned to scan the skies to the east.

Shielding his eyes from the glare of the sun, Bellman was one of the first to pick it out. It was several seconds before he realised what kind of curious machine was buzzing towards them. It was a helicopter.

The word passed from mouth to mouth amongst the straining crowd as the awkward machine, travelling with surprising speed, drew closer.

" Well I'll be darned . . . d'you reckon they're going to try it with that? "

Bellman shook his head, not attempting a reply until the helicopter had roared over their heads. When it was possible to speak he said:

" I shouldn't think so. They can't climb high enough. I asked the pilot whom I went down to the Valais to interview. The best the Swiss have got can't get much higher than eight thousand feet or so."

Wilson exclaimed excitedly, " Johnny, that wasn't a Swiss machine! Didn't you see its markings? Look, it's coming down to land. Man alive, we've got to get over there, this may be something big! "

He turned and thrust his way through the excited crowd. After a second's hesitation Bellman followed him.

As they ran, they saw the helicopter hovering over a small flat plateau several hundred yards away. Then it sank in a noisy but controlled vertical descent. The ground sloped upwards towards the plateau in undulating curves. As they reached the lip of the last slope the machine had settled and the engine was cut. It was immediately surrounded by a small knot of eager tourists. Several crates containing spare parts and a number of large petrol drums, guarded by three men in denim overalls, formed a circle round the machine. The main three-bladed rotor swung lazily to a standstill, a cabin door opened and the pilot eased himself out. There was another man in the machine. As Wilson and Bellman raced up, he too stepped out.

It was Chipperfield.

His face was lined with exhaustion, but his eyes shone with an unnatural brightness and the habitual smile lingered at the corners of his mouth. Attempting a show of nonchalance, he pulled out a packet of cigarettes, and was in the act of lighting one when he realised that the mechanics were commencing to refuel the helicopter. He threw the unlighted cigarette away and began conversing in low tones with the pilot.

" What's it all about, Paddy? " shouted a breathless reporter who had doubled across from the Scheidegg. Any hope of an answer was drowned by the barrage of questions that began from all sides.

Chipperfield pretended not to hear them for a while. Then he turned and faced the exploding flash cameras and the stream of questions.

" What the blazes are you up to, Paddy? "

" Where did you get this kite from? "

" You going to have a shot at rescuing him yourself? "

Chipperfield smiled complacently and held up a hand to stem the flow.

" What *do* you imagine, my dear fellow? " he said. " Did you think I was just going on a sightseeing trip? "

" You mean you're going to try and get the poor devil yourself? "

" That's the rough idea," Chipperfield answered with a bland smile. His fatigue-rung eyes glowed with ill-concealed triumph.

" Do the Swiss know about this? Have you O.K.'d it with them? "

" My dear chap, since when did one have to apply for permission to try and save a man's life? "

" How are you going to manage it? " challenged Wilson.

" Wait and see," came the curt reply.

Chipperfield obviously intended to say no more, but the questions poured at him from all sides, heedless of whether an answer was obtained:

" Where did you get this helicopter from? "

" Who's behind this stunt? "

" How the hell d'you hope to do it? "

" It's just another stunt—these kites can't fly that high unless——"

" It's one of the new Sikorskys, they can get up to fourteen thousand feet."

" Where the devil did you get it from, Paddy? "

" Who's paying for this circus? "

The pilot had finished his inspection of the machine, refuelling was complete and minor adjustments had been carried out by the tight-lipped mechanics. Muttering a word to Chipperfield the pilot climbed nimbly into the cabin and settled himself at the controls.

" I hope you know what you're doing, Chipperfield," said Saltash, who had just arrived.   " That's a man's life you're playing with, not a circulation figure."

" Won't you tell us what you hope to achieve? " said Ferguson eagerly.

Once again Chipperfield held up an authoritative hand and the frantic questioning died.

" You can hardly expect to get your information quite so easily, gentlemen. As I always say, read my stories and you'll keep abreast of the news. Now if you will excuse me, I have work to do. Stand back, everyone . . . *Weg, bitte !* . . . So long, be seeing you."

He gave a truculent wave, flashed a broad smile at the press cameras and paused for the split second it took them to snap the shutters, then turned and climbed into the machine.

The small knot encircling the helicopter retreated as the motors sprang into life. The air was filled with the roar of the 450 horsepower engines, thunderous at such close quarters, the huge three-bladed rotor whirled above them like the beating of a giant bird's wings. In a few seconds the helicopter had risen from the ground, climbing straight upwards with steadily increasing speed.

"Goddammit, what a ham!" exploded Doug Wilson.

"Take me back to those good old Lyceum days. Irving himself couldn't have done it better," commented Bellman dryly.

"Just read my column, you poor boobs," mimicked another journalist, "I honestly wonder whether Paddy hasn't gone right round the bend these days."

Some of the reporters turned away with bitterly sarcastic comments, others stood gazing in awe at the clumsy silver machine's ascent above their heads, whilst a few descended like clamorous wolves on the three tight-lipped mechanics and began fruitlessly pumping them for details. They learnt little, except that which was obvious—that the men were there to service and refuel the helicopter, and that they had been hired by Chipperfield and told not to talk.

"Another exclusive for the maestro," Bellman said, as he made for the Hotel Nordwand with Doug Wilson. "Where on earth do you suppose he dug that helicopter up?"

"I'd guess it's from one of the NATO bases. I think they've got a few Sikorskys in Europe. Could be from France, or from Germany. Some newspaper will be putting up the dough."

"That's likely. But why all the petrol up here?"

"These crates have a pretty short range. They're no good over long distances, you have to service them from right up in the front line. I learnt all that when I was covering Korea."

"It's a fantastic idea. What chance has he got?"

"If anything can get Stringberg out in time, it'll be that crate. I've seen 'em do wonders."

     ★   ★   ★

To Chipperfield, the moment of his ascent from the circle of open-mouthed onlookers had been one of intense, ecstatic triumph.

He knew what they had all been thinking. Everyone had assumed he had run out, had got cold feet because of the talk of an inquiry tribunal. Instead, he had fooled them by coming back—and coming back in a fashion so spectacular it must have taken their breath away. For a brief moment he allowed himself the luxury of reflecting on their utter bewilderment, the frantic flood of questions, the picture they had made as the powerful rotors had plucked him from their very feet. It was a moment of glorious triumph, the fruit of intensive thinking, planning, travelling and cajoling during the previous thirty-six hours. It was a feat which only a man of his flair and connections could have pulled off.

Then he shut the scene from his thoughts and concentrated all his mind on the daring venture he had now irrevocably embarked upon.

Visibility through the bulbous Perspex nose of the helicopter was excellent, far surpassing the comparable view obtained from a normal aircraft. He could see around and above him in a three-dimensional arc of almost one hundred and eighty degrees. They were climbing steadily, and one after another the peaks of the Oberland swam into sight. But still the Eiger soared above them. The rate of climb was supposed to be a thousand feet a minute, but the pilot had warned him that in conditions of heat or at high altitudes the density of the atmosphere was likely to rob the machine of some of its performance. The needle on the altimeter flickered over ten thousand feet as they drew level with the second major icefield on the North Wall. He could see six figures roped together, laboriously cutting steps and crawling like snails up the sheer wall of gleaming ice. Some of them turned and stared at him as the machine struggled steadily higher. He felt that there was something symbolic in the contrast between their tortuous, plodding progress and his own bird-like ascent into the powder-blue heavens.

Down below the world had taken on a toy-like aspect. The few buildings such as the Nordwand and Scheidegg hotels had become children's wooden playblocks, and the crowds were tiny black pencil dots scribbled on a vast sheet of green paper.

The temperature in the cabin grew stifling. Sweat eased its way in trickles from his armpits. The pilot's face was tense, and no word came from the tight line of his mouth. The sun beat down on the Perspex roof, almost blinding them, until the pilot eased the machine forward into the shadow of the massive north face. The altimeter needle climbed steadily, ticking off the hundreds at jerky intervals.

Suddenly the pilot gave an exclamation and pointed above them. Shielding his eyes, his pulse racing wildly, Chipperfield stared, as slowly the man on the end of the rope came into sight.

Was he still alive? He must have heard the roar of their engines, yet he gave no sign of reaction. His back remained towards them, his feet were dangling without any purchase on the ugly bulge of rock, and his arms hung limply at his side. His head was sunk on his chest, only the tip of the helmet visible.

But as he studied the ugly strata of rock from which the man hung, Chipperfield realised with a surge of triumph that one factor was in their favour—a factor that no one looking from the distorted viewpoint of the slopes below could have known: the rock to which he was lashed bulged out from the sheer surrounding strata, bulged sufficiently clear from the vertical plane to enable them to fly close without smashing the rotor-blades on the mountain's face. What everyone had scorn-fully dismissed as impossible, now, at close quarters, bore the appearance of possibility.

If only the injured man were still alive . . .

And then he seemed to stir.

As the helicopter closed in, gaining height slowly but surely, Chipperfield saw one arm stir in a faint, listless movement, like a branch stirring in a gentle breeze. Chipperfield's heart missed a beat. He crammed himself against the burning hot Perspex, keeping his eyes glued on the hanging man. Again! This time the head moved a fraction, as if trying to rise up against some terrible burden. He had not imagined it.

The man was alive!

He wanted to let out a scream of exultation. The man was still living—hovering on the brink of death, dying by inches, but nevertheless, *alive*!

He would have to hurry, it was clear the tortured creature could not last long. But he would get to him, before the last faint breath expired from the shattered body. He would snatch him from in front of the astonished faces of the plodding rescue columns, save him in front of an audience of thousands. He would succeed, where all else had failed, and the threadbare accusations they planned to bring against him would evaporate into thin air. And, he thought with a surge of triumph, he alone of all men would hear the whispered dying words, his alone would be the power to conceal them or to reveal them to posterity.

And he had one more surprise in store, a brilliant twist that would enrage his dull-witted competitors: he would not land at the Scheidegg or Alpiglen. He would fly past them, with his priceless possession in the back of the helicopter cabin; fly past, and land at some quiet spot where no one could beat him to the telephone with his sensational and completely exclusive account of the news the world was waiting for. It would be a scoop without equal in newspaper history.

The pilot eased the machine nearer the mountain. It rocked alarmingly in a momentary pocket of turbulence. Gradually they climbed the remaining few feet that

brought them level with the hanging man. Chipperfield's mouth was dry and sweat was streaming down his
face as he saw the swaying figure reach feebly forward,
scraping with spiked boots to find a purchase on the rock.
As they hovered no more than twenty feet away, the man's
foot found a hold, the second leg came up with the leaden
torpor of a dream, the uninjured arm stretched out and
touched the rock, and the man gently thrust himself sideways to stare full face at the roaring craft a few yards
away. Chipperfield uttered a convulsive cry as he stared
at the upturned face.

It was a face with no name.

Hideous open sores and straw-like stubble covered
those parts of the flesh not concealed by goggles and
crash helmet. It was a face that had been lacerated by
wind and rain and hail and snow, burnt by heat and
slashed by bitter cold: a face etched in torment, the
mirror of a human soul driven beyond the utmost limits of
mental and physical endurance. The mouth gaped open,
a black gap in the straw-coloured stubble; it worked, as
though in speech, and then closed with an agonised
grimace. The head dropped, and the limp body swung
loose from its feeble hold on the rock, as though exhausted
from the pitiful effort.

Chipperfield remained as though hypnotised by the
terrible thing he had seen; his body was racked by
spasms of icy horror.

Vaguely he realised the pilot, ashen-faced, was shouting
something. He became suddenly galvanised into action.

" For God's sake, get cracking with the hook! " he
yelled. " There isn't much time."

He slid the Perspex panel by his seat open and a blast
of air rushed in, rocking the machine violently. The
pilot fought the controls and shouted a stream of impre-
cations above the roar of the engines. Somehow he
managed to right the craft and achieve a measure of
stability.

Chipperfield grabbed the retractable arm of the rescue winch and thrust it out into the open. The pilot began operating the winch and slowly the heavy clip-hook dangling on the end of the wire swung downwards towards the hanging figure.

"You've got to get closer!" Chipperfield shouted frantically.

The pilot pointed to the bulging rock alongside, so appallingly close to the great sweep of their rotor. He had gone as near as he dared, incredibly near. It seemed as though the blades must inevitably smash themselves against the mountain and send men and machine plummeting to the valley below.

The hook dangled above the trapped man's head, and then it reached a point level with him. Level, but not within reach. It was impossible to get closer to the mountain. A gap of perhaps ten feet separated them, and though he made a feeble effort to clutch it, it was clearly too far away.

"Closer, man, you've got to get closer!"

"I can't. We'll be smashed against the wall."

"For crying out loud, man, try rocking the machine—it may swing the hook so that he can grab it."

The pilot shook his head vigorously. Sweat was coursing in rivulets down his face, and the hands that gripped the controls were dripping wet.

"It's no use. We can't save him," he shouted. "Even if he could get hold of the hook he's much too weak to hang on."

"Try, man, try!" Chipperfield screamed. "We've got to get him out, it's his only chance."

"There's nothing we can do, I tell you. I can't take her any closer to the wall, and the wire's not heavy enough to swing like a pendulum."

Chipperfield caught the last words above the din of the engine. In a flash he saw how it could be done.

"Wind it up! Wind the wire up. I'm going down."

" Are you crazy? "

" Wind it up, for God's sake! "

" You're out of your mind," the pilot screamed.

But he rewound the wire on to the projecting arm, as Chipperfield frantically buckled the rescue-girdle round his waist. As the heavy hook came up he snatched at it and clipped it on to the ring of the girdle.

" Don't you see? You can swing me, like a pendulum. I'm heavy enough. That way I can reach him."

" And what then, you raving maniac? How are you ——? "

Chipperfield did not bother to listen. He was already half-way out of the panel. He thought he heard the pilot shout something about a safety catch, but the rushing air and the thunder of the engines drowned the words. As he eased himself out into the open a blast of air plucked at him; in the nick of time he regained his balance.

" O.K.," he yelled. " Let me down! "

The pilot shouted something but his words were hurled into the vortex and lost. Slowly the wire began paying out.

Chipperfield glanced down, and for a second the enormity of what he was attempting struck him with awful clarity. A wilderness of rock and ice spun below in one great rushing sweep, thousands of feet into the distant valley. The earth seemed to reel and he fought with shut eyes to stem back the waves of nauseous fear. The rescue girdle at his waist had slipped up around his chest and was threatening to suffocate him; the thought flashed through his brain that he had not fastened it properly. He fought the waves of nausea and panic. There was no going back. When he opened his eyes he kept them glued to the top of the helmet of the man below.

Inch by inch he swung closer and closer towards the spent figure on the end of the rope, until they were level, with only a distance of some ten feet separating them. His grip on the wire above his head was slimy with the sweat of naked fear. He let go of each hand in turn and tried to wipe them on his clothing. His mouth was dry, and the breath in his lungs under the crushing grip of the girdle was like the churning of sharp-bladed knives.

Gripping the wire afresh, he began trying to swing his body, to gain movement as a child gains momentum on a garden swing. At first his body refused to budge. Then he rocked gently, countered the movement with precise timing, and swung forward a foot. He swung back, and gained further momentum. On the return swing he gained even more, until at the end of each arc the distance separating him from the other man visibly diminished. All fear had left him. Every nerve in his body was screwed to the point of attaining his objective. He knew he could make it. He had to. There was no alternative.

The listless figure awaiting his approach watched him with half-raised head. God alone knew what thoughts were passing through his mind. It must have seemed to him like the climax to some dreadful, long drawn-out nightmare. He seemed to know it was an end of some kind. Wearily a feeble hand came up and pulled the goggles free. His eyes stared uncomprehendingly from huge sockets of utter despair and exhaustion. Feebly he tugged at the strap fastening his helmet: he would need it no longer: the hail of stones and jagged blocks of ice would now come to an end, the terrible agony of the rope cutting his body and the throbbing pain of his crushed and useless arm would soon be over. The helmet fell on to his shoulders and toppled drunkenly into the void below. Long blond hair streamed in the breeze.

Chipperfield gave a shout, a great rebounding peal of triumph that swelled from the very depths of his soul. He had been right, even from the very beginning! The lacerated face that stared vacantly at him was the ghastly caricature of Baron Wendelin Mandoza.

Victory surged like a mighty song through him,

mingling with the pounding of his blood. Once more he checked at the end of his swing and with every muscle and nerve in his body strained to the utmost, swung back in one supreme effort, lunging wildly at the Baron's rope as he reached the end of the arc.

He missed by inches.

Despair welled up in him and he grabbed frantically as the wire began to pull him back; and in that wild movement he knocked free the safety catch that he had failed to secure when he had clipped the girdle to the heavy iron hook.

In a blinding instant of revelation he knew what he had done, and fought it. The pilot had tried to warn him but he had not heeded him. The wire from which he hung parted from the clip at his chest, and he snatched at it as it shot above his head. He was screaming, screaming with fury and agony and despair: he could not fail, in this, the moment of his supreme triumph.

For seconds the racking pain shattered his body as the thin steel wire cut through his hand.

Then the pain became unbearable, and it was a queer kind of relief to let the evil slippery thing snake from his blood-covered grip.

He fell soundlessly, for almost one mile, to the green slopes that reach the foot of the Eiger near Alpiglen.

CHAPTER XIV

THE PEOPLE in the valley saw Chipperfield fall. When, a moment later, they saw the pitiful figure on the end of the rope double over and sag like a sack drawn tight at the middle, they knew it was all over.

The six-man rescue team, which by then had reached the third icefield, had halted, mesmerised by the extraordinary drama being enacted a few hundred feet above them. They watched as the helicopter returned to base, and awaited instructions from the Swiss headquarters.

The men on the Scheidegg knew there was no point in going on with the operation. There could be no further justification in risking men's lives, now that the man they had tried to save was clearly dead. The rescue teams were recalled. The team on the third icefield, the French-led party on the north-eastern ridge, and the lone man in the Spider icefield, received signals telling them to withdraw. Weary, treacherous hours of climb or descent faced fifty-six men from seven different nations before they reached the safety of the green slopes below. Their day was by no means over; but for the vast throng of onlookers, the story was finished.

They streamed quietly from the scene, some by foot, some by train, down to Grindelwald and Lauterbrunnen, back to their interrupted holidays, back to their homes. To some it was merely the end of an exciting drama, the highlight of a fortnight's holiday abroad, a topic of conversation for months to come. With an ease that seemed like callousness they were able to take up their lives once more, to laugh and to play and to drink and to love, within a few hours of the final tragedy. Life went on, as it always does, no matter how great the disaster.

For others, stirred to the roots of their being by what they had witnessed, there could be no thought of immediately picking up the threads of a carefree holiday. Silently they paid their hotel bills and with scarcely a furtive, pitying glance at the lifeless body that hung doubled up on the rope, hurried to the railways and travelled in stricken silence to their homes.

The journalists and radio reporters stayed, to learn the full details of the story's end and file them back to head office. That too was not callousness: it was their job, the means whereby they earned their bread and sustained their families. Only Ferguson, the corpulent reporter for a famous British Sunday paper, was heard to express a thought whose sheer bad taste verged on the mon-strous:

"Oh, boy, am I glad to-day's only Saturday. I was getting worried about meeting my deadline to-night."

Those nearby who heard him walked away in silent disgust.

*   *   *

John Bellman phoned a brief, factual report to his Hamburg office, slowly packed his bag and then paid his bill. His friend the unctuous clerk thoughtlessly expressed the routine wish that he had enjoyed his holiday, then blushed a deep red as he realised the implications of what he had said. Bellman felt sorry for him, the fellow had meant well.

Late in the afternoon he walked over to the Hotel Nordwand for the last time. His footsteps were heavy, and it was all he could do to keep his gaze averted from the North Wall.

As he entered the hotel he met Claire coming, white-faced, from the director's bureau. He felt certain from the expression on her pale face that she had just quarrelled with Hügi, or been dismissed her post.

Trembling slightly, she shook her head in answer to his question.

"No," she said. "He wants me to stay, and I think I should, if only for Papa Borgwand's sake."

"Something's happened, hasn't it?"

"Nothing that should surprise us, after the carnival they've been running for the past few days. Hügi has just been in touch with some travel agency or other, somewhere abroad. They want to organise pilgrimages."

"What?"

"Coach tours . . . to visit the scene of the tragedy. They're going to call them 'Baron Mandoza Pilgrim-ages'."

Bellman's face twisted in a grimace of repugnance and disbelief.

" I thought we had finally plumbed the full depths of human greed and vulgarity, but it seems I was wrong," he said. " There's always be someone like Hügi to think up something new."

They walked to the hotel steps and stood looking at the terrace. The giant telescope was deserted; the old woman in black who had sold tickets was no longer at her post. Chocolate wrappings, paper cups, squashed cigarettes, a glove, crumpled newspapers and discarded scraps of food littered the entire area. Heinrich pottered out from the hotel with a broom and began leisurely sweeping up the debris. He kept his back to the mountain, and did not pause in his work.

They heard a roar of engines, and a moment later the silver helicopter buzzed overhead. In the back, behind the pilot, a second figure was hunched. Bellman thought he caught a glimpse of a Red Cross band on the man's arm. The rumour that the helicopter was being used to transport the remains of Chipperfield's body seemed to be true. Remarkably little time had been lost in reaching the spot where he had finally come to rest.

Unconsciously thinking aloud, Bellman said:

" The ironic—you could almost say bitter—thing about it is that he was right all the time."

" Who? Chipperfield? "

" Yes. It would have been the greatest triumph of his career."

" He paid a terrible price for being right."

" The irony doesn't end there. God alone knows if they might have succeeded in saving Mandoza with one of the rescue columns, but if Chipperfield had only remained on the ground he would have learnt that his story was vindicated. Word came through from a little fishing village in southern Italy, just before midday—Kurt Stringberg has turned up."

" They've found him? Where was he all this time? "

" Sailing an open boat in the Adriatic. The rumours that he'd been seen in Venice were perfectly true. He must have been frightfully surprised to hear of the hue and cry all over Europe for him."

" You mean he knew nothing about it? " Claire said in astonishment.

" Nothing at all. He was six days at sea, in a boat without radio—only a tiny yacht, I gather. He couldn't have been more cut off from the world if he'd been stranded on a desert island. So I was wrong, and all those who thought along with me, and Chipperfield was right."

" He was plain lucky."

" No he wasn't. He was a damn' good journalist who followed his nose, despite the scorn poured on his head from all quarters. I certainly hold no brief for the man's character or methods, but as a reporter and hounder-out of news, he was incomparable. By comparison, I'm a failure."

" I don't agree," said Claire hotly. " There are other things in life besides being a huge professional success and making pots of money."

Bellman smiled wistfully and took her hand.

" Say that softly, or a lot of people will think you are mad. Thank you for your support, anyway. And thank you for all you've done during the ——"

" No, I want to thank you. I don't think I could have borne all this cheap nastiness if I hadn't had the feeling all the time that I could rely on at least one person."

They looked at each other in silence for a few moments. Then Bellman pressed her hand and said:

" Well, I'm afraid I must be going. My train——"

" Now? This afternoon? "

" I'm afraid so."

" Will you write to me sometime? " she said in a small voice, blushing slightly. " Or shouldn't I ask that? "

" Of course. Why ever not? "

" I thought perhaps . . . your wife would object."

" I very much expect she would," he answered, to her mystification smiling broadly at the same time. " However, she is far too busy at the moment, arranging to divorce me in a curious town called Reno in America. I'm afraid I don't consider it any longer her business whom I write to."

" Why is she divorcing you? " Claire stuttered.

" Because I proved unable to keep her in the style which her many male friends assured her was her due."

He took her other hand and pulled her gently to him, kissing her softly on the lips.

" I will write, Claire. And I will come for you as soon as possible . . . that is, if I may? "

Her eyes were shining with tears of happiness as she whispered, " Please do. I shall be waiting."

She watched him go, down the steps and out along the cinder track that led to Alpiglen Station. Once he turned and waved. She watched him till he was out of sight. Then she went up to her room and cried, though whether from sheer happiness or in order to release the pent-up emotions of the long, nerve-racking week, she did not know.

*　　　*　　　*

The story did not end as neatly as that. No story in real life ever does. It disappeared from the world's headlines, but rumbling echoes were heard for many months afterwards.

The bitter dispute that had been occasioned by Zellwäger's venomous article continued for some time in German and Swiss mountaineering circles. It was to some extent scotched by the verdict of the independent board of inquiry set up to inquire into the conduct of the rescue operation. The professional Swiss guides were vindicated entirely, and were publicly praised for their part in the whole operation. At the same time generous tribute was paid to the volunteers from Munich, from France, and all the other countries concerned, who had so selflessly risked their lives in the common endeavour. All that it had been in mortal power to do, had been done, without thought of reward or glory.

The coach tours bent on their salacious pilgrimages came, were satiated, and left, Hügi returned to Zürich at the end of the season a richer, wiser, and if possible, harder man than before; he had learnt that there was practically no limit to human greed and gullibility once the baser emotions had been aroused and fully exploited. Jasmine the mannequin received fabulous offers from film and television companies to star in a story of the late Baron's life, but being at heart a very shrewd young girl, she turned them down in favour of a solid proposal of marriage from a middle-aged Johannesburg diamond merchant who had seen her photo on the cover of an illustrated magazine.

Zellwäger, headstrong with the limelight that had briefly been his as a result of his highly effective articles, offered his services to Global Features Syndicate, and was turned down. It was explained to him that talent, rather than a mere poisonous pen, was the principal qualification needed to force an entry into the higher flights of his profession.

Klaus Borgwand climbed the slow hill back to health, and found himself penniless and without a job. For a while he obtained work as a travelling salesman for a firm manufacturing kitchen fat, but all the time he longed to be back in harness again, doing the job he loved—running a hotel. Fate smiled on him, in an ironical way, and led his path full circle back to the hotel he had once owned. The Zürich Finance Company, its new owners, realised that quite a large part of the fame that had come to the Nordwand was likely to stick. Casting around for the right man to put in charge as director, and realising that Hügi's methods were a trifle too ruthless for normal conditions, the shrewd Zürich businessmen could hit upon no better choice than the hotel's erstwhile owner. At first he refused, fearing that memories of those fateful days would prove too heavy a burden. But gradually he began to find in the idea a strange kind of justice; he came to terms with his own queer destiny, and accepted the offer of the post.

The fickle summer came to an end, followed by an autumn of glory. Sycamore, beech and mountain maple burnt with a flame of colour across the windswept slopes of Alpiglen, spruce and pine clung bravely to their hues of jade and bottle green, and soon the first snows sprinkled the soft alpine pastures with a thin white powder. Cutting winds swept up from the Grindelwald and Lauterbrunnen valley, heavier snow fell, and soon the first winter skiers arrived, filling the air with their ebullience.

The man on the end of the rope was forgotten. Few realised that he was still there. For they had not been able to reach him in order to cut him down. Deep winter came and bitter storms lashed his lonely rock, but the rope on which he hung withstood all onslaughts.

With the arrival of spring the boisterous skiers departed, and another season, another year, loomed ahead for the hoteliers of the Oberland.

Methodically, quietly, and with a touch of sadness now that Claire had received her long-awaited letter and departed for Hamburg, Klaus Borgwand set about the task of reopening the Hotel Nordwand for the new season.

Every so often he would stop and look up at the mountain that dominated the huge windows of his *Saal*. Others might have forgotten, but he had not, and never would. The man was still there, though one could not see him with the naked eye.

For those whose appetites were not fully assuaged, he was visible through the giant telescope, his body stripped by the wind, bleached and burnt by the sun, picked in parts to the bone by wild birds, hounded by the elements and yet free of them: a terrible testimony to human folly, human bravery, and human greed.

THE END